Copyright © 2024 Kevin Farrington
All rights reserved
Version 1.2

www.kevinfarrington.com

Facebook: Kevin Farrington

TikToK: @kevinfarrington

Instagram: kevin_farrington_1976

Twitter: @KevFarrington76

Chapter 1
Edward

Grace photographed by Howell Conant in 1955

You'd think with the Internet being the Internet, with the whole wide world at your fingertips and all that, you'd get at least a few offers when you post in online groups asking for someone to please read what you've written, and if they could give some feedback. I got one. She read the first page and said, "A book that starts in bed is so cliché." Maybe she's right, but I'm not going to go down the route of the first line being like, "He emerged bloody and battered through the car wreckage." If I keep largely to the truth, even if nobody reads this, I'll be happy. Just for the fact of having done it. Grace Kelly, the princess of Monaco, in a swimming pool. Back in the day, to me anyway, she was undoubtedly the most fantastic looking person that ever lived. It was the Girl Next Door quality that appealed to me, as well as obviously being very good looking. I cut it out of a newspaper and stuck it up. We did that sort of thing back then. Things weren't as accessible then as they are now. Vinny used to say, "What have you got Grace Kelly on your wall for? She's dead." I never knew what difference it made. I can't see how somebody's being dead can interfere with their looks while they were alive.

I was lying there, in two minds about what to do over the summer – to get the J1 visa like so many of my friends were doing and going to America for a job for a few months, or staying at home and getting a job here. Here, as in Ireland. Edward, one of the blokes who'd been living with us since the previous October, he'd been at me for weeks now, telling me I should go on over. He was American. The "United States", more specifically. I saw a Brazilian dude on teli a while back, upset how there's lots of countries in "America". He was lamenting how they all get lumped into one. So, in case he ends up reading this, as small a chance as that might be, I wouldn't want to offend him again. Edward was from "The United States". He had been studying in Ireland since the previous September. He'd be going home soon. This day I'm telling you about was in June, the following June, the last day of college, the first day of the holidays. Edward said I could go over and stay at his place, or his parents' place more like, for as long as I wanted. He had a pool table in his gaff, and lots of other cool things. He showed me a photo album. It was certainly tempting. I'd never been to America at that stage. He was a well of kindness, Edward was. As for his parents, who would've actually *owned* the house... well, I'm not so sure. I imagine they'd be keen for you to get going quick smart. I know I would, if it was my kitchen, where you can't even walk in a circle without banging elbows, in my flat here in Dublin that hardly has a window. Strolling around in your boxers, interrupting my cornflakes. No thanks. Even if I had a Cribs style mega kitchen I'd be keen for you to get going.

 I suppose I should tell you about him first. Edward Brophy. It makes sense. He's the reason I'm writing all this in the first place. All this story is set here in Ireland but just to fill you in about him, he lived somewhere not far from New York. He was a student in Columbia University, doing banking and economics or something. His family don't live in that house anymore. This is a long, long time ago. The world has changed a lot since then; or, at least one part of it has anyhow – the Internet. Thank God for the Internet. It definitely deserves a capital 'I'. I wouldn't be doing this were it not for the Internet, no way. I'd be too scared of the consequences. With the Internet, I can zone in specifically on his old home and see those same things he used to talk about. The big tree he built a swing on with his sister. The park with the tennis courts down the road. I'd love to go *in* to his driveway and see more but... Google Street View doesn't let me do that. I looked up the address on Google and some property register says the house was sold in June of 2002, to whom I don't know. Maybe I could find out where the Brophy family live now, with a bit more research. I'm sure I could in fact. I might try that someday.

It was 11 in the morning when I heard a big "Ow!" from downstairs. I jumped out of bed and went down to him. It's funny. I used to wear a watch back then. It's all phones now. We did have phones in those days too but mine wasn't nearby. It wasn't like now where your phone is practically glued to your eyes and fingertips 24 - 7, it was just simply a mobile phone, pretty much. One of the early, sturdy Nokias, a 5110, I remember. The only game you'd play was "Snake". No internet access back then, that's for sure. This is all way back in Nineteen Ninety something, let's just say. I'm not going to tell you what year. Friday the 5th of June. I remember it all so clearly.

That's the ironic thing. I'd be lying if I didn't admit that for years, *decades*, I've pushed myself to the limit to try forgetting everything about that day. I cut contact with friends. I came up with lame excuses to not go to weddings. If I wiped every little detail of what happened that day from my mind, I seemed to be telling myself, it would be as if it never happened. And for years I was successful, I had forgotten it... but lately it's resurfaced again. I've forgotten a lot of the *names* of people, and the places, but as for what happened... that's something I can never forget. And anyway, it would be pretty dumb of me to go around giving real names and places. I might be stupid but I'm not *that* stupid. I've mixed things up a bit, on purpose. A long time ago it was but you could still land yourself in a spot of bother if it all turned out arse ways. And that's something I'm not prepared to risk. I mean... just so much has happened. Yet so much stays the same. I'm still here thinking about it yet life has moved on. I'm not going to get into names and personalities. I've too much to risk. I'm too much of a coward.

I'm so much of a coward I can't even write it anonymously. Even with that cloak I can't write what happened. I can write *around* it but I can't write it down directly. Whatever about writing it, I can't even *say* it. Even when I'm completely by myself in the middle of the countryside or something and I've had a good look around first to be sure I'm alone. Even when I'm out there like that I can't say it. Nobody anywhere. All I want to do is yell it out, to scream "I did it!" at the top of my voice – what a liberation! – but all I can do is whisper it, and even then, before I've finished saying his name... it peters out to nothingness. Why? It's a question I ask myself all the time. All. The. Time. I mean I get the whole, "Oh if he says it out loud it will be such a psychological blow and his conscience won't be able to deal with it." angle... but that's not it. I know I did it like I'm holding the pen in my hand now. There's nothing that screaming it out loud is going to solve, or ruin, just like screaming, "I've got a pen in my hand!" isn't going to fix anything. I know I did it. I'm not going to go having a nervous breakdown by simply saying, "I did it."

And yet... and yet there is a chance... There was a lot of booze and drugs involved. Already, I realise I'm making excuses now. I remember my feelings at that point in time, on the road. I'm not fooling anybody by saying I don't know what happened.

I actually did write about it once before. On that same night. I burnt most of it. I'd totally forgotten about it, but then I found a few sheets, some of their edges singed. For years it had been charred and buried, but it's back now. So here I go again. Putting it on paper will help. Writing is the deepest form of thinking. So here it goes, here goes what happened on that day.

When I heard that yelp, I ran downstairs to him. I didn't know he was back. I must've been asleep when he came back in. We hadn't seen each other in a few days. We'd all been all over the place the past week or two, the proximity of exams necessitating protracted cramming sessions in the library, breaking the pattern of what had been our intersections every evening in the front room, when we'd watch tv and chill out and talk. I'd finished my exams the previous day. I was waiting for these two head cases who'd been living with us, the Boys, to return home. I hadn't seen them in two days, which was as long as I'd ever gone without seeing them, unless I went to Dublin for a long weekend. They were always there, part of the furniture, glued to the sofa, watching TV. We'd made plans to hit the town, and they owed me some money. 10 pounds, which went quite a way for a student in the nineties. They were from Tip, the Boys. Before I went down to Edward, I remember I was reading this flyer or pamphlet. Some Students Union dudes had handed it out a week earlier to everybody at the end of a lecture, a sort of advice guide on how to find a job for the Summer. It was mostly common sense stuff - look sharp, make eye contact with the person interviewing you, shake hands, and so on. There was a part saying about being careful to choose relevant adjectives to describe yourself at the interview stage, like be conservative instead of risky, and I laughed at the thought of someone going for an accountancy job and describing themselves as "creative", or an art director being asked at the interview for his best quality and him saying it's being "punctual". Yes, sad to say but those are the things that make me laugh.

 He had a pained, angry look on his face. He was inspecting his knee. As I suspected, he'd banged his leg on the table. It was one of those stupid glass rectangular tables with edges you can't see. It takes either a sadist, or a person who should be fired instantly from their job as a designer, to be a designer of tables like that. It was Edward's table. He'd bought it in some charity shop. Only God knows why he kept it. Most of us just sat in that room, watching TV. Edward hopped about, doing stuff. He put white masking tape all along the edges, yet continued to bang his knees on it more than anybody. I stopped there for a second on the last step of the stairs, trying not to laugh at the stupidity of it. He was on his hands and knees on the carpet with a sponge, soaking up a spilt coke can. It had been on the table. He looked like he was in the middle of a war zone. There was a greasy frying pan on the brick hearth of the fireplace. There were half empty cups of tea scattered here and there.

"Hi Edward, how's it goin'?" He looked around him, transfixed on the rubble and bombs of cups and frying pans, his eyes wide open. He always had his eyes wide open – these big green eyes, wide open and inquisitive like a kitten's, burning with energy and craving for knowledge. There was a sofa in that sitting room, running the length of the window, adjacent to the wall. I dived over the arm, landing right in the heart of it. "Isn't bed just great, Edward.", I said, from my comfy spot in the sofa, delving my shape into it, losing myself in it. I knew I should be helping him, but I didn't feel like getting up just yet. I knew that once I got up, and active, it would get easier. "I think people should be paid to stay in bed. What do you think, Edward? There'd be no crime, no war... Bedism. It's the way of the future. If you commit crime, your punishment is to stay awake. Then when you go home – exhausted, you can sleep for as long as you want. It's a win-win. Cool, eh?" Normally he partook in a conversation, no matter how silly or inane, but not on this occasion. I didn't really give a second's thought though because Edward was one of these people who, when he got in the rhythm of doing something, it was impossible to break him away from it; he got so absorbed in stuff, only happy when the sink was polished with a silver sheen, or the garden freed from the weeds that choked it, or the coke properly soaked up from the carpet with a sponge. He never got diverted from the particular task he was working on, which was, the majority of the time, a task that involved tidying the mess the rest of us had made.

He was no schmuck, mind you. Lately he'd been making the point he was nobody's maid. I mean he was very kind and he contributed more than his fair share, which he was happy to do, but he did have his limits. That's why the house was so messy the last few weeks. We didn't have time to clean. In the meantime, the Boys, who made all of the mess, had more time to mess. They'd pretty much commandeered the front room, leaving their crap everywhere. They'd finished their course days, if not weeks, earlier. They often fell asleep on the sofa and chair in the front room. When we got up in the morning, having our breakfast and pottering around them, getting ready for lectures, trying not to make noise, they'd ask us to please keep quiet, the cheeky gits, after keeping us up for a lot of the night. The smell of hash around the house lately was so obvious. One weekend, Edward went away on a hiking trip or something, and all that was left in the house for the rest of us to eat was rice and bread, pretty much. We complained about Edward a lot that weekend – how he could have done this, or done that, like at least leave some food in the freezer, like we were used to him doing. We did try keeping a kitty, in the beginning, but it fell apart when the Boys moved in. You know that poem by Rudyard Kipling? Edward reminded me of the boy who keeps his head when people all about him are losing theirs and blaming it on him. He was always in a good mood. We took the kindness from him for granted.

So, it came as a shock when he stood up suddenly and said, "Look at this place! Look at what they've done!" – his once wide open green eyes now vacant black dots, contorted with anger and hatred, and he threw his arms up hopelessly. "They've ruined fucking everything!" Where one saw no redeeming features in a person, Edward normally saw a blizzard of virtues, but now his eyes were hard and cold, like he had been reduced to those people he so often lauded. My tummy swirled with that horrible feeling that something terrible is happening, or about to happen. First, the language: Edward was not a man for curses. Prior to that moment the only ones I heard him say were, 'Damn it!' or 'Gosh!' – not really curses at all. He often went out of his way to rebuke people for swearing. Secondly, he wasn't tidying the room, he was actively messing it up! I sat bolt upright in my seat. He was throwing magazines onto the floor. He looked under the pot with the haggard flower on the shelf besides the neatly aligned books except the books weren't there; they were thrown on the floor. He wasn't just messing up the house, he was thrashing it. The latch on the door of the little cubby hole under the stairs had been busted open. It had been locked for months with a padlock since someone lost the key which, the padlock evidently being too difficult to remove, had caused him to prise open the plating holding the bolt against the door jamb, leaving gnarly screws exposed, and gnarly holes exposed in which screws had been burrowed deep in the wood. I don't know how he managed to do such damage. He was such a contrast to the gregarious, peaceful Edward I had come to know and love. I got up from the sofa and went to look out the window, feigning interest at what was going on outside. I didn't feel safe lying in that vulnerable position on the sofa. My imagination played tricks on me. The only explanation I could think of was that he had been taken over by an alien. What else could it be? A small crack would appear on his forehead. The crack would grow and grow all the way down to his pelvis, leaving a gaping hole. An alien covered in blood and guts would crawl out his stomach and chase after me. It would have been a pretty big alien, too, about six-one. He'd have killed me.

Chapter 2
The Departure

Outside the window it was grey and cloudy and drizzly. It matched the mood. Coming down the twist in the Dublin road was a J.J Kavanagh bus full of students. I expected it to be bursting with energy, thinking it was off to Clare for the Two Mile Inn, but they looked too sedate, most likely off home instead. Right now I felt like going home too. I can't believe I was in the sofa before I noticed it. I was the only one in the house the night before, the last one to go to bed, and it hadn't been that bad, nothing like now.

I ventured by him quickly into the kitchen, happy to see it was still intact. I was happy to see the mop I'd been trying painstakingly to fix the night before was intact too. It was a present we'd all chipped in together for Edward. The guy in the shop said it was high tech with a built-in steamer but it wasn't high tech enough for the handle not to snap when I tried it out on the brown lino kitchen floor to see how good it was, some months earlier, before Edward even had the chance to use it. I'd been planning on fixing it, and the previous night, having no money to do anything else, seemed the opportune time to do so. To fix it, I'd used superglue on the plastic handle, reinforcing it while it dried with a plank of wood strapped on with several tight layers of masking tape.

"Holy shit, man. Relax. Chill out.", I said, when I eventually managed to say something. Relax. Chill out. The completely wrong terminology. Edward's being on the verge of a nervous breakdown, or whatever it was, was largely due to everybody being so "chilled out" the whole time.

"I'm sick of it, sick of it, sick of it."

"Sick of what?"

"Sick of everything. Sick of... tidying peoples' crap."

"Don't be worrying about cleaning up peoples' crap. Although to me it looks like you're messing the place up. We'll give it a quick whip around before we leave, and we'll get our deposits back grand, if that's what you're worried about. Or some of it anyway, after what you've done. You are aware you're making it worse, right?" I alluded to the banjaxed cubby hole door. I noticed his suitcase and rucksack and guitar packed there against the wall. He used to frequently play the guitar for Vanessa, his girlfriend. Some Saturdays or Sundays when the others were out I'd pass by the 2 of them on the sofa and think how cute it was - Vanessa singing along to some INXS song, her voice quiet and gentle by nature but growing in confidence with the accelerating strums and thrums on his guitar strings. He used to sing for us, too, when we were having cups of tea in the evenings, but our lack of reciprocal goodwill over the months made intimate performances like these difficult for him. We were like a bunch of new-born babies - so wrapped up in our comforts, incapable of understanding a universe outside ourselves and, like the baby not being able to comprehend their parent's single minded love and attention - the feeds, the nappy changes, the long rocks to sleep, we took the kindness from Edward for granted.

"You're leaving?" It sounded stupid as soon as I said it, like him departing from the house, like him going away for good, on this last day, with college finished, was the most unusual thing in the world. I just didn't think he'd be leaving right now. Up to that point it just hadn't hit me. "Right now?... I mean that's just... insane. What are you looking for?"

"If you'd come down an hour ago like you said you would, I might have told you."

"This morning? Sure I'm only just up."

"When I called in and asked if you wanted a fry. You just went back to sleep. Have you ever heard of a thing called a phone? They're these little black things that people carry around with them. You should try it sometime." Yes, I remembered it now. It was a bleary haze of a memory but he had indeed called in before I'd even started reading that brochure, and when I looked at my phone, there were 2 missed calls from him, from the previous day.

He put some final objects into his rucksack and clicked the plastic latch into place, his departure imminent, despite the room still being such a mess. I wanted to say something, but I just stood there. I couldn't believe how I was faced with this situation. I wanted to tell him I'd miss him when he was gone. Over the weeks and months our bond of friendship had taken a serious dent. I'd sided with the others, particularly the Boys, over Edward's penchant for cleanliness and tidiness. I could have made life easier for him. I racked my brains through all the fun we'd had together and was sad to acknowledge that in the past month there'd been a dearth of memorable occasions like the ones we had up to then been accustomed to. He'd been studying for exams and I'd been studying for exams, although me studying a lot less than he'd been doing, and we hadn't seen much of each other. In all the time we'd been living together in that house, we hadn't been "out out" together. We'd done stuff during the day, like played kerbs on the road or went to the cinema, but we'd never really gone out together, like going out on a good, mad, gender bender session.

Seeing him there with his bags packed reminds me of a time at my then brother-in-law's wedding, which happened years later. I was 38 at the time, and the wedding was in May. My 39th birthday would be that August, and all of a sudden I realised, just taking a walk in the garden, "Next year I'm going to be 40!" It was like a smack in the face. In an instant I was converted from a child with the world at his feet to an old man. That Sunscreen song... up to then I always pictured myself as one of the kids he's giving advice to, and suddenly, in the garden taking a walk after the wedding ceremony, I'm the man who should be singing the bloody song, to kids. It was a, "You didn't know you had it so good til it's gone" kind of feeling, where nostalgia and unrealised dreams merge into one. It really did hit me with a jolt, realising I'd be 40 so soon, and seeing Edward now, with his bags packed, made me feel the same way. Edward, who'd been living with us for months, who I'd become good friends with, wasn't leaving tomorrow, or the next day, he was leaving right now, right this minute.

"Right, well that's me almost finished around here.", he sighed, and reached for his rucksack, which was against the wall. "Better go. Have to be up early tomorrow."

What I wanted to say was, "Don't go. We can't leave like this." But I was afraid he'd say "No". Damn Pride. It's the root of all things that could happen, but don't. I'm always just noticing a very important occasion when it's gone. I looked from him to the books on the floor and the broken latch. He smiled knowingly, incapable of suppressing a little laugh of old, as infectious as a syren's lyre. "Don't worry. I'll be back tomorrow, early, before Myles gets here. We'll tidy the place up and fix it up as good as new. But now I'm taking all my stuff to Vanessa's, and staying over there. I'll buy screws and a similar latch in the hardware shop. Myles said he'd be over by 1 so if I'm here by 9 that gives us plenty of time to get the place ready. I'm not going to leave it all for you to do." I helped him lift the rucksack so he had both straps over his shoulders. "See you tomorrow." We shook hands awkwardly.

At last I mustered the gumption to say, "Listen, Edward, why don't you stick around a bit longer? Seriously. I mean, you just can't leave now. It's just... wrong." I just kept talking. I don't know why I was so nervous about it. "We'll go out to town tonight! The cinema first, if you want." He loved films. "Bring Vanessa too. What do you think? It's the first day of the holidays! You're going back to America! We might never – " I hated saying the words, "Never see each other again.", so I didn't finish that sentence. "Everybody is going to be out. What do you think? You just can't leave like this. It's such a... it's just such an anti-climax. Go on, Edward. Go out tonight. We'll have feckin' mad craic."

From my first word to the last I could see the tired and worn out shell of Edward's face, brought on by whatever had suddenly happened to him, unbeknownst to me at this stage, gradually transform to one reminiscent of earlier days. It made me happy.

Instead of him going back to all his friends and family in America and telling everybody what a shower of rude and impertinent scumbags lived in Ireland, he'd tell them that we were actually an alright bunch of people. It made me feel good.

But despite that kind flush returning to his pale cheeks and those eyebrows, knitted with suspicion in the form of a sharp V becoming the welcoming ones of former times, and his grey eyes underneath those eyebrows brightening like they were filling with green sparks, and his lips curling upwards once again from a death cold purple to a lively red, he said that it was best he didn't go out, that he still had so much stuff to do, and then all the work to be done the next day, too. "It's not a good idea, man. With all this tidying up to do, and then our car in the evening."

"Just come out for a while then."

"Fuck!" He put his hands to his head, like the pressure of it all was too much for him.

"If they do come back... you tell me, ok? You tell me."

"I will, yeah. Of course I will."

"You've got my phone number? Check you have my number."

"I do, definitely. Sure you just rang me. And all the times we're texting each other when "The Prisoner" is on."

He swept his hands over his face. "I'm so stupid, stupid, stupid."

"I know that. But what happened to you? It's like you're on speed."

"I'm sorry, Kev, I don't mean to be rude but... I can't talk about it. It would just be... I don't know... it would just be disrespectful."

"Ah man, you have to tell me something. You can't just leave me hanging like this." He came up with an analogy to express what he couldn't say plainly. "You remember that time we got that takeaway? The four of us sitting right there?" He pointed at the sofa. I nodded, as I remembered it clearly, a few months earlier. "We were saying the most important thing to do in the Lotto, if you won and all."

"Vinny was saying the most important thing is, make sure you say to the taxman you chipped in for the Lotto ticket with the people you plan giving money to, otherwise they'll have to pay a ton of tax on the money you give to them. It's a way of avoiding tax."

"Tell nobody, not a soul, you'd won, until you'd informed family first of all, is what we said the most important thing is. Just don't go blurting it out to everybody. Likewise, as much as I want to, I can't blurt it out. I have to say it to the people closest to me, first."

"You always have such a fecking roundabout way of saying things. Are you saying you won the Lotto?"

"You think me acting freaked out like this is how I'd be if I won the Lotto? I'd hate to see how I look when I'm happy. No, I didn't win the Lotto. I'm just saying, some things you have to keep secret, until you tell the respective people, and that's why it would be wrong of me to go into detail about this... this... this... Fuck! It would have been perfect. I'd booked tickets for the Opera. A real Italian opera. I have to talk to somebody. Come on. Let's go. I need to talk to someone about it. Let's go to Giovanni's. Vanessa is not going to be happy at all, not one little bit."

Chapter 3

Giovanni's

Giovanni Rossi's was a family run café-restaurant on the Dublin road, next to the Hangman. That was the pub near our house, just through the alley way. You'd have sworn it was Italian with a name like Giovanni's, you'd have expected some sallow skinned beauty with long wavy silky black hair to come running to your table and serve you saying, 'buongiorno!', but all we ever got was "Laura" and the reason we couldn't understand a lot of the words coming out her mouth was because of her indecipherable Limerick accent, not some mellifluous Italian lilt. It was a handy place to go for a quick bite to eat, like a sausage roll or, if you really felt like spoiling yourself, a full Irish breakfast. It was just around the corner from our house which was in the nearby estate, Sycamore Park.

I didn't bother getting dressed, just stuck a hoodie over my T-shirt and went there in my pyjamas. And no, I'm not a pyjama head, walking about in my fluffy cotton pyjamas and slippers all day. I don't think walking around in your pyjamas was a thing back then. It's only more recent. It was an old tracksuit from around the late seventies I'd say, which my Dad used to wear. Respectable enough. They were navy in colour, tight around the thighs and then turned to flares at the bottom, with two white lines running down the side of each leg. Very funky. My mother bought them as a gift for him, back in the day. She was receptionist in the place he used to work. Everybody says there's a striking resemblance between me and my Dad in photos, when he was younger, which is true: we both had heads of thick brown hair, blue eyes and what my aunt calls a 'Roman nose'. Every time she'd call over, she'd comment on that nose.

In any case, Edward would not have allowed me the time to get dressed even if I'd wanted to – he was keen to get going ASAP, tugging me along by the sleeve.

I remember Edward and me found a table in the corner, beside a couple with two young kids and an even younger kid in a buggy. Giovanni's was pretty busy, young parents stopping in for a chat and coffee with other parents after picking up their kids from the local primary school, and stopping in for a break from the drizzle. I looked intently across at Edward and waited for him to start his tale but rather than any words passing through his lips his green eyes shot back at me like arrows, with the unease I had seen for the first time only that very afternoon, like he was expecting me to *guess* what he was about to say.

A waitress approached our table. Not "Laura", for a change, a "Helen", according to her name badge.

"Two beers", I ordered.

"Tut tut tut", Edward said, wagging his finger. I'd forgotten. He once told me he'd have a glass at Christmas with his mum and dad and relatives but that was it. Up to then, I'd never seen him take a drink. He looked at the waitress. "A water for me, please, a full Irish breakfast, and a...?" He looked at me, asking what I wanted.

"How much is a full Irish?" I was calculating whether the meagre few coins in my pocket would cover the total, but Edward, being the kind-hearted and generous person he was, went ahead and ordered for me regardless.

In the intervening period until Helen arrived with our fries I met a friend from my year, Seamus Fogarty, who was buying a pack of crisps at the counter. To say Edward was less than happy I invited him over is an understatement. I could feel his eyes burning into my head, asking how could I be encouraging visits at a time when he needed to discuss matters with me. I pretended I didn't notice. He was like a child in school with his hand up trying to catch the teacher's eye to go to the toilet. It was the right and polite thing to do though, as Seamus was going to Germany for the summer, and I wouldn't be seeing him until the following September.

Seamus headed off when our fries arrived, but not before nicking one of my hash browns. I kicked into a sausage with my fingers. I was pretty hungry. The last time I'd eaten was the previous day. "These sausages are gorgeous.", I said, still not looking up at Edward. "They're as close as you can get to Superquinn sausages." It was an artery-blocking platter of sausages and eggs and rashers and hash browns, beans, mushrooms, black pudding and white pudding and toast... the Real McCoy. "All I need now is a bit of feckin' ketchup. The cardinal sin in so many of these places, Edward, why don't they just feckin' get it.", I said, lowering my voice, as there were little ears around, "A fry is not a fry without fuckin' ketchup." Edward nodded in appreciation of my pain. "You know in the students' canteen they charge you 15 pence a sachet? I bring in my own bottle now. They look at me like *I'm* the stingy one. Freaks. But anyway, Edward... what's this all about? What has you so freaked out? I just want to say first of all, and I know you're sick and blue hearing about this... that I'm sorry about the mop. Seriously, I swear to God" – because he was shaking his head again like the mop was of so minor significance, yet I wanted it off my chest – "me and Vinny had taken it out of the rack, we had money in our hands, we were walking towards the counter to pay for it, and this bloke stops us and does a sales pitch, full on, for like... twenty fecking minutes. We were already set to pay for the bloody thing. Me and Vinny were too nice to say anything. We missed our bus in the end. It's not the mop I'm sorry about. It's that we got you a mop for your birthday. What a shitty present." He said the mop right now was the least of his concerns which hurt my feelings a small bit, as I'd put quite a bit of effort into repairing it the previous evening and I'd given quite a bit of thought to buying it, selecting the one I thought he'd like - a serious machine with a sleek handle and an impressive weight.

"I'm pretty sure the other day I caught the Boys in the act of having sex with each other."

"Sorry what!?"

"You heard me. The Boys." He saw the confusion in my face. "It's true.", he nodded. "I saw it with my two very own eyes. About the mop, just for future reference you need to wait for the steam to get going and then you don't need to push as hard. There's a red light and when that goes green it means the water inside is hot enough –

"Fuck the mop. Sorry, you saw who having sex together?"

"I thought that would get your attention. You heard me. The Boys.", he nodded, loving my gobsmacked, inviting expression. "I saw it with my two very own eyes. Now don't get me wrong." He jolted upright in his seat and raised his palms outwards, to deny making any judgement. "I'm not gonna hold that against them. Whatever they wanna do in their free time is up to them. It just surprised the hell out of me, that's all."

"Fuck off!", I said, louder than I'd have liked, and shut my mouth. A little boy looked at his mum in that questioning way when adults say unsuitable stuff for kids' ears. It was such an outrageous thing to say though! To be sure we were on the same hymn sheet I said, "We're talking about Dave and John, the Boys, the same ones we've been living with for months, having sex together?" He nodded regretfully and reached into his pocket, not breaking his knowing, level gaze from mine. He certainly looked confident in what he was saying. He threw across two sharp cornered squares of plasticky paper at me, the second one first, which I quickly realised were Polaroid photographs. "That's the second one I took, the one that got me caught." It was nothing of the salacious details I'd concocted in my head, I was happy to see. It was mostly the glare of the window. Behind you could make out two figures lying on their backs on the ground, who seemed to be laughing. The top of one of the heads was missing. It was taken in the heat of the moment, not with the laborious, painstaking attention which he usually applied to taking photos.

That was one of the things about Edward. He was sort of eccentric. By today's standards, he'd probably be labelled "autistic" or something. But he wasn't. He was just quirky. Like how he liked the mat perfectly square with the door, or how he liked arranging the cushions propped neatly on the sofa. As for that one, arranging the cushions, it didn't endure too long. After the Boys moved in, if he'd kept it up, he'd have spent the whole day arranging those cushions.

Or how he liked putting his photos on the fridge with his little magnets – lots of photos, and lots of little magnets. Vinny and me talked about that before. Vinny was one of the other lads living with us. There were six of us sharing that house. It was about two weeks after Edward answered the ad we put up in the canteen for a new tenant, way back in October. I'd known Vinny before coming to college. We met Ciaran in the first week. Edward asked if he could put photos on the fridge. We said no problem. We did think it a bit mad though when we found out he carried a camera around campus, and took random photos. In his room he had a proper SLR camera which he used on special occasions but in his bag he often kept a Polaroid camera. We just didn't know anyone else who did that.

Only recently, just a few weeks ago, I found a handful of those Polaroid snaps in my room, ones he'd given me, in the flat where I'm living now, in Dublin. There was a cardboard box full of memorabilia and crap at the end of my bed which I'd been meaning to sort out for years, and they were in there. One of the photos is of a sandwich. That's all it is, a sandwich on the counter-top in the kitchen dated March 3rd 199- on the back. Suddenly I remembered everything. It was rag week, just before they'd be doing the bungee jumps for charity. Vinny, me and Ciaran, we'd stupidly missed the deadline for handing in our sponsorship money. Those photos, and those notes, are the catalyst that got me to write all this. I wish I'd never found them. I'd just walked into the kitchen. The sandwich was there on the counter-top. I told him thanks very much, he shouldn't have. It was for himself obviously. He asked if I wanted it. I asked if he was serious, he said of course he was, he took a snap with his Polaroid and gave me the photo. That's as close as I was getting to that sandwich.

Anyway, we were sitting there in Giovanni's, and he passed me across the table these photos of the Boys, which I was glad to see were less saucy than the picture in my head. "That's it?", I said, acting less than impressed, but secretly delighted. I had gotten to know the Boys well. I'd have felt betrayed, the three of us laughing outrageously at Dave's dirty, sexist jokes the way we did, if it was more than them just getting cosy. It looked like they were helping each other pull off each others' hiking boots.

"They're practically butt naked." That was a huge stretch - you could hardly see what was going on. Even a good quality smart phone of nowadays, with pinch and zoom, wouldn't have captured a good image. It was always dark in that front room. "And the music from inside. It sounded like a satanic ritual or something."

"They're taking off their hoodies. Just getting comfortable, man." It was more camera flash on the window than bare belly. "But anyway, who cares? What the hell makes you think they were having sex? It's just nuts!" I tried to study the photo diligently as he looked so serious on the other side of the table but I felt a sudden urge to laugh - just the sight of him with his Polaroid camera at the window, prancing about taking photos.

"What's so funny?"

"Nothing. Niggaz Wit Attitude, Cop Killer... it's not far off." It was pointless. I tried to smother it with my hands, but laughter spewed out the sides. "Oh man, oh man.", I said, "If Vinny was here... oh man, this is funny. You frightened the life out of me, you know that?"

"I'm glad you find it so amusing."

"The Boys having sex... it's hilarious! You'd sooner see... I don't know... a mouse have sex with an elephant. What the hell were you taking photos for? It's just... insane."

What happened was, the previous afternoon when I was doing exams, he was on his way back from the travel agents in town when he got his bag stolen, which contained his passport and the car rental details and plane tickets and train tickets for Europe they'd bought, and more. They were going travelling around Europe for a few weeks before Edward returned home to America, and Vanessa to Ireland. Or that was the plan. Mostly Italy, but maybe France too, depending on how money went. Edward told me that part was a surprise, so he asked me to keep quiet about it, in case it didn't happen. He said he was taking out his key to enter the house, when he heard this noise from inside. He peeped in the window and when he saw the Boys on the ground he got his camera from his bag and started taking photos. When the Boys looked up, or he thought they looked up, he got flustered and ran away, forgetting his bag on the doorstep. When he remembered and promptly returned to the door, the bag was gone.

"Why were you taking photos?"

His response to this was less than clear-cut, because he was probably embarrassed to tell the precise truth, but from what I could deduce the photos were some sort of face-saving mechanism, where he could go to Myles, our landlord, with "proof" and ask how could he be expected to keep a house clean with these animals sharing with him? Losing our deposits is something Edward would have taken personally. He collected the rent from us every two weeks and called over to Myles' house and handed it directly to him.

"Did you confront them about it? I mean what did you do when your bag was gone?" He said Dave answered the door when he called back 2 minutes later. "'Did you see anything John? No? Sorry, Edward, can't help you.', he said, playing dumb. I know they took it. It's so obvious. I know they fucking took it."

I suggested ringing them. He concurred. It turns out I didn't in fact have the Boys' number, but maybe Vinny, or Ciaran. Ciaran didn't answer. When the phone was ringing for Vinny, Edward changed his tune and said, "No, wait. We need to think this through.", but Vinny picked up just at that second. Edward glanced left and right, like checking Giovanni's for spies dispatched by the Boys. I have to say, the way he was looking at me throughout that phone call, with a mix of relief and respect, made me feel like a seasoned hostage negotiator; ruthlessly efficient, with a touch of compassion, conscious to minimise embarrassment and distress on the part of the aggrieved. Mention of photos and sex would have made the call descend into comedy, or farce. I was succinct and to the point. Edward was about to interject. I put my finger to my lips, urging silence. He sat back, letting me talk. Vinny asked why I was looking for the Boys' number. I looked at Edward, soliciting permission and promising discretion, to which he nodded his assent. I gave the overall gist of the affair, divulging only necessary details - Edward's bag with passports was missing, we suspected the Boys took it, I needed to ring them pronto. He sounded like he was keen to get back to bed. He reminded me to get his and Ciaran's deposit and he'd get it in September or maybe earlier, as he also lived in Dublin.

Unfortunately, Vinny didn't have their number, so my negotiation tactics came to nil in this instance, but Edward had perked up, seeing clearly he had a brother in arms to guide him through these troubled times, and buzzing off my effusive optimism on the matter in general. "You see? They'll definitely be back." Vinny had concurred with my supposition that taking the bag was their idea of a practical joke. "If they're not back today, they'll definitely be back tomorrow. There's no way they're going to lose out on a £50 deposit."

"There's that... and I have something more valuable, too. To them." Before any explanation could be offered to sate my curiosity as to what this might be he'd gestured to Helen at the cash register who took a piece of paper from a pin and made her way over to us and handed it to Edward who paid it and wouldn't accept reimbursement of my paltry smattering of coins when I offered them. I'd hardly mopped the egg yolk on my plate with the last of my sausage and rasher and black and white pudding on my fork when he was getting out of his seat and putting on his leather jacket, a stylish brown one which was the envy of so many of us. He said we had to leave Giovanni's and go to the house. He had to show me this thing he'd stumbled upon. He walked briskly up the Dublin road, me struggling to keep up with him.

It was a real West of Ireland summer day. The rain had stopped. Patches of blue were bursting through the grey clouds which had golden contours and scudded across the sky. A cool breeze was blowing. "The seagull shitting on your head, remember? Ok, at the time, not the ideal thing – a seagull shitting on your head, but looking back on it, it will be the thing you remember most." Man, he was walking fast. It was a conversation we'd had months earlier where basically I said he worried too much. "There's no point worrying about it til tomorrow."

We passed a bus stop and he gave the bus timetable on the stand an aggressive spin. "I'd rather have an elephant shit on my head over what's happened. Really, sometimes I think you know me, and then it infuriates me how you don't at all. You really think I sit around all day worrying about grass grow? You don't have a clue." I let him rattle on, which made me feel surprisingly satisfied, forgoing a rash proclivity for self-defence and instead biting my tongue and focusing on being a good listener, as the occasion demanded. "If it needs to be cut, I'll cut it, but I'm far from Mr. Perfect. 1% perfect, my life is, if even. And you say I'm perfect all the time. We have the car booked for 5, but I can postpone it til Sunday if I have to, I suppose. I should have walked right in that door past them and started turning everything inside out right away. What the hell am I supposed to do though, Kev? We're flying to Italy on Tuesday evening, I have no plane tickets or passports, I've no idea where the Boys are, and I don't even know for sure if they took them. What I found at the house could be turned to my advantage. All I know is, I need to get that bag back. Otherwise, I'm screwed. We just *have* to be in Rome for the 12th. It's not negotiable. We *have* to be there."

Chapter 4

Hash

He headed straight for the old green sofa along the side of the wall, on which I had been lying earlier. He placed both hands on the corner of that heavy sofa and as he prepared to lift it and give it an almighty shove and reveal the dark secret underneath he gave me a look that said, "Prepare yourself for the horror you are about to witness."

I have to admit, I was pretty nervous. What could it be under there? Edward had mentioned satanic music or chants. I couldn't dispel eerie images like a human heart, or a pair of chicken heads. When he pulled the sofa away I saw... a sort of brown package, wrapped in cling film. It didn't take long to realise it was a big block of hash. "I found it a few minutes before you came down earlier.", he said with a sigh, eyeing the hash like it was a harmful reptile that needed to be disposed of.

Years later, when a chef I knew brought me into his kitchen to show me this amazing thing called Wagyu steak, it reminded me of that block of hash. The hash had a more golden appearance, light from the window playing on it in a mysterious way. It had cling film tightly wrapped around it, which gave it a veiny texture, like the steak on the plate had. It was like the prized possession in an art museum, its own spot in the clean rectangle where the sofa had been, unencumbered by the stains and debris on all sides.

Joy and relief gave way to greed. I'm no expert on ounces and pounds – I'm a metrics man through and through, but even at the usual swift rate the Boys smoked, it was a humongous amount. It was about the size of a small kid's shoe sole. I could also see, which lifted my spirits even higher, resting against the wall behind where the sofa had been, two amber coloured, bulging bottles of cider, their caps and shoulders standing proudly over the edge of the crumpled plastic bag that contained them. Labels emblazoned with the familiar "Linden Village" were visible through the thin white plastic of the bag. The Boys drank that cider. They must've forgotten they existed. I ran over and picked up the hash and held it to my nose, cherishing its putty pressure on the tips of my fingers as I looked fondly at the bottles of Linden Village, and relishing the big, long, glorious sniff which brought on, I remember, a touch of pleasant dizziness.

"Ahhh! Better than the smell of napalm in the morning!", I said. Even come the worst case scenario of having to stay in the house alone with no money, by myself, should the Boys not come back, like we'd planned, and Edward not want to go out, it would be far from a boring night, as getting blasted on hash and cider and music, even by yourself, is rarely non-eventful.

Edward wasn't amused. "We shouldn't touch it, Kev, is all I'm saying. We should keep it as evidence." That cracked me up. He was actually considering calling the guards!

"Do you not think the guards have more important shit to do? People are out there getting murdered." Before reverting to a more sombre tone, I took another long sniff, enjoying how it made my head swoon with giddy excitement. "I don't mean to be making light of the whole thing. But you do know who owns it, right?", I said, because he continued to look at me in that disparaging way, for even holding the hash. "It must have slid down the sofa. If the guards got involved, I mean... keeping it as evidence? Really? If they took your passports and the bag, you'll get it back. Maybe just give them a fright back or something, saying you'll call them, instead of actually calling them."

"Did you ever stop to think they could have just given *me* a 'fright' and given my bag back?" He blew an imaginary pile of dust from his hand. "Phoosh! Vanished into thin air, never to be seen again. They know I know. They know I know they have it."

"You checked their room?" He said he did, but we went in again anyway, for one last check, two eyes being better than one, and then we checked upstairs in Vinny and Ciaran's room, just in case.

I always hesitated before going into the Boys' room. It was downstairs, the room next to the kitchen. The door was always slightly ajar. It was always so dark inside, and cold. The door handle was missing. It used to be a box room, before the Boys moved in. Everything was thrown in there by Myles or the previous tenants before the Boys made it their bedroom: old suitcases, chairs with velure coverings worn thin and shiny, framed paintings with mouldy freckled stains on the glass... and it all stayed there after they moved in, too. Two sleeping bags lay on top of two single mattresses on the floor, mattresses which had been in the box room all the time. They'd never put bed sheets on the mattresses, just slept on them like that, in their sleeping bags. Their pillow cases were filled with clothes. A bulb dangled on a long lonely wire in the middle of the ceiling, with no lampshade or anything. A window that didn't let in much light, with the overgrown hedge in front of it, was wet with condensation, and the sad green curtains closed over. There was a radiator behind some of the stuff but the knob was so stiff it was never turned on so it was always cold in there.

We had a quick yet efficient search about the room. We looked at each other, double-checking if there's something we'd missed. There were books on the shelf, there from before the Boys moved in, judging by the titles, which we leafed through, in case tickets or passports or something were hidden between the leaves of them. There was an old wooden set square against the wall. "You want to check under those?", I said. On one of the sleeping bags, there was a pile of Y-fronts and socks. I felt if anybody should be ruffling through the Boys underwear with their fingers, looking for plane tickets, it should be Edward, as the tickets were his. He laughed, saying he was prepared to take the risk and leave it, which made me laugh too.

He collapsed onto the sofa in the front room. His tensed muscles gave way to limpness. His head fell back over the edge of the sofa, like he was at his wits end, trying to think of solutions. Nowadays you'd be WhatsApping, Facebooking, Googling their names and maybe find home addresses and dm them or a landline number, I don't know, but here there was nothing. I couldn't even call to Admin and come up with some spoof that I needed to contact them because the Boys weren't students in the college. If they were students in the college, we might have tried that. Not that they'd have given me that info even if they *were* in the college. We thought of calling to or ringing the college the Boys had been studying in but we didn't know the name of it, or where it was, or even if it was a college. All we knew was it was some woodwork thing. I tried Ciaran again, but there was no answer. I sent him a text telling him to ring me.

"In the ten months or so I've been here, living with you guys, I think I've done my fair share around the house, right? I've cooked some meals, I've lent a helping hand around the place -

"Damn right, man. More than your fair share."

"Thanks Kev. I appreciate that. You're right. What was I even doing taking photos? What was I expecting to achieve? If I'd just been more… I don't know… " He gave a long sigh. It sounded like air leaving a punctured tyre. "I rang the car company and explained what happened. They said as long as I had photo id it would be ok. I don't know. Drive to Galway tomorrow evening and if you're sticking around a bit longer, like a few more days, check in with you maybe, see if there's any sign of them back? We'd have to skip the cliffs of Moher, and high tea in the Great Southern. We were going to go for a jog along Salt Hill. I called back to the travel agents this morning. They said it would be Monday before they got new tickets from Aer Lingus, if they're even *able* to do that. I looked so stupid. *Stupid*. What are you thinking, Kev? You look like you have an idea."

"I'm thinking I can't believe you're going to Galway for only two days and doing all that stuff." I sat on the sofa beside him. I told him he was tying himself in knots by thinking ahead. I was sure the Boys would be back. It was the worry they mightn't have the bag that made it excruciating. I racked my brain to see if there was anything I could do to help. He didn't even look at me, just straight ahead, contemplating all his vanquished plans. It really was a sad sight, to see the Edward I had known and loved, a titan of a man, reduced to this wreck I'd never witnessed before. Like my nephew. He reminded me of my nephew who hurts his knee after he falls off a swing and needs a cuddle. I went into the kitchen to get him a glass of diluted orange, for which he was very grateful. "Here. Take some peanuts." I brought out a dish with the last of the roasted peanuts and handed him the bowl.

"Cheers, Kevin. I really appreciate this. You're a good friend." Part of my bringing out those peanuts was to alleviate his mood, yes, but I'd be lying if I didn't admit there was an ulterior motive. In that story of the frog and the scorpion, I'm the scorpion. I wanted Edward to stick around, I was going to miss him, I wanted to party with him like it was 1999, for him to go wild for once, fostering a final wild memory of this place into the future, but also, I knew he had money, and I had none. As I said, I'm a scumbag.

"Edward?"

"Yes?"

"Eh... I might have to ask you for a small favour."

"Sure."

"Would you be able to lend me some money, do yeh think? Just a few quid. John owes me ten quid. Hopefully he'll be back - and he will be back, believe me, you've no worries there, but if he's not back today, I have nothing, and tonight's the big night. I'm getting a job over the summer so what I can do is pay you back when -

His hand raised slowly with the palm facing outwards like a Cherokee Indian Chief saying, "How!". In his other hand emerged a big hefty brown leather wallet and shortly later from that emerged a more than generous wad of notes. He plucked out a wad of pink notes intermingled with blue ones, which I think totalled 60 quid. For the briefest moment, just watching him, a pang of sadness gripped my heart. Suddenly I was poignantly aware that in front of me sat the greatest of the altruistic and it saddened me immensely that, notwithstanding the fact that humility would not have allowed him accept it, the world could never repay Edward for the generosity he had to offer. The Edward before me wasn't of that chiselled chin and thick fair hair and neither were his eyes lively and glowing with that eternal energy. All I could picture, in my mind's eye, was him old and frail, a beautiful creature on the verge of extinction. It morphed into that of my neighbour's old dog. Sally was her name. She belonged to my sister's best friend, Deirdre Keogh. We used to all take her out for walks together - I mean Caoimhe – my sister, Deirdre and me, and throw tennis balls for Sally to fetch. For years later when I'd be at home in my folks' house in Dublin just chilling out there in front of the TV I'd see Sally walking up the driveway and into our front garden. She'd sit there on the grass and stare in the window, staring vacantly. I'd wave, and she wouldn't respond. She wouldn't wag her tail or jump like the younger dog she was. If you threw a tennis ball she probably wouldn't even see it. Yet somewhere in that mind that was once sharp and fresh and whose body was young and agile I'm sure there were memories of us taking her out for walks through the estates and throwing balls in the field. Some things you just don't forget.

"Edward." I said to Sally. "I can't take all that. It's a... it's an abuse of hospitality." Torn between guilt in the face of Edward's unconditional kindness on one hand, and the glorious chunk of cash in his other hand, I could sense my ruthless instinct ratcheting up to the next level, overshadowing the guilt. Normally I'd have been delighted with a tenner. "40 is more than enough." I soon wished I'd taken the 60.

The notes in his hand which he'd plucked out went back to join the more numerous quantity of his plump wallet. "I've done all my pound spending, apart from a few presents. When you get your job you can post it out to me. And besides, I do have something to celebrate, in spite of all that's happened."

I was so engrossed with my new fortune between my fingers which would not only sustain me on this current night but several more to follow that it took me longer than normal to notice that last sentence, how it was left hanging in the air like a ripe fruit asking to be picked. Then I asked the question he was dying to hear. "What do you have to celebrate?"

"Vanessa's coming to the States for the Summer."

I nearly dropped the money out of my hand when he said that. I was thrilled for him. It would have been a shame for it not to progress to the next level between them. They were a natural team. I could see that ever since a day in December one Saturday afternoon when the 3 of us went to the Hangman for a few games of pool. Vanessa and Edward had common lectures together. They met each other early in September. They were both members of the Irish instruments or Music society and they remarked how they were in the same class and from there magic happened. He kept hiding under the table, behind the pocket she was aiming for. What a distraction. He kept sticking his head up, peeping over the edge when she was taking her shot. He was annoying me, and I wasn't even playing. She did the same to him. I saw that being able to laugh together is so important in a relationship. He was all competitive against me, mind you. He made it like a personal battle between Ireland and America. If I moved the white ball a tiny bit by accident he'd insist on two shots.

If Edward had been worried about the future state of play between the two of them, going their separate ways and not seeing each other again, he did a good job of hiding it. The perils of a long distance relationship, the seas that would soon divide them, seemed to be the furthest thing from his mind. I thought as the months rolled on into Summer and imminent departure loomed he'd be a bit disagreeable, or worried. Sometimes, when sitting there and reading something on the sofa, I'd keep my head still but move my eyes to where he was sitting to judge any involuntary tick or sigh that might be a mark of irritability, but there were none; every day seemed to roll blithely into the next. One day, in early May, I felt comfortable enough to ask what the story was between them, going forwards. We were having a laugh. He showed me the picture next to the recipe of a "Jerk salad", with Caesar sauce. He just smiled, saying it would work itself out. Outside the times when he was justified in being upset or annoyed, like if we took food from the fridge that was labelled his or we'd borrowed stuff that was his and left it lying around, he remained his usual, chirpy self. Until today, there had been no signals of emotional upheaval; he maintained that goodwill that was so common to him, like the prospect of him and Vanessa departing for good was no bother to him at all.

"That's fantastic news! That is massive."

"I know. It's awesome. Sinead and Meghan are going to Boston next week. Vanessa's going to join 'em in the end of June. She was pretty smashed after this European trip but they'll get jobs in Boston no problem. Her parents gave her a loan. She bought her tickets yesterday too. Luckily she held on to those ones herself. The 29th. She'll meet my parents."

I remember now the sister of a French boy I went on exchange with in transition year giving me a roll of sellotape for some of the stuff I was bringing back to Ireland. I found her letters in that box at the end of my bed I told you about, with those old photos from Edward, and the notes I made that night. There were lots of things in there. It was a trove of things I'd forgotten existed. There were 3 letters from her, each one thinner than the preceding one that had arrived. The envelopes were a dull pink. Chloe was her name. One of them was ripped the length of the top, as were some of the pages inside, like I couldn't open it fast enough. Reading them again, in the days following my newly discovered relics in the box, decades after I'd first received them, decades after all this is happening here with Edward - at which stage Chloe was probably already vanishing from my mind, I felt a faint deja-vu kind of feeling. I sensed fingers trembling with excitement at how she'd been holding the same pages I was holding. The paper, 30 odd years older, was softer than it had been. Maybe it had been fancy paper. There was only the smell of paper, but it was old.

If I'd had to take a bet I'd have said Edward and Vanessa would go the same way me and Chloe went. When I received those letters, I was unstoppable; no doubt writing back straight away with the pen shaking in my hand, the words coming out in torrents on the page. I would have written at the desk in my room under the warm glow of a directional lamp, which I brought with me to my flat and still have today. Gradually though, the big bad world does its work on you. The voyage you'd make through oceans to be with the one you love is crushed by realities of long distances and school starting again. The precipice of an ardent future with your soulmate becomes flat and dull. The letters get shorter, the intervals between them longer. You tell yourself, as it looks like me and Chloe did after the third letter, that you're young, every day is a new adventure. A comfortable numbness sets in. All good things come to an end.

When he told me Vanessa was going to America, the image of them holding hands on some street in Boston took a solid form. It was harder then, too, I think. There were no instant texts. Landline calls were so expensive. You'd hear from them once a week, if even, not a thousand times a week.

"So, you're coming out to celebrate tonight then? You might as well stick around and make the most of it." The moment was ripe again to cajole him to hang around a bit longer. He leaned forwards on the sofa. I could detect the beginning of the return to his typical, cheerful self.

"I'm staying in Vanessa's tonight.", he said, calculating the mess in the room that needed to be tidied. He looked up at me, wide-eyed. "How about I cook a meal for the three of us – you, me and Vanessa? In her place. A coconut curry."

It sounded delicious but the three of us sitting around a candle lit dinner wasn't the valedictory send-off of madness I had in mind, at all. I wanted to *really* go out and party, rather than staying in for a meal. Edward noticed because straight away he said, "Or else we can go to a nightclub or something, if you want. I suppose it is important to make the most out of your last night in a place."

"Now you're talking!"

"I'll have to ask Vanessa about this." He appeared doubtful, rubbing his chin with his thumb and drumming his lips with the tip of his forefinger and index finger. "I'll talk to her. We just have to get up so early. I'll have to tell her everything that's happened, anyway." He nodded his head reassuringly. He was growing more confident that she would be accepting of the new arrangements. "Vanessa knows we're going to Italy but no idea what's lined up... or *had* lined up. You're right, the Boys are gonna be back. They'll have looked inside and seen it's important. They're annoying, but they're not evil. They'll know it's important. Jesus, I hope they've looked in the bag. You think they did? Imagine they didn't even look inside the bag. Their deposits though. They'll be back for their deposits." He peered towards the fireplace with a wistful smile on his face. "She says she has to know where we're going so she'll know what to pack. How cute. I told her I'd pack for her. You should have seen her face. We're staying in her parents house Monday night and then onwards to the airport. Yes, she'll understand. She'll be on for going out." He looked at me. "There's this nightclub I've heard so much about. Chez Bobby's. You ever hear of it?"

I told him I had indeed heard of it. It was up by the roundabout closer to town, near Dunnes Stores.

"We could go there – provided it's ok with Vanessa, of course.", he said. "What do you think?"

"Sounds good to me!"

"It will be *awesome!*"

His eyes widened and a broad smile followed. Then he started clicking his fingers as if there was an inaudible beat coming from somewhere. "You hear that?", he asked, with a hand cocked behind his ear. "I hear it and I like it!" The old Edward was back! I joined in with him, clicking my fingers too, and before I knew it, both of us were dancing around the room, full on, with no music playing or anything. It was just one of those moments. We both recognised that this sudden turn of events, this prolonged stay, was a real bonus, something that may easily have passed by, our last memories of each other being sour ones, and we were grateful that it was happening.

"Ok.", he said at last. He straightened himself up. He was out of breath, as was I. We'd been dancing around a good bit, really getting into it. "So, I'll call to Vanessa, put the changed plans by her, and then we hit the town." He nodded his head, staring into space, playing her response over in his mind. He bit his lower lip, the way he often did when he was concentrating on something. "Space", in this instance, was a spot on the wall by my head. He smiled as if an image of Vanessa were projected on this part of the wall. I tried to picture what he was thinking. Sometimes, when Vanessa was over in the house and he wanted something from her, and she said no, he'd lean over her on the sofa with both hands raised. She'd recoil at the other end of the sofa. He'd wiggle his fingers and ask her again. She'd say no but she'd struggle to hold in the laughter. He'd tickle her in the ribs, the tummy, the neck – everywhere, and finally she'd give in.

He nodded his head more fervently, with a growing certainty that her response would be a positive one. He looked at his watch and said he'd be back to the house at around four. He gave me a nudge on the shoulder and soon later he started to proceed out the door.

Edward Brophy. What a character. He could have picked any university in the world for that year of study, and by good grace and fortune he came to Limerick. In spite of the hassles, the being taken for granted, he had a good time in Ireland overall. He'd never have met Vanessa if he hadn't come here. He had such an optimistic streak, he'd have been happy anywhere.

Chapter 5

The Boys

When he was gone I went about tidying up the house, so we'd at least get some of our deposit back from our landlord, Myles. He was always looking for an excuse, that fella. Looking mournfully at the walls, "Oh those are going to need to be repainted", or the carpet, "Oh that's terribly worn down, that'll cost a hundred pounds." He was a clever, quite devious person. He capitalised on Edward's benevolence for his own gains. Like the way of the boiling frog theory, he gave Edward jobs to do, which he'd praise him for doing, and the way Edward's mind worked - being naturally thrilled he was making people happy, soon he was doing lots of stuff, and was honoured to do them, too. From the moment Edward offered to drop the money over to his father's house rather than Myles having to make the walk over to our house to fetch it himself, which was a chore, some of us having the rent, some not, he knew things would go swimmingly.

I scoured the cooker and oven with brillo pads. Under the sink, in the cupboard, I found a pint glass full with gunk, or treacle. I didn't know what it was at first, but then I remembered John used a pint glass in a filtering operation or something on his car a few weeks earlier. Edward told him not to pour it down the sink, in case he blocked it, so John stored it in the cupboard. I poured it in a plastic bag and then into the bin and cleared out the fridge. I put away the pots and pans on the rack beside the sink. The floor needed a clean. I put the electric mop to the test. The upper part of the handle, which had snapped, stayed stuck to the main body of the mop, I was glad to see, when I unwound the masking tape, very slowly, pressing the piece of wood tight against the handle with my other hand as I did so. I took a deep breath and pushed with a small bit of pressure which worked ok, but then, to my disgust, it snapped in the same spot where the glue was when I was in the middle of using it. I got down on my hands and knees and pushed the steamer along the floor. The plug was connected to the steamer part, so that worked. I took the superglue out of the drawer and threw it in the bin with a vengeance. I was going to put the mop in the big bin outside, but thought I'd better ask Edward. The fridge was cleared off of photos now, I'd noticed, only the magnets there, all the photos I tried to recall I'm sure packed away in the luggage Edward would be bringing home with him.

 When I'd finished the kitchen, I surveyed it all from the door with a sweat on my brow. I was pretty proud of myself. Edward would be happy. Myles would have struggled to find a reason to not give us our full deposit back - based on the kitchen. As for the TV room, that was another matter. He'd have kept our full deposit and asked for more. I'd tackle the front room later, not just now. I'd go for a quick power nap, first. Before going upstairs I looked at the door into the Boys' room, feeling sad. It was occurring to me that perhaps they mightn't be coming back after all. Maybe they'd forgotten their deposit. The Boys were doing a cert rather than a degree so they were finished now, gone for good, not coming back in September. I'd see Vinny and Ciaran, but not the Boys. When I was walking up the stairs which I'd been up a million times I sensed an echo I'd never noticed before. Perhaps it's because the room was emptied now of so much stuff, and emptied of people, too, who'd once filled it with joy. I tried to dispel silly notions that they'd done a runner with the money they owed me. We'd become friends. We'd never even said bye. We got on quite well. Or at least I thought we did.

I couldn't help but smile and shake my head fondly on the bottles of cider I'd discovered by the wall. "Linden Village" had become that most important staple of household grocery items, the centre of so many good laughs together. I was thinking how the name "Linden Village" had transformed into "Village Idiot". I still remember the night it started, in the driveway in John's old beat up Volvo, the 5 of us just back from the off-licence. John called it "Little Village" by accident, to much laughter by the rest of us, which made him angry at first, but soon he was laughing with us. The trajectory of names continued, "Village Idiot" cider being the one that stuck.

The next thing I knew, I was lying in bed, and my bedroom door kicked open like it was being kicked off its hinges. The sight of the two people at the entrance of my door, staring down at me, was hard to comprehend. It was the Boys!

Dave came over with a big smile on his face - he always had this sort of devious smile - and he sat on the side of my bed.

John stayed standing there against the door. He pointed his finger at me and started to laugh hysterically.

"This place looks like a bomb hit it 'n' shit.", he said, "dirty cacks 'n' shit all over the place, you lazy bollox."

I hadn't completely packed yet so there were clothes and stuff strewn around my room. Not as bad as he was making out though.

"3 in the feckin' afternoon 'n' shit. We haven't slept in 3 feckin' days."

I didn't like the way he said hello, and perhaps being crankier than I would have been had I not been woken up so abruptly, I leaned on my elbow and said, "You're not exactly Mr Prim and Proper yourself, with that ratty old green coat you haven't taken off in 6 months." - he always wore this sort of green army jacket, John did, with hot rock holes or moth holes on the sleeves. "When's the last time you had a fuckin' shave? I don't remember seeing you walk into that bathroom at all - not once - since you moved in with us."

In my waking stupor I'd forgotten how touchy he could be.

"What's with my personal life 'n' shit, huh?", he said.

He had an inferiority complex, John did. You'd tell a story and he'd tell one twice as crazy. Most of the time it *was* twice as crazy - and true, too, but he still had an inferiority complex. Dave approached and gave my leg a slap through the duvet. "Wake up, man.", he said. He peered out the window over my bedhead, at students streaming by the house.

"The Kremlin is going to be mobbed tonight, lads. It's going to be great craic."

"That's why you should hurry up and get dressed."

You'd have sworn they were the most organised and punctual people in the world.

"How come you're back so late anyway? Where were you yesterday?"

"Got caught up. Where's Edward?"

"He'll be back later."

Edward. The word elicited a growl from somewhere in their throats. "What the hell happened your eye?'", I said to John. He had a big black eye.

"Playin' hurling 'n' shit. Got hit with the sliotar." He rolled ten pounds into a ball and tossed it at me. Everybody who had a black eye in that neck of the woods, you could guarantee it's because they got hit in the face with a sliotar.

The Boys were both twenty-one, two years older than me. Dave was from Cloughjordan and John was from Borrisokane. I'm not surprised Edward was out of the house so often. If we'd been living with them any longer, we'd probably all have moved out. I'm not saying they weren't nice blokes or anything - they were, they were alright - but they were just a bit on the dirty side, that's all I'm saying. They were crude, too. That was the funny thing about them, half the time. Especially Dave, he was the crudest. To show how crude he was, take this good friend of Edward's, Fiona Lynch, who used to call round to the house quite often. She was one of Edward's best friends, and the whole time she'd be talking about study and economics to Edward beside the big red fire, drinking tea by the pot load and eating toast, both of them worried about exams, Dave would be talking about something ten times cruder, like rods and arses or something. Fiona quit calling round to the house about two weeks after the Boys moved in.

John and Dave both got up at the same time every morning, they both had their corn flakes and their pint of tea together every morning, and then they both headed off to work in John's rusty grey Volvo 740 every morning. You'd never see them one without the other. They were either both in the house... or they both weren't. Then, when they'd come back from their day's work - I'm not sure what they were at - nobody was; some FÁS course or other - you'd find them relaxing on the sofa and chair in the front room, watching t.v and smoking joints and drinking tea or Linden Village, with the curtains drawn. On warmer days, they'd be in their jocks and t-shirts. Even if it was the sunniest day of the year, the curtains would be drawn. Sometimes you would see them in the open fresh air. Just outside the door, hitting a tennis ball to each other with hurleys. Both of them in their slippers. That's all they ever did - smoking and drinking and watching t.v and playing hurling. What a great life, I can say now with the benefit of my years. It's because they were always together we treated them as if they were just one person. If we wanted to know where they were, we wouldn't ask, "Where are Dave and John?". We'd say, "Where's the Boys?"

Right now, Dave was all crouched forward on the side of my bed, and he was platting or plaiting his fringe. He had quite a long, grey fringe. His hair was black, but his fringe was completely grey, for some reason. He didn't dye it, either. Anyway, it was just when he was looking at me with that madman smile, something dawned on me. Right that second. Ever since the Boys moved in, Vinny and myself were trying to figure out what cartoon character Dave looked like. We both had the same character on our minds alright - it was some dog character - but we just couldn't figure out the dog's name. It just snapped right there, just when Dave had his fringe platted up. It was Muttley. Muttley the dog. Dave was small and chubby, and he had a strong, lower protruding jaw, like Muttley. His mouth was frozen in a grin, regardless of whether he was smiling or not. He often had a cigarette pinned behind his ear. He had small ears, yet the cigarette never fell. He was a very kind person, in his own way. He wouldn't be the first to offer you something if he was making it for himself, a bowl of Pot Noodle or a cup of tea, but if you asked him to make you one, he'd do it. That mightn't sound like much – sticking you on a cup of tea when he's making one for himself anyway, and you having to ask for it, but he was reliable, that's what I'm saying. If you asked him a favour, he'd do it. You'd be waiting a while, but he'd do it eventually. He had this self-destructive nature. That's what was so intriguing, so appealing about him. I sometimes thought of him as some demented maniac sitting on a cliff overlooking a burning city. He'd be laughing out loud and inching closer and closer off the edge of the cliff. He got a thrill from knowing he could jump over any time, but he decided to stay sitting there, enjoying the view.

    Dave had these very blue eyes. They looked even bluer than they were because his face was so dirty. It was like looking at diamonds in a coal bin. He had a way of looking at you that made you feel he was disappointed in what he was about to hear. It was only for a split second. You'd wonder about it afterwards, questioning if you'd said something foolish. It was like he feared it could be a trap he was walking into. He had a hilariously cutting wit, although not such fun when you were on the end of it. He was softly spoken, rarely raising his voice, which made his humour all the more effective. John was taller than both of us. He was about two inches taller than me. I'm five foot nine - or so I tell myself. John was a very nervous bloke. You wouldn't have thought so straight away, but he was. I mean, whenever there was someone in the room with him - someone he didn't know - he'd be fidgeting the whole time; tapping the arm on the sofa with his fingers, or the ground with his feet. He'd be doing that the whole time. You wouldn't notice it right away. It's funny. You only realise these things when you're living with somebody.

John opened the zip on one of the pockets on the arm of his army jacket and took out what looked like a small white square. He passed it to Dave. He held the square by the edge. A line suddenly dropped from the little square. For a while I thought it would spring back up like a yoyo but it stayed down. It was a strip of something like blotting paper divided into lots of squares. Dave detached a square from the strip and leaned over me in my bed - on top of me, it felt like - and raised it closer to me in the palm of his hand.

"Go on, Kev, take it.", he said. I took it by the edge and studied it. There was a picture of a penguin. I don't know what it was - if it was just the expression on Dave's face or the way he talked in that spooky low voice or the three of us crammed together in such a small room, but I didn't feel like doing it anymore. We'd been planning it for days and now, with it only a few inches away, the last thing I felt like doing was swallowing it. It was like being dared to jump across a narrow crevasse. So easy to do, yet so easy to fall into, I don't know.

"You won't know where you are after one of those.", John said in a way that made me even less enamoured with the idea and which made Dave laugh. It was one of those laughs that frequently turns into a coughing fit, as it did now. There was a pint of water on my bedside table and he took a gulp and then looked at the glass. Maybe it was too warm. It was there for a few days. "Get him a fresh glass.", John said. He's standing at the door, beside the bathroom. I'm in bed. And he tells me to get the water. If he didn't smoke so much, he probably wouldn't have coughed like that. The Boys smoked like troopers.

He recovered soon enough, as he always did, and swallowed one of the acid tabs himself. He passed one to John and he swallowed it, too. They both stared back at me. With grins on their faces. I was the only person left to do some swallowing. I weighed my commitment to Edward against indulgent pleasure seeking. We had come a long way together, me and Edward. We deserved one last hurrah together. The small times we had left together were to be cherished and what we'd done would resonate forever but on the other hand... the Boys! The sun came in the window behind my bed. Its rays invigorated everything in the room. Their eyes yearned and pleaded with me to join them on the trip ahead. Dave's clothes and cheeks were tinted with an orange hue. John was cheerful and fresh faced with a childlike grin. They looked like little kids, more clean and innocent and joyful than they really were. How happy I'd have been to caress it between my thumb and forefinger and let it tempt me forever with its charms. Who was I to squander this night, which we'd talked about and looked forwards to? Edward would understand. In the long run, his enduring memory when he got home to America would be of me as a decent person, not some scumbag who didn't turn up at a nightclub. The nub of the matter boiled down to this: what would be the most craic on this last night of nights, mayhem with the Boys or the club with Edward?

The thought process was shattered with Dave's voice. "Are you going to sit there all day looking at it or are you going to swallow the fucking thing?"

I swallowed it. It happened so quickly. Forbearance got lost in the blinding light. Nobody said anything for a while. They both just stared at me in bed.

"Well done, Kev, welcome to the club.", Dave said.

"Okay, we're gonna grab something to eat. Haven't eaten since yesterday", they said. And then they were gone.

Chapter 6
The Front Room

Obviously, shortly after the Boys left me in my room, I ran down after them, because I knew Edward would be home soon. I wasn't crazy at the idea of the three of them being together, alone. In fact, nothing terrified me more.

John was sitting on the sofa and Dave was sitting in his chair, both of them eating baked beans from the microwave on toast. Everybody called it his chair, a comfortable, nondescript armchair that used to be green whose arms were worn down and sunk a mile deep, which made it all the more comfortable, as he was the only person who ever sat in it. We were just so used to seeing him there the whole time. We heard Edward's key rattle in the door. He came in from the porch, Vanessa by his side. Dave threw his eyes to heaven at that instant, annoyed his peace was broken. At the sight of the shadows before him, Edward froze like a hare in headlights. He was as stunned as I'd been to see them. He went upstairs, followed by Vanessa. There's no way she was going to hang around in that room without Edward and just the Boys there, especially if Edward had told her about the incident with the plane tickets, as he said he would. "Would anybody like a drink?", I said. I told the Boys about the Linden Village I'd found and they agreed now was the opportune time to crack into it.

I went into the kitchen and poured three glasses. The Boys practically knocked it back in one fell swoop. "Maybe I should bring the whole bloody fridge into the room.", I said. I went to get them a refill when the kitchen door opened again. Edward was standing there, blocking the door, inert as stone. His piercing green deep-set eyes fastened on my own. He closed the door with his foot. His hands were behind his back, like he was concealing a weapon. He stepped closer.

To my relief what followed were words for my ears rather than blows to my head. His hands emerged from behind his back. He was holding a small white metal box, with a keyhole in front, like a safe would have, which I had seen before in his room. He held the box in front of me.

"What the hell is this?"

He knew damn well I was very eager to find out, but rather than tell me straight away, he indulged in one of his few, annoying traits. He grinned, for ages, refraining from telling me. "What the hell is in there? Can I have a look?" They say travel to a destination is half the holiday, or anticipation of an event is as much fun as the event itself and, likewise, Edward wanted to preserve the suspense, he wanted to withhold his big secret for a bit longer. "It's the hash, isn't it? The block of hash from earlier?" Any imbecile could tell from his expression that's what it was. He handed it over. It was locked with the key. It made a muffled rattle when you shook it. It had the same weight, and sound. "You went into my room and got it without asking me?" It didn't bother me as much as I was letting on. I was enjoying looking at him squirm.

"Well I mean I..." He had an embarrassed look on his face, choking on his words. "The Boys... the Boys..."

"The Boys... the Boys...", I mimicked, "I can't believe you went into my room without asking me.", I said, shaking my head, feigning insult.

"The drawer wasn't locked. It was wide open. If I'd called you up it would have been so obvious... we're always going into one another's rooms! The Boys would have –

"It's fine, Edward, it's fine." I'd had my fun. All I had in that drawer anyway was loose change and spare pens, pretty much. And a big block of hash.

"What's with the box?"

He glanced over his shoulder in case of being overheard – totally unnecessary, he'd already been speaking quietly and he'd closed the kitchen door – nobody could hear us. "You didn't say anything to them about my bag, did you?"

I told him I hadn't, that I thought it best he deal with it rather than me mess it up.

"Can you help me with something? A huge favour?"

He'd given me a ton of money, we'd given him a ton of abuse over the months, and I said, "Of course, Edward. Anything at all."

"I propose we play a Good cop Bad cop strategy. Me and Vanessa will be, 'look outs'. I will focus on Dave. Dave is more shrewd. On my signal you get the box and hold it clearly so the Boys can see what's inside. When I start the interrogation -

"Interrogation?" It was the craziest good cop bad cop strategy I'd ever heard. I was regretting saying I'd do him a favour. "I'll do it on one condition. Instead of all this fancy pantsy signal crap, just say, 'Kevin, can you get the white box in the kitchen, on top of the fridge?', or wherever it is. I'll say, 'Eh... ok', like I'm only a casual partaker in the whole thing, which I am, because I don't want to make it look like I'm out to trap them, I'll hand you the box, and you open it."

"Ok then. You get the box and give it to me. Can you do that? When they see what's inside, I think that's gonna rattle them." I gave him my word. He made a fist and nudged me on the shoulder, took the box from me, put it on top of the fridge, and we went back to the front room to join the Boys. Vanessa came back down the stairs when she heard us coming out of the kitchen.

"So, lads, you have a good few days, yeah?", I said, trying to make small talk. I turned on the teli, its low din giving an air of reassurance instead of a cold, numbing silence. The alien could return. It could get nasty. I opened the curtains to let in more light. "Edward, Vanessa, take a seat there." I pointed at the empty space beside John in the sofa, knowing it was unlikely to be filled. They stayed by the bannisters.

"Finished the exams yesterday. French. Last one."

"Yeah? How did it go?"

"I made a balls of it. Fucked up."

"We're all fucked up.", John said.

"Everybody's fucked. We're all doomed. Life's a bitch.", Dave said. They said that sort of thing a lot, the Boys did.

Things went quiet. I glanced at Edward. He kept crunching his ice cubes. I regretted putting them in. He in turn was looking at the Boys. He was probably thinking what a dope he was for having agreed to Ciaran's proposal all those months ago. We were either all in, or it wasn't happening. That was the agreement. In a nutshell, Ciaran had a friend who had two friends thinking of doing a course in Limerick, they were looking for accommodation, we had a spare room downstairs, the rent would be cheaper with more tenants... we were either all in, or we were all out, and the four of us chose in.

Dave asked, without a hint of sarcasm or irony, "So, Edward, Vanessa, are you looking forward to the Italian holiday then, huh? Everything arranged?" John couldn't resist a chuckle at that comment. The Boys had arguments occasionally but most of the time he considered Dave a comic extraordinaire, chuckling at every joke every step of the way. "A very strange thing happened the other day, Kev.", Dave continued, still in his jaunty tone. "Me and John were chilling and some dude came right up to the window and started taking photos. Can you imagine? Some dude taking photos of us. We have our own feckin' Paparazzi crew. Vanessa, if you see me or John in 'Hello' or 'Vogue' or one of those magazines, let us know, will you?" John was slapping his legs and rocking hysterically. Nothing thrilled him more than the quick wit of the man in the chair beside him, who he had the honour of calling his best friend. In his mind Dave's prodigious talent and battering comebacks would wilt the most hardened of comedians, reducing them to bumbling wrecks.

Edward wasn't laughing at all. He moved closer to Vanessa, practically hiding behind her, which made the Boys laugh even more.

"Ok, so it sounds pretty obvious you took my bag."

"What bag?" Another yelp from John.

"Look, I can't force you guys to do anything. As with everything else over the months, all I can do is ask. I will... pay you for the bag back. A hundred quid. Two hundred quid. Keep the plane tickets if you want. I just need the rest of that bag intact."

"Where did you say it is you're going?", John said, his interest suddenly piqued.

"Italy."

"Italy. Huh." Disdain dripped from his lips, probably picturing all these swarthy Italians doing their fancy things, eating their fancy paninis... He said out of the blue, "You might be loaded, man, but you haven't lived." We looked at him. He was jealous of Edward, how well travelled he was, with his pretty girlfriend. We were all jealous of him, but probably John is the only one who'd ever say anything. He took a lung-ripping drag of his smoke and stood up and paced around the room in his typical, provocative manner, fetched the hurl by the door and embarked on his trip down memory lane. He started by tapping the tennis ball back and forth against the wall, a bit angry at first, but soon his tone lightened. "Some people think money is the be all and end all of everything. It's not. Most people with money are miserable – that's a statistical fact. Poor people are the happiest in the world. I hate money. When I was a kid, we had loads of money. I used to do plastering with Da. He used to run his own business. Years ago. I was his helper. His apprentice 'n' shit. We were loaded, man. Going to Kerry in the caravan every summer. He'd be up the ladder and I'd hand him the tools 'n' shit 'n' mixin' cement and polyfiller. Ah, yes, those were the days."

A dimple formed in one cheek and then the other and a delicate smile extended between them, stretching bigger and broader the more vivid the memories of halcyon days became. "The auld lad was a master of the craft. Himself and Mr Rooney, a part-time taxi driver down the road, used to work together. You remember Jo Jo Rooney, Dave?"

Dave chuckled. "How could I forget."

"Years ago one of the restaurants they did in the town won best prize for innovation, some shit like that. Straight after Dessie was born Mr Rooney drove all us kids into the hospital to visit Ma and the baby. He kept saying to us, 'Now, are you all ready to visit baby George?'. Baby hadn't even been named yet. When we were getting into the taxi he counted us on his fingers and said, '1, 2, 3, 4, 5, 6 – ok, everybody in'. We said back, 'No! There's only five of us.' He kept counting six and we shouted back 'five!'. Gas man. Good sense of humour. I saw Jo Jo at the garage years later and he asked me how 'George' was getting on. It took me a while to twig what he was talking about. Poor old Mr Rooney."

"Anyway" he continued, snapping back to life. "the auld lad would be up the ladder and I'd be handing him bits and pieces when he needed them, learning from experience 'n' shit. It was an A grade reputation we got for ourselves, travellin' the length and breadth of the country from town to town. Word spread through the counties like wild fire 'n' shit, the father and son team." The funny thing with John, you always knew how his stories would end up. "Some people are born great. Others have greatness thrust upon them. I'm a bit of both.", he said, totally serious, looking vaguely out the window, contemplating the vast breath of his life's achievements, lost in lofty thoughts. His chin was raised proudly and solemnly like the sun was doing a dance in the sky just for him. He always ended up being the superstar. His Dad wasn't even in the story anymore.

A yelping sound from someone else's mouth wrenched him from his happy cocoon of glorious days past. It was from Edward. John glared at him.

"Are you laughing?"

"No." He tried to suppress what came out his mouth which made the yelps and yowls more scathing and insulting than had he let them come out naturally. Tears welled in his eyes. A yelp like a kicked dog escaped his mouth. It was like he'd been told a dirty joke and was trying not to laugh in case the teacher made him reveal to all what was so funny.

It was a charade that fooled nobody. His secret was out. "I'm sorry. I know, I shouldn't. Oh man, I just can't." Vanessa poked him to stop. "The greatest architect that ever lived. How can you make a definitive statement like that?"

"I didn't say I was the greatest. I said I'm a bit of both. Don't talk to me about feckin' derivatives." Vanessa stepped in. "Please, there's no reason we can't sort this out as adults. We can all come out of this situation better than how we came into it."

Edward went to the shelf by the TV and shook it. "Fixing stuff the length and breadth of the country, eh? Look." It wobbled like mad. John had put it up a few months earlier. "You can't even fix a shelf. You should have used those... what do you call them... those things that reinforce the screws in the wall."

"You're a handyman 'n' shit now too, yeah?", John chortled derisively. "Look at you, hiding behind your girlfriend. If she was blonde she'd be a dumb blonde. If you can find something better than screws to hold up a shelf, you'll be a rich man.", he said, looking at Dave and waiting for him to return an affirmative laugh of his own, in acknowledgement of having said something extremely wise.

"Rawl plugs.", Vanessa said.

"Kevin, would you be able to get me a small white box in the kitchen please? On top of the fridge?"

"Sure.", I said. I came back and handed him the little white metal box. He stepped into the middle of the room and held the box in his hands in front of Dave, horizontal with his line of vision, to draw his complete attention to it.

"What's in the box?"

"Oh, you will see. You will see." His eyes never left Dave's, like savouring the shock he was about to cause in the one who'd ridiculed him for months. A worried countenance washed over John's face. He covered his mouth with his hand and leaned over on the sofa and whispered in Dave's ear, and then he was worried, too.

Edward reached for the key to open the lid.

"Don't open it!", Dave said. But when he saw what was inside, worry was supplanted by joy. "My hash!"

"I'll make you a deal. You give me my bag... and I give you your hash."

Dave said it was a deal. He leaned forwards for the box but Edward pulled it out of reach.

"Bag first."

"Seriously? That means I have to get up." He reached forwards again but Edward pulled it out of reach.

"Off you go then."

"I'm in the middle of a smoke and a beer. Actually, I'll keep the bag. You're making me suspicious. You don't even smoke cigarettes and now you want the hash."

"If you really understood what you were saying, I think you'd have a different view. I went to the guards about this. As soon as I found it, off I went. Just in case a scenario like this arose."

"Ha! Bullshit!", John said, through a burst of laughter, slapping his lap. Dave anxiously shifted his feet and sat up more in his chair, but his nerves abated somewhat, realising everything wasn't as bad as it sounded.

"We'll just deny it."

"I thought you might say that. What I have in here is pristine. It's unadulterated. I looked at it in the lab in college. It is teeming with fingerprints. I didn't bring it in with me to the guards, obviously. I just told them about it. You know what you're looking at? You're looking at up to six months in jail. Detective Callaghan. He's the head honcho on Henry Street. I spoke with him myself. Here, look. He gave me his number." He pulled a piece of paper from his pocket, on which we could see scribbles of ink. A satisfied smile like the glint of coffin plating flashed on Edward's teeth as the colour drained from Dave's cheeks. "What's wrong? Cat got your tongue?". The hue on John's face started to sink to the green pallor of Dave's. Moments earlier he resembled a hermit crab recoiling into a shell. Now he strutted about the room like a legal prosecutor in a soap opera, full of confidence, happy to see the effect his grilling had on the defendant. His fingers tapped along the box like a player doing ripples on a piano.

"I've done my research, believe me. And I will go back to Detective Callaghan and tell everything, and give him this box, if you don't give me back my bag."

I was impressed at the depth of his acting skills, and at how he'd managed to stay so calm. I had witnessed yet another string in the bow of his many talents. Don't ask me where he'd hid it, but Dave came back with Edward's red bag. Edward ran up to his room and seconds later he returned as happy as Larry, obviously relieved all the contents were intact. I'm totally sure they would have returned that bag to him in any case, hash or no hash. It was just their idea of a practical joke.

After that, for the last time in that house, all of us got on like a house on fire, before all going our separate ways over the summer, and the rest of our lives. You'd never have guessed the room was full of tension just a few seconds previously. John zipped about the room re-filling glasses of Village Idiot, and coke for Vanessa and Edward. Dave put on AC/DC. He burnt off a piece of hash and crumbled it to a fine sand. He mixed it with tobacco to make a fat coned three-skinner. John told Edward how dare he criticise his shelf after what he did to the cubby hole door. Edward challenged him to do a better job. John said it was a challenge and marched out to his car and came back with his toolbox, saying he'd show him how a cubby hole door is fixed. It was all in good jest. He unscrewed the old gnarly screws from the wood and installed the new bolt and plate which Edward had bought in the hardware shop on his way back to the house with Vanessa. Edward said he was honoured and humbled to see the greatest architect in the world at work. John said that's what doing architecture the length and breadth of the county, 24 hours a day, can do for you. I'd tell Ciaran and Vinny about it the next day. They wished they were there too. I really don't know why they had to leave so soon. Especially Vinny. I was blue in the face telling him he really needed to chill out and hang around a bit. He went back to Dublin every weekend.

I asked Edward if he was happy once again, now that his plans were back on track. "You bet!", he said. The flames in his eyes ignited with the intensity of matches under a gas stove. He patted Vanessa tenderly on the lap. He stared into her big hazel eyes. They shared a lovers' fit of the giggles. He pulled her close and gave her a kiss. She smiled, revealing a perfect set of teeth. "Rome, Venice... you name it, we're goin'!" Thoughts of adventure simmered through his voice. He spluttered his sentences like he couldn't get them out fast enough.

Then there was a knock on the door. It was Myles, and not even he could dampen the enthusiastic spirit pervading the room. He partook in it, in fact. Myles' Dad is the one who owned the houses, three or four of them, maybe more, and Myles is the one who made sure the rent was collected on time, and that the tenants were pulling their weight. We implored Edward to not answer the door, concerned with the stink of hash among other things but, of course, he did. We heard his voice in the porch. We waved the air in front of us away frantically with our hands. I ran into the kitchen to open the door and the window. Could he come in? Edward could hardly say no. Myles owned the bloody house. He did his usual thing, walking in slowly and morosely, eyeing the room and its contents. We were all trying to not crack up laughing. Myles was in his mid-thirties, I'd say. He was a hard person to feel sorry but I frequently managed to. He was always so suspicious of you, and morose. He had long, thin, greasy hair, I think to hide the fact he had a thinning bald patch on top, but it just made it more noticeable. He struck me as a person whose main diet was chipper food. He was cursed by a dogged loyalty to live up to his dad's expectations. At the base of it all I think he had a naturally good disposition - too good, and he had to be on his guard to keep it under wraps, otherwise he might slip into being Mr Nice Guy and let us away with things and end up disappointing his Dad. When I looked at him, I thought of a boy who rarely felt his father's love. I thought of a man who hoped someday a rent collecting expedition would transform into a social visit, and here it was.

John did his magic and offered him a glass of Village Idiot... and he was transformed. The relish with which he devoured that Linden Village! It vindicated in my mind my theory about Myles. I couldn't remember him smile before now. What he really yearned for, more than anything, was to be part of the gang. Me, Vanessa and Edward talked about the nightclub we'd be hooking up in later, the Boys said they might join us, and I headed up to get dressed so I'd at least be ready for the Kremlin when he was gone. I said I'd meet Edward later. I was still in my pyjamas, technically speaking. The Boys more frequently went to the Hangman. That was the pub just next door to us. But the Kremlin is where the action would be tonight, it being the start of the holidays and the student pub. I put on my jeans and hoodie and went into the bathroom and threw some water in my hair to mould it into shape and brushed my teeth and put on some deodorant. For a while I thought Myles was going to ask could he tag along too. But he didn't. That's a bar he wouldn't stoop below.

Myles said he'd call in before Edward headed off on his journey out west the next day, sometime in the afternoon like 1 o' clock, to check up and, hopefully, give us our deposits back. The Boys, me, and Edward agreed we'd do a big clean up and have it ready by then. As it turned out, we did no cleaning the next day at all, we'd leave the place a mess and we would all get our deposits back, except Edward.

Chapter 7
The Kremlin

We took the shortcut to it. Through the fields. We hardly talked on the way. It had stopped raining but the grass was still wet and it's this very long grass – up to your knees - so the three of us were pretty soaked by the time we got there. "This is great weather for magic mushrooms", Dave said along the way, "Straight after a good drizzle."

The Kremlin was packed. *Really* packed. We stood on the hill for a while, the three of us, and surveyed the pulsing, living swell of bodies struggling to get in the door below us. Ah, yes. The sweet smell of Friday night. Teen Spirit. The evening was rolling on and summer was rumbling around the corner, about to explode.

"Screw this, let's go to the Hangman.", Dave said.

I looked at him in disbelief.

"After all we've just walked? You must be mad." I started down the hill, the Boys following behind me. The thought of walking back to the Hangman made them weak at the knees. And anyway, why would you go there? It was an old man's pub, which has its place, but no mayhem like now. The crowds here at the Kremlin, the shouts! I inhaled a deep breath, like the sweetest flower was being held below my nose. I wanted to consume it, to *be* it. Youth and indulgence and pleasure, all rolled into one. With relish, I made myself the latest attachment to the growing blob of life at the door of the Kremlin, an ordered chaos that squashed and squeezed in the general direction of the bar. There was stamping on toes and pointed elbows in rib cages. But nobody cared. We were all in this together, every single one of us, all of us followers of that forlorn god called alcohol, and we would do anything to sup from his cup.

Dave and John were right behind me in the tight queue. "Sit down anywhere, Kev! Sit down anywhere.", Dave yelled over my shoulder, evidently failing to see the place was full. His hot breath rankled on my ear. His shoes stomped on my heels. Someone poured a pint on my chest. Dave had a coughing fit on the back of my head. For the briefest instant I wondered why people bother getting dressed up and socialising at all in a crowded and uncomfortable environment. Why not simply stay at home beside a hearth fire, where you can have a civilised conversation? But then through the small holes between elbows and over shoulders ahead I caught a glimpse of the growing white shirt behind the bar, the beloved gatekeeper, the barman, and all doubts evaporated into the smoky sweaty air.

Needless to say the first round was on me, due to my newfound fortune from Edward. I ordered pints and shots of tequila. We grabbed our drinks off the counter, about twenty minutes after I'd eventually made the order. We took those lifesaving first few gulps of cold beer, like shots of Nirvana to the brain they were, and started heading towards the terrace for a bit of fresh air where it was always a bit less packed.

The terrace was my favourite part of the whole Kremlin. It was this big courtyard and it was especially brilliant in the summer because on warm days, which rarely occurred, but were special when they did, you got people sitting on the ground and lying against the walls in their t-shirts and drinking and relaxing, with their sunglasses on. That was nice to see. The terrace was completely paved with these grey and terracotta bricks, a bit like the way Grafton street used to be in the old days, and there were long green stretches of ivy clinging to the granite walls. And today, as the Boys and myself ambled by the small fountain in the middle, with the greeny-bluish copper fish squirting water out his mouth into the open sky, the sight of the Ents Crew, who were setting up sound equipment on a stage, heightened my anticipation for the evening ahead. The Ents Crew were a bunch of volunteer students who did jobs like organise concerts and gigs on major events. It was just a great place, the terrace, especially in summer time, and it was like another world when we got there after all that pushing and shoving through the pub.

Right now it wasn't sunny but the place was packed nonetheless as it was the last day of exams. We managed to find a table to ourselves – that surprised me - the rain must have put people off or maybe it was still early – and we wiped the little puddles off the benches with our sleeves. There was actually another crowd, five or six of them, racing for that table also, but we just managed to clinch it. There was no problem if they wanted to share with us but they smiled and decided to move on. The Boys sat on the same side, across the table from me.

We wallowed in our pints in silence, enjoying every moment of it. "There's going to be some dancing tonight, lads.", I said. Two exhausted members of the Ents Crew wheeled amplifiers by us on a trolley. The only music now was coming from inside the pub, but soon it would be blaring outside too.

There was no response. I turned to face them. They were both crouched forwards with their chests against the oak table and they had their hands wrapped around their pints like it was a pot of gold and their heads almost touching.

They were deeply immersed in conversation. I crouched forwards with them, to hear what they were talking about.

Dave was recounting to John the first time he ever had sex. Which wasn't surprising. He was always talking about some sex thing. I can't remember the story exactly but I remember it happened on a tractor in his uncle's field. I'd believe him, too. He struck me as that sort of a person the moment I set eyes upon him – the sort who has sex for the first time on a tractor. "She was a sicko in the sack.", he said. A lot of the time it was bullshit but you never knew with these guys.

You should have seen John the whole way through the story. He was listening like a madman with his eyes wide open and attentive. Every time Dave paused for a second or two John would say, "Yeah? Are yeh *serious*? What happened next 'n' shit?" He loved it.

But there was something else he kept doing. Dave would be talking away and telling his story, without taking any notice, but every few seconds John would take a very quick terrified hissing gulp of air between his tightly clenched teeth and straight after it his whole body would quiver and shudder from head to toe. Drugs kicking in. His eyes bulged like a rabbit's caught in a snare. His teeth were shut tight and his lips were stretched in a grimace across his face and when he took that terrified quick inhale it would release again slowly, like air hissing from a balloon. I didn't ask if he was ok or anything. Not right yet. I just watched him for a while, without making it too obvious.

Then *he* started telling some story. About some guy he knew. "Some black guy 'n' shit", he said – he was always saying *'n' shit* at the end of every sentence. It was just a habit he had. "This black guy, friend of my cousin's 'n' shit... real cool bastard down in Ranelagh, in Dublin... had two birds in bed at the same time 'n' shit." It was a good story. He told us how the girls were twin sisters and he told us it was the first time he's ever met a bloke who had two sisters in bed at the same time. I told John I've never met a person who's had two women in bed at the same time, full stop. Let alone them being bloody sisters. He couldn't believe it.

Then things went very quiet, for a while. Nobody said anything. Everybody just sat around the table, staring into their pints. I couldn't think of any stories myself. Sometimes you just can't think of stories.

"You know who I'd say gives a great little ride, Kev?", Dave said.

"Who?"

"I'd say that Fiona honnie – that friend of Edward's – gives a great little ride."

I agreed with him. "Yeah but she's not that way inclined.", I added. That crowd who raced us for the table managed to grab another one nearby. "It's not her style. She's too... sophisticated. She's not going to jump into bed with the first bloke she meets."

"What?" He ripped the pint of Stella from his lips, sending gushes over the edge. "I'm not talking about riding her style. Are you telling me that if you were locked in a room with her you wouldn't do sex with her? If you were both lying naked on your big single bed?"

"If we were both stark naked in bed, yes, of course I'd go the whole hog with her. Because if she wasn't on for anything then she wouldn't be lying in bed naked with me in the first place. But if we were just standing in a room I wouldn't hop on her unless -"

He wasn't listening. He got distracted by three girls who came into the terrace and took a spot in the middle of the courtyard, standing near the fountain. He got up from the bench to approach them. Me and John followed his lead, bringing our pints with us.

He could be quite charismatic, Dave could. Talking privately among a familiar bunch of lads is a different kettle of fish to talking to a bunch of girls you're trying to impress. He came across as a suave, sensitive, mysterious, even erudite type of guy. He had a presence, a classiness about him. To these three ladies we were about to become acquainted with, me and John sauntering towards them through the courtyard behind Dave, our leader, with his leisurely swagger and his mouth half open in a dazed smile as he locked them in his sights, he was the quintessential gentleman. Smiling back on their part was irresistible. In spite of his somewhat gruff appearance, he oozed charm. His first words conveyed a person who had a fun quirky wicked side; he was an open book, non-judgemental, willing to share his own story, and his heart. That sentiment disappeared as soon as you got to know the fella, but those were the first impressions; a charming, caring guy, full of empathy, with an intriguing, alluring bad boy side. He didn't care what people thought about him, was partly it, he just went with his heart and gave it one hundred percent.

"Enchanté", he said, strutting over with a beaming smile. Enchanté. He was a real Don Juan, all of a sudden. Girls love that stuff, a bloke genuinely walking all the way through a courtyard especially for them and saying romantic stuff like, "Enchanté". He went straight to the really good looking one, Stephanie. She smiled back – she was smitten with him. For a while I thought he was going to reach for her hand and raise it to his lips and kiss it, but no, he didn't do that, just stood close to her and asked her name and what she was studying.

To cut a long story short, we really got played by these girls. With the antics of me and John 'ogling' over Stephanie, as no doubt Carol and Rebecca would have construed it, which were the names of the other two girls, and Dave 'lechering' over her, and other blokes in the courtyard making discreet glances at her too; how she was an exquisite gem you stumble across once in a million years, ultimately they said – screw these guys, let's get our own back. I think they thought we were sexist chauvinist pigs. Maybe I should have been more polite and chatted with the girls but being a splendid conversationalist wasn't highest on my list of priorities at that point in time. I was feeling very mellow. I was happy to sit back and listen. I was looking at Dave rather than Stephanie, to be honest. Seeing how he was progressing, learning from his tricks of the trade... He was a pleasure to watch. I never had a big belief in the saying that opposites attract but opposites they were and Dave was charming the hell out of her. Yes, he definitely had a charisma about him, looking at him now.

She had eyes that glistened like emeralds through water on a sunny day. Her tanned arms and wavy long black hair suggested a provenance from some faraway, colourful land, far beyond the shores of Limerick. He never took his piggy blue eyes from her enchanting green ones. She had pristine white teeth. When Dave smiled – more like a deranged leer, a lot of his teeth were crooked and yellow, like kernels of corn. She had a gold bracelet on her wrist. Dave had hot rock holes on his sleeves. He was short and fat, like a defunct shrub. She was tall and slim, like a proud poplar tree, made even taller by the silver stilettos that held her high. The icing on the cake, for me anyhow, was that sometimes Stephanie's heel would flick backwards – a timid gesture, I thought. To me it suggested a humble, sincere beauty, not wishing to draw attention to itself. She giggled demurely at her two friends when Dave was looking elsewhere. Like a brilliant diamond, she had no knowledge of how special she was.

She was wearing a simple white silk dress that kissed her figure perfectly, curving with her voluptuous hips. Below the hips it got loose and swayed and flowed freely and lightly in the courtyard breeze. Her bosom was supported in a ribbon that was tied on the back in a bow. It looked like that bow supported the whole dress. Her wardrobe sense suggested chic and elegance. A more lavish display of cleavage might have been borderline vulgar, but here, the optimum quantity of boob was revealed, swelling pleasingly above the ribbon, just enough to induce a vague tingling sensation in the loins; pitched perfectly, simple and beautiful and innocent like two bronze eggs in a hanky. Any more would have made lapses in eye contact more awkward. Nothing made me happier than to stand there on the sidelines and admire with unguilty pleasure, my lust pleasantly checked.

Out of the three of them I chatted mostly with Carol. She had square rimmed glasses, an eagle beaked nose, and rarely smiled. How Dave had practically barged through and ignored Carol and Rebecca, making a beeline straight for Stephanie, how John's and my behaviour could have been construed as rude, particularly some of the things John said, might have intensified her desire to take us down a peg. John chatted with Rebecca, or "Becs", as he was calling her by the end of the evening. They were studying art and design in the NCAD, in town. That's what they told us at *that* point, anyway. I'm sure of it. By the end of the evening they were saying something different. John disagreed with me. I'm quite sure I'm right though – one hundred percent in fact – because I remember being impressed by how focused they were on their careers, knowing exactly where they wanted to go, like fashion houses and stuff, years before their current course had even finished. When they left college the three of them wanted to go to London or New York, where the action was, they said. It's always impressed me, people knowing exactly what they want to do in life, and how to get there, years before their course has even finished, so that's how I remembered they were studying fashion, or something along those lines.

So, suddenly, John was in a seething rage against Dave. This competitive streak had emerged between the two of them. Man, was John furious! Rebecca was trying to make conversation with him. It's like he didn't even realise she was there. At one stage he said something like, "I'm sick of this. Sick of it." He was staring at Dave, angry as a raging bull. Dave was the taunting matador. "Sick of what?", Rebecca asked. John didn't even look at her. He was too busy staring at Dave over her shoulder, seething, racking his brain on how to give him his comeuppance. His answer was something like, "Sick of second best. He drinks the fine wine and leaves me the plonk." Stuff like that was hardly going to endear them to become our bosom buddies. "The rhythm of the night" started blaring on the speaker. Dave led Stephanie out to dance. John sprung to action. He couldn't stomach the possibility of Dave winning her hand, and him just *standing* there.

"Do you want to dance?", he said, or spluttered, at Rebecca. Spittle flew from his mouth like pebbledash on her face. She blinked. "No thank you." He turned to Carol and asked if *she* wanted to dance. "No", she said.

Dave could smooth talk but he couldn't dance. He had no sense that she didn't want to move at the same tempo as himself. She'd been roped into dancing, rather than going of her own volition. I wondered if the DJ saw what was going on; it was like he changed the music to slow sets, like he wanted to slow things down and rescue Stephanie from the madness. When they returned to their spot with us by the fountain it was evident by the dreamy infatuation that had left Stephanie's eyes and her deflated body language after being tugged around that the brightly burning flame of their relationship was extinguished. John watched Dave with a beady eye, plotting how to get his own back, in repayment for the insults Dave had thrown his way. He took gulps from his pint and mumbled to himself. His shaking hand ensured quite a bit of beer poured over his jacket, rather than into his mouth.

Chapter 8

Rebecca

What caused the fury to boil over in him was when, before Dave and Stephanie went out dancing, all of us standing there in the courtyard, Dave insulted his Dad. Dave took a break from staring into Stephanie's eyes and said, "What was that film we were watching a few days ago?... John?... with the Mexicans and the cowboys?... John?" We were all standing there in the middle of the courtyard by the fountain, the place getting more and more full. John grunted, no idea of the film Dave was talking about. "There was a line in the film that said, 'If you want the food, you take the food, if you want the cattle, you take the cattle, if you want the woman, you take the woman.'"

"Huh?"

"You're in your own world, man." He turned to the girls with his hands extended outwards for them to assess how stable they were, and then back at John. "Am I that bad? You're like Michael J Fox sitting on a washing machine and masturbating."

"You see, ladies and gentlemen", John said, "I won't name any names, but someone in particular – I won't say who" – he tilted his head towards Dave – "keeps giving me drugs the whole time. Isn't that right, Dave? Makin' me paranoid 'n' shit. I wonder who that person could be? Any ideas, Dave?", he said sarcastically. "Go on, take a wild guess. Edward's right about that drugs shit. I go a bit hard on Edward sometimes."

"You use the past as a... what's the word I'm looking for..." He knocked his forehead with his palm as if it would click into place. "A crutch... the caravan... you mind if I tell 'em that caravan story John?" John looked at him with vacant eyes like a fish in the supermarket and his mouth hanging open as he didn't know what caravan story Dave was alluding to and by the time he did it was too late, not that Dave would have stopped anyway. "John's Da, God rest him, used to sleep in the caravan in the garden. Two local lads, Jimmy Byrne and Smelly Murphy... one evening they put black bin bags on all the windows with masking tape. It was two days before John's Da came out. He thought it was night time!" Dave gave one of his wheezy laughs that degenerated into a coughing fit. He leaned on one of the tables to control his laughter and catch his breath.

So this put Dave in John's bad books for the remainder of our time in the Kremlin. He gritted his teeth with chagrin as he listened to Dave embellish the Princess, Stephanie, with compliments, and watched them out dancing with malice in his eyes. Rebecca was asking him where he was from, but he barely answered, his thoughts far away, shaking his head in dismay and eyeing Dave and trying to plot revenge. Gradually, though, with her kind, persistent advances towards him, that thick bleak rage that encapsulated his sensibilities started to dissipate. His social awareness began to filter through. The hard contours of doubt on his face started to break into those of jubilation. Yes, Rebecca had earned his trust. He sighed and told her that Dave ridiculed him all the time and made him the butt of jokes. He was always being teased. What he would love more than anything, would be, just *once*, to come up with a trick or quip that would leave Dave stumped and speechless. He told her about the "triangles", a 5 pound bet they'd made some weeks earlier. We were all sitting in the front room. Dave said he could blow smoke in the shape of a triangle. John betted he couldn't. Dave moved his head in a triangular motion and exhaled at the same time, so that he was indeed blowing smoke in the shape of a triangle. He told Rebecca he wasn't too happy about that.

"That's terrible.", she said, shaking her head in sorrowful understanding at the tribulations poor John had suffered. She was drinking from a flute glass of something red and sparkling in her hand, some cocktail or other, with a straw to her lips. As she listened to John her head was tilted to one side, motionless as the undivided attention a bird gives to worms moving underground; for his part, he was singing like a canary, pouring his heart out to her, a confidante to whom he could express his deepest woes and fears.

Then, out of the blue, she stood on her tiptoes, light and leisurely as though the breeze propelled her upwards, and kissed him on the lips. Man, she was good. It was a carrot she could dangle all day. The donkey would be assured to take the bait. It was merely the touch, the *suggestion*, of a kiss. There was no enduring or lingering. It was pitched just perfectly – ephemeral, like if John didn't act on it quickly she could forget it had happened. As if it were an accident, a dream. "What do you study?", she asked. "I study…I study…", he said, his mind all over the place, jingling from foot to foot. He could hardly get his words out. Rebecca laughed – not a nasty laugh but a kind, effeminate one. The kiss! She had him wrapped around her little finger! Her piercing blue eyes stared straight into his and said, "I am looking for Mr Right. I have met so, so many nice men in my time, but they have proved fruitless." She was saying that maybe, just maybe, John was the man to assume that role, to be Mr Right.

The way she sucked on that straw, too, I'm sure, accelerated temptations in John's mind.

His first instinct was to look at Dave and see if he had witnessed his success. It was a reflex action. He forgot about Dave, and the Princess, immediately. He lunged forwards to try to kiss Rebecca again, displaying nothing of the deft, subtle technique with which she had kissed him. His legs and even his neck seemed to wrap around her, like an octopus surrounding its prey with tentacles and trying to ingest it, but just before his mouth approached hers she swung her head aside and squeezed out her arm between the space of their tightly sealed chests and wagged a cautioning finger under his nose, the way one scolds a puppy. Far from an outright rejection there was a coy smirk on her face and a devious twinkle in her eye, saying, "not just now, but later in the night, who knows what might happen?" Every ounce of energy, every breath, every step, revolved around this new mission; Rebecca was the fulcrum of his existence, the food of his soul.

I was looking straight at his overjoyed face when fear struck in his eyes. "What? What?" He shuffled uneasily from foot to foot – he didn't know whether to approach her or run. He probably thought he'd gone too far, the potential for love was squandered.

Rebecca wiggled a finger, urging him to come closer. Man, she was good. A total winder-upper. He probably thought she was about to deliver his worst nightmare: "I don't love you but my friend is madly in love with Dave."

At last he stepped forwards and she stood on her tiptoes and she placed her mouth at his cocked ear and she covered her mouth with her hand and she whispered and he listened fearfully to what she had to say.

A look as vacant as the grey autumn sky, devoid of joy, shock or confusion, washed over his face. Then he said, determined that what he was hearing was ludicrous, "No, I don't believe that. Impossible."

Rebecca was nodding, insisting whatever it was she was saying was indeed possible. "Yes, it is possible, I'm telling you…" I leaned in closer, to hear what it was they were talking about.

She was saying that the best way to get back at Dave was to give him the challenge of drawing a square circle. I laughed out loud when I heard that! I thought she was obviously joking, but no, she was coming across as dead serious. "Yes, I'm telling you…", she said, full of alacrity. "I study theoretical physics and it's a conundrum that has the entire class stumped but it is possible… I have *seen* it, it is probably the most amazing thing I have ever seen." John was having none of it either, shaking his head with scepticism, but not too much as he didn't want to offend her. When we made eye contact on the sly you could see we were both thinking the same thing; she'd clearly lost her mind.

"If I show you will you believe me? You don't trust me, John?", she said, pouting her luscious lips, her long eyelashes batting over her sad, offended blue eyes.

"Ah Becs, of course I do.", he said, throwing his eyes to heaven with an embarrassed rosy hue growing in his cheeks, like a little boy telling a dear friend his mum wasn't allowing him play with him anymore, that there were bigger forces at play than things between them personally. "I'm not saying that. Of course I do. I do believe you. It's just..."

"It sounds to me like you don't believe me.", she said.

She suggested they exchange phone numbers, the intention being that herself and John meet up the following day. John almost toppled over with glee at that suggestion. When he was inputting her number into his phone he recited each digit loud and clear and pressed the buttons on the keypad very deliberately and slowly. I thought it was because he was stoned and wanted to be sure not to mess up. He wanted to be cautious in case he inputted it incorrectly. But he kept looking over at Dave. I realised he wanted to prolong the experience and be sure Dave would be witness to the success he was having in getting her number. He rang the number after he'd entered it. He was a little bundle of blushing joy when she answered and talked back, both of them giddy and giggling like love-struck teens how the conversation took place when they were just in front of each other.

Before they left, he leaned over to hug her again but she put pressure on his shoulders to release her. "You're the best, Becs, the best. I'm dying to see you tomorrow." He wasn't at all jealous of Dave anymore; on the contrary, Dave was more jealous of him, as he could see the astounding inroads he was making. Whatever infatuation Stephanie had on first meeting him was dead now. That smile as natural as the crescent moon was dimmer now than the night sky. That was the big difference between Dave and John. At the outset Dave came across as a warm, charming, considerate and caring bloke, but the more you got to know him in fact you realised what a dirtbird he was. John was the opposite. You'd be sceptical of him at the start, but the more you got to know him, the more you realised he was just a child in a man's body.

At around this stage I went to the toilet and when I got back... I was amazed to see he'd been indoctrinated 100% into the school of square circles. Dave was a complete convert too. The girls were gone. "What are you doing?", I said. They had managed to squeeze into a space on one of the benches a bit further up. Dave had his head cradled in his hand, deep in thought, with a pen in his other hand. On the table in front of him was a beer mat. On the beermat he was doodling little shapes and patterns. John had a thrilled expression on his face – growing more thrilled as Dave's face got more and more intense.

"Don't tell me you're trying to draw a square fecking circle? It's impossible, man."

He had an expression of concentration which I hadn't seen on him before. "They're astrophysicists. Everything is possible mathematically, Kev." He made a pattern on the edge of the beermat, the solution to the world's problems a mere scribble away, he was sure.

John couldn't resist taunting him, smiling proudly at the progress he was making, which was zero. He took a reassuring gulp from his pint. "You're like

Master Yoda in everything but brains – short, fat, hairy –

"Shut up. Even Stephanie said it can be done, Kev.", Dave said.

"Oh well then, Stephanie." I said, and threw my head back. "Then it must be true. She's winding you up. Did they not say they were doing interior design or graphic design or some shit? Going to London and all? I don't know where this metaphysics shit is coming from."

"No Kev, definitely astronomical physics. Don't know where you're getting your London shit from."

"And for your information, loads of things can't be solved mathematically.", I said. "Like two plus two equals five can't be solved, or the speed of light. You can't go faster than the speed of light no matter how hard you try. You can't make a square circle!"

"Actually that's not true.", John said, taking a delightful swig from his pint as he observed the waning efforts over Dave's arm which were coming to an end, as he was running out of space for new scribbles to draw. "With quantum physics they've solved that one, with electrons 'n' shit." I didn't know if this was true or not so I said nothing. "Anyway, a square circle isn't like saying two and two is five, it's more along the lines of blowing triangles. If you didn't know the answer to that, like someone making a bet and saying, 'I bet you can't blow a triangle', if you knew that was impossible you'd say, 'No way, I'm not going to make such a stupid bet and lose my fucking shirt.' and we saw how that went for me – I lost my shirt 'n' shit. So far out shit really does happen, Kev. Becs is right. It's all about... lateral thinking 'n' shit.

That's what she said. Lateral thinking. Thinking outside the box."

I didn't say anything more about the girls studying art or design, which I'm sure is what I'd heard. As for square circles, if they wanted to believe it was doable, I just let them at it. I had better things to be worrying about. And besides, who's to say the joke wouldn't be on me, if I got involved? That idea did cross my mind – that I could be the victim of an elaborate wind up, them trying to make me go through the hoops of actually drawing a square circle and then saying, "Haha. You idiot, can't believe you fell for it." I'd have looked like a right eejit and I was too paranoid to be looking like a right eejit at that point in time.

Finally, because he was bored of the idea or to get some inspiration maybe, Dave stuck his hand in his pocket and whipped out a big fat chunk of hash, his tobacco and his Rizla papers, and started skinning up a joint under the table. He asked me to keep sketch because occasionally you got these bouncer type blokes in green suits roaming around the place and they'd kick you straight out if they caught you at it.

But rolling a joint was the last thing he could do right now. This bloke had been rolling joints since the day he was born, probably, but the last thing he could do right this minute was roll. Usually he could roll with one hand, even – like a cowboy, but he'd lost all sense of coordination. His hands were trembling all over the place. He even dropped his pouch of tobacco on the ground. He spread everything on the table, scratching his stubbly chin and wondering where to start. He looked at me. He didn't *say* anything, but I knew damn well what he wanted. He was desperate.

"Don't look at me, man", I said. "You know what I'm like." I was terrible at rolling joints. One of Dave's favourite pastimes was timing people roll joints on Ciaran's stopwatch. It took me ages. The result always looked like a tampon rather than a joint. It was just Dave's form of entertainment, timing people do things like that. He must have remembered how bad I was because he took his gaze away. He looked across at John.

"Don't look at me, man. I'm even worse than Farrington. Me hands are in bits."

So instead of doing anything, Dave just sat there at the table, bewildered, looking up occasionally in the vain hope he might recognise someone walking by who may be able to roll him a joint.

Chapter 9
The Guy with the Teeth

Looking back on it, it really started happening before we met Fiona. Only I wasn't aware of it back then. When I look back on it now, though, I'm sure the ball was rolling before we met her. It must have been. Fiona, like I said already, was one of Edward's friends. She was a real goody-goody, just like the man himself. They cracked me up a lot of the time because they were always rushing in and out of the house to be on time for things. They spent a lot of their time swapping secret ingredients for secret meals, and studying. Apart from a handful of friends, hardly anybody, other than Fiona and Vanessa, called into our house. The Boys were mad about Fiona. She wasn't too crazy about them. They were always taking the mickey out of her, right in front of her face. Most of the time they'd be sitting in the front room with the curtains drawn, using bad language and smoking joints. Fiona wasn't into that sort of thing. She almost stopped calling round completely, after the Boys moved in.

A lot of the time Edward preferred being sprawled out on the floor, leaning on his elbows, when he was studying. Right in the middle of the room, in front of the fire. You'd feel guilty walking into the room. I once asked if he wouldn't be more comfortable upstairs at his desk. It wasn't a *hint.* He just looked uncomfortable, with his elbows leaning on the ground, and crackling logs from the fire, and people walking around. He'd even tell you to put on the teli, if you wanted, and after five minutes you'd forget he was there. Partly, I think, he wanted to make his presence felt. It was his idea of a deterrent against the Boys, coming in and turning up the radio and drinking all day and making noise. Marking his territory. Not that it ever worked, mind you. Most of the time, despite the stubborn resistance, he got up eventually and left to go study in the library or in his room.

Before we met Fiona, we just stayed sitting at that same table in the middle of the courtyard for a while, beside the fountain, drinking our pints. That is, me and John did. Dave wandered off somewhere. I don't know what he got up to, but he disappeared on us. I was sipping my pint rather than gulping. I wanted to knock it back but the thought of having to walk through the throng of bustling activity in the pub to buy more drinks terrified me. A mysterious girl was lingering or loitering around our table. I thought she wanted to know the time but was afraid to ask. "Are you ok for drinks?", she asked. I ordered 2 Carlsbergs. I'd never seen it before. I thought it was clever to have a girl taking orders and bring the drinks rather than lots of people squeezing into the pub. She didn't have the formal attire of white blouse and black dress. She didn't even look like a member of the Ents crew. She was most likely genuine but I was happy I hadn't given her any money in advance and I can't remember if she came back with the drinks or not.

I looked at my watch shortly before Dave left or I realised he left or shortly after and I remember it being around six o' clock. There was still plenty more light in the evening, it being Summer. The courtyard was getting pretty crowded, with everybody laughing and screaming their heads off. To make things even noisier, those big speakers and noise equipment the Ents crew had been setting up earlier, it was blaring away now. Real techno music. The Ents crew were out dancing in strength. They all wore the same red and black outfits and had to stand in the middle of the terrace and dance together – about ten of them – so people would build their confidence and dance with them. They were all crap dancers – and they knew it – so they were all pushing each other on the shoulder and laughing about it, to make it look like it was all a big joke.

I was just looking at the Ents Crew again and then I turned back towards the Boys. That's when I realised Dave was missing. "Where's Dave?" I asked.

"He's gone lookin' for someone to make him a jay 'n' shit.", John said. Through clenched teeth. He was crouched forwards against the table very rigidly and looking down at the wooden surface with this very concentrated, worried look on his face. His arms were taut and rigid and his fists were clenched into tight balls on the table and he kept doing that grimacing business with a vein like a worm protruding on his forehead and every time you said something he'd answer through clenched teeth. Locked jaws. He looked like he was about to explode or something.

"Hey John. Are yeh alright? You're looking kinda -" He cut in on me but I couldn't understand what he was saying. He was talking through clenched teeth. "What did yeh say?"

"I'm rushin' man……rushing. Trippin' 'n' shit. Don't know if my heart is beating too slow or too fast 'n' shit." He had his mouth shut tight whenever he said anything – he was hardly even moving his lips – and occasionally he'd take a quick gulp of air between his teeth. Every time he took one you could hear it going *tsssst...*, like a rattlesnake, and you could feel the table vibrate, with his arms and elbows pressed on it. His fists were clenched into knots. It was like he was expecting the table to suddenly shoot up into the sky and he was trying to apply as much pressure as possible to keep it down on the ground.

"I'm going for a walk.", I said. I didn't want to stick around with John making those spooky sounds. I just *felt* like moving, too.

The very second I stood up from the bench, John jumped up like a shot and grabbed me by the arm and said "No. Wait. I'll go with you." It half scared me and half amused me, the way he looked. He was scared to be left alone. He followed me around, bringing our pints with us.

The first bloke we bumped into was some bloke I'd never met before. It's funny the way you just bump into random people like that. It was right beside the terrace door into the Kremlin, I remember, and he had a pint in his hand. Like me and John. He had a pimply face, a big nose and very bad teeth. They slurred up his speech. I could hardly understand what he was talking about. I'm not sure how we got talking to him in the first place, exactly, but I think it's because he asked John if he was a soldier, just with the combat trousers he had on, and the army jacket. He was only trying to be friendly, but John was too paranoid to see the humorous side of things. He was looking at everybody with this about-to-explode look on his face and he was holding my bloody hand. He was standing against me, brushing against me, and every now and then he'd clutch onto my hoodie as if expecting me to rush off from him, and his hand would slide down my arm and slowly onto my sleeve and then into my hand. Anyway, I answered for John. I said he was a soldier, just joking, and then this guy said that he was a soldier, too – because he was wearing green trousers like John's, so then I said I was a soldier, as well. We were all soldiers. We talked about Vietnam and where we fought. None of us had ever been anywhere near the place. I'd never even been out of bloody Europe. He asked me what part of Nam I fought in and I made up some bullshit name right there on the spot. I asked him what part of Nam he fought in and he said he fought in the Congo. He was full of it. But his teeth were in bits, and they were totally destroying his pronunciation. I felt sorry for him. Food was falling out of his mouth the whole time – into his pint glass and onto his t-shirt and on the floor. He didn't know that was happening, I don't think, so that's why I felt sorry for him. He wasn't even eating anything. It was probably pieces of food that had been in his mouth for weeks. Anyway, we were talking for quite a while, just the two of us, and then he asked John, "So wud part of Num d'you fight in?" He was only trying to be friendly. But John hit the roof. He was just so bloody paranoid. He had the collars of his army jacket up over his ears – to hide his face – and he never cut out that grimacing business. He was just so suspicious looking. With his black eye and all. He took a step closer to me – hiding behind me, almost – and said in his very panicky voice to the bloke with the teeth, "What do yeh want, man? What the hell do yeh want... don't even know yeh... wanna do a deal or somethin'?" He was looking at me when he said it but he was talking to the bloke with the teeth. I don't think he knew what John meant so John said again, "Yeh wanna do a deal or somethin'?"

He was looking at the guy when he said it this time. His voice crackled, his nostrils flared.

"What do you mean?" the guy with the teeth asked.

"Yeh wanna do a deal or what yeh want?... sell us some drugs 'n' shit? ...We got no fuckin' money, man."

"Hey John", I said. "Take it easy will yeh?...He's only trying to be frie-

John cut in on me before I could finish. "Never been to Vietnam in my fuckin' life. Don't even know this guy." The guy with the teeth said he didn't want to do a deal. I tried to cover up for John being so rude. "Don't mind my friend. He's not himself tonight. He's had a lot to drink.", I said, and gave him a wink. "Awwwww right.", the guy with the teeth said. He laughed, and half a mouthful of food fell out over his old t-shirt. You should have seen the state of his t-shirt. It was mouldy.

After that, John and I sort of walked off somewhere else. I didn't just walk off without saying bye to him or anything. He was a nice bloke, and I really did feel a bit sorry for him. He was alright. We even shook hands and said we'd see each other again some time.

Then we bumped into Fiona. With a friend of hers. We said hello. Straight after it Fiona moved her face a bit closer to mine and said, "What's wrong with your face?" She didn't ask John what was wrong with *his* face, with all his grimacing, she asked what was wrong with my face.

"Nothing's wrong", I told her. Then she introduced us to her friend. I can't remember her name – I think it was Pollie – but I've never seen a girl wear so much makeup. Even on her earlobes. Maybe all girls wear makeup on their earlobes, I don't know. We just stood there in the terrace for a while, the four of us, smoking our heads off and talking. The girls kept raving about exams and trying to predict results but I kept changing the subject. Everybody was chatting away. Except John. John didn't say a word. Not one. He was standing behind me the whole time – right behind me – and he had his head over my shoulder. He kept gripping and ungripping my arm. We must have looked so stupid. Anyway we were just standing there for a while, and then it started to rain again – not too heavily though – and Fiona had the idea of going into the video room. That was a room opposite the main bar, where all the video freaks hung out and watched videos, and played video games. On nights like this night, though, when the place was very busy, they'd bring in wooden benches and a few kegs and change that whole video room into a bar, just like the main bar, so that's where we headed. You could hardly find a bench the place was so crowded and when at last we did, Fiona and her friend sat on one side, and John and myself sat on the other. Then - we'd been sitting for about five seconds, I'd say – John stood straight back up again. He almost overturned the bloody table, he jumped up so suddenly. We all just looked at him. "I have to go for a walk.", he said in his panicky voice. I have to go for a walk. Just like that. The girls must have thought he'd dumped himself or something. He took off like a lunatic, barging his way through the multitudes.

    If he'd stuck around to keep me company, nothing might have happened. I don't even know if I remember all that happened. I kept hoping he was beside me, at the beginning, but then I got in this very analysing mood, and I completely forgot about him. They've got this distinctive orange wallpaper in that video room, with little yellow patterns – it'd been there for years, and I'd been in that video room a million times – but what I'd been thinking while I was sitting there, right that moment, waiting for John, I didn't know what colour it was. I did *now*, when I was right beside it, but if you'd asked me only the day before or something, when we were back at the house or something, "What colour is the wallpaper in the video room?", I wouldn't have had the faintest idea, despite being there a million times. I was analysing the whole room like that – the roof, the kegs, the pictures... even the people. There was a girl with a mole on her cheek, and I was staring at it. The only reason I knew I was doing that is because Fiona interrupted me.

"What did you say?" I wasn't even looking at her. I was looking all around me.

"I said 'When are you going back to Dublin?'"

"Wha-, oh...a few days, yeah.", I said. I could hardly even hear her.

"Have you a job lined up?"

"What?"

"I said are you working over the summer? Have you got a job lined up?"

"No, no. Not yet. I'll find one about somewhere. As lounge boy in a bar or something."

"Are you drunk, Kevin?", Fiona said. I looked at her, when she said that. She was looking at me like my mother would. She was a very motherly type of person, Fiona was.

"What... yeah. I am, yeah. We started early today. Straight after breakfast." If you think I was going to tell her what was really happening, you're mad. She wouldn't have been impressed. She wasn't into that sort of thing.

Then John came back. I didn't bother asking where he'd been because I wasn't interested, to tell you the truth. He sat down beside me again. Exactly where he was before he ran off. Sweating. All crouched forwards and rocking in little jerks, a juicy, wormy vein embossed on his forehead which I was sure I'd feel a pulse on if I pressed on it with my finger and another vein bulging on his neck. His eyes were watery and red. His pupils looked like they were popping out of their sockets. He was letting out that rattlesnake noise more than ever, now. Fiona asked him a question. I don't know what it was – I wasn't listening – but you should have heard what John said. Straight after she'd asked him, he looked at her with this terrified look on his face, and said, "Who the hell are you!?" I swear, the poor bastard didn't even know who she was! Fiona stared at him, with her mouth hanging wide open. She didn't say anything, so John asked her who she was again.

"Why... I'm Fiona.", she said. The rosy colour in her cheeks dissipated and she was as pale as snow, like she'd seen a ghost, like she was a ghost. John leaned right over to me, quivering, with his army collars up above his ears; like he was embarrassed, wanting to conceal his face. Leaning in so close, I could see the eyelid of his black eye was twisted in the middle, giving it a more angled, lozenge shape compared to the other eye which had a wide, startled, frightened oval shape. It gave me a chill, like a dodgy beggar had sneaked up on me in a bad part of town. "Kev, who the hell is the girl on the other side of the table?", he said. He was terrified.

I know I shouldn't have, but I cracked up laughing. The whole thing was sort of funny, if you thought about it. I just couldn't help it. I stopped as fast as possible, though. I didn't want to hurt John's feelings. He could be very sensitive. I looked over at Fiona – just to make John happy – and something hit me. Like a brick across the back of the head. It was like all the blood in my body had suddenly rushed to the top of my head in the same vein and it was exploding off my shoulders. *I* wasn't even sure if the girl on the other side of the table was Fiona or not. All of a sudden, I just wasn't sure. It could have been someone who just *resembled* her, like her twin sister or mother or someone. I'd seen her a thousand times but right now I wasn't sure whether or not Fiona was Fiona and it was driving me mad I couldn't say for sure that it was Fiona. You can't be one hundred percent certain of these things. You can never be one hundred percent certain of *anything*.

John was still looking at me, waiting for an answer. "Who the hell is it?", he asked again.

"I don't know", I said. I was telling the truth, too. I didn't know.

He laughed. He moved his head closer to mine so that our faces were almost touching, his deep brown eyes staring into mine. His pale and damp forehead and cheeks glowed with the sheen of a statue's head of alabaster. The sweat running down his forehead had its source deep in the bird's nest that was his greasy clotted hair. When the cascades of sweat hit the stubble on his cheeks they split into runnels and ran down his throat into the heavy blue and white checked shirt under his army jacket, which I imagined was pretty damp at this stage. His eyes weren't laughing. It was the laugh of a madman. Laughing through the grimaces.

Then, before I knew it, I was laughing too. I was laughing at John laughing. We were in *hysterics.* Our faces burning up all over and our laughs turning into a cough and back to a laugh and the hot tears streaming down my face and people turning around to see what was going on. But then all of a sudden he stopped. His whole face just dropped. He wasn't even smiling anymore and he grabbed me by the shoulders and said, "Kev, who's the girl on the other side of the fuckin' table!?"

I stood up from the table like a shot. I shrugged his rigid hands off my shoulders and stood up straight and knocked my pint over because everything was dizzy and hazy. It was boiling hot air everywhere and they were all roaring and shouting and jeering me. The Hall of Fame. A big glass maze with glass doors and pictures of Michel Jackson and Ronald Reagan and you kept banging into them because you didn't know where the hell you were. Banging into everybody. Everybody standing right over me. Even that girl with the big brown mole getting her revenge. All of them forcing my head back beneath the water so I couldn't breathe. I ploughed my way through the crowds. I got out of that whole Kremlin place like a bloody rocket.

Chapter 10
The Library

I stopped running when I got to L-block. They've got these red parking pillars all over the place and I sat on one. There was a wall in front of my pillar and I picked out a single brick on the wall, at random, and focused on it, to try and steady my blurred vision.

Then I heard, "*Je*-sus Kev." John was standing over me. "Next time you run out like that, tell me, will yeh." Under his shrunken, bloodshot eyes, his cheeks were swollen and puffy, like those of a man who'd had 50 shots of tequila rather than the single one he'd had at the bar. He brushed his hand anxiously through his hair, terrified by the prospect he'd narrowly avoided - having to face the world alone. His hair stayed standing on end when he took his hand away, matted and clotted as it was. He sat on the pillar beside me with his hands on his knees, out of breath. His collars were still up. People were walking by us into the Kremlin, giggling and laughing in their little groups. I was envious of them. I was incapable of doing that right now. All I wanted was to sit in a room by myself and watch TV. Or lay down on the sofa and listen to classical music or something with my eyes closed, no fear of these ideas racing around my head making a fool of myself. No, classical music wouldn't do it at all, I thought. I never listen to classical music. I wondered where classical music came from. I was too shaky, too full of energy; there's no way I could sit still through classical music.

John lay his cold hand on top of mine and said, "Don't worry, Kev. There's no need to be afraid. I'm with you, and I'm not going anywhere." Wow. That really settled my anxiety. He, who couldn't be left alone for even a minute, telling me to not be afraid.

He stood in front of me and looked at me, shaky and unfocused, like he was building up to something very important to say, like a great revelation was about to issue from his lips. "I need a joint, man. Come on. Let's do this." Up to then, they were the wisest words I'd ever heard him say.

We headed to the James Joyce entrance, near the Kremlin. We stood in the shelter and between the two of us we managed to skin two one skinners, no mucking about with licking rizla papers that blow away on you. They were messy as hell and we were spitting tobacco from our lips with every toke but afterwards, we felt great. I remember John was looking wistfully at the Kremlin when he was taking that last lung-collapsing toke. "Tomorrow is going to be a good day, Kev." The joint had transformed him. He paused and repeated and nodded to himself slowly, reflectively. "Yeah. A good day."

"The future's so bright you gotta wear shades?", I said, because it really seemed at that instant a pink flush had come into his cheeks, the future was indeed bright. His positivity rubbed onto me, making me feel better, too.

"Come on, let's go back to the Kremlin and find Dave.", he said. "Are you mad?" I wasn't ready for the Kremlin just yet - with all those funny people with funny moles walking around. "How about you follow me?", I said. "There's something I want to show you in the library." I set off in the opposite direction.

"The feckin' library!?" He wasn't crazy about the idea at first. Then he said, "What is it? The herons?" He followed me.

The herons were these birds we sometimes talked about back at the house when we were altogether in the front room in the evenings. John and Dave had never seen them. The library sporadically had these very tall glass windows and directly in front of one of the windows there was the top of a tall tree. And near the top of the tall tree there was a nest with three white birds with long beaks and they'd start squawking when they saw you. It was fascinating to look out at them and see them looking back at you, making that sound. Vinny used to say they were herons, but I don't know if they were or not.

Before John mentioned those birds, the thought of showing them to him had never crossed my mind. But the way he said it now and the way he was staring at me wide-eyed with that eagerness I smiled and said, "Of course, the herons.", like there was no way in the world I could have meant anything else.

We headed into the James Joyce entrance and took the lift. What I'd been thinking about while we were smoking that joint and in the lift was this old photo album I'd found by accident one day, way up on top of the shelves, when I was helping a friend of mine, Tom Malone, do a search for some economic reports he needed for a project. Sometimes you'd come in that library when you'd had a crap day and you'd glance through a few photos in that album and you'd always leave feeling a bit more cheerful. I found it hidden under a whole bunch of those reports, with years of dust on the cover. It left a clear trail with your finger. Somehow it got mislaid up there. I put it in the right place where it was supposed to be. I think of that book now and it makes me think of Edward. It's obviously the photos that's the link. It was like I'd *saved* it or something, just the way nobody might have ever discovered it, stuck up there by itself. There was one photo of Muhammad Ali's fist, actual size. It was impossible, every time you were looking at that photo, to not put your own fist on the page and compare sizes.

When we were in the lobby John said, "Do you know any good recipes, Kev? Something romantic 'n' shit." He had Rebecca on the brain again. We walked by the reception area where the ladies behind the desk scan your books. There were a few people in the queue, way less than normal. "I'm cooking dinner for her tomorrow. We should have got food 'n' shit in the Kremlin. I'm hungry."

"You're going to cook a meal? What are you going to cook?"

"I don't know. That's what I'm asking."

"Lasagna is always good."

"Is that the one Edward made with the crispy shit on top?"

"Shhh, let's keep our voices down." The lobby with its high ceiling and airy space had instantly helped me relax, but now, going through the glass doors into the library, the ceiling was lower, the lights brighter, and there were groups of students scattered here and there, which immediately put my senses on high alert and put me on my guard. We were talking a bit loud. We veered away from them until we were in a quieter section through which to walk. "Invite her out to Eddie Rockets or something, seriously. The most I've seen you make is a rasher sandwich, and the rashers were burnt." In case I hurt his feelings I said quickly, "Don't get me wrong, it was tasty, but lasagna is a whole new ball game."

I noticed the cease of his marching steps. He'd stopped walking. I immediately saw what had captured his attention; on a vacant desk surrounded by scattered open books and pens lay a pack of Taytos. He licked his salivating lips and reached for the pack. I waited til a group of students walking by were out of earshot and said, "Ah, John. Leave it there. It's someone's snack. They're just on a break. *Leave* it." I noticed a head of bright yellow hair bobbing over the edge of one of the partitions, watching us, spying on us. He would be looking straight at me, then he'd turn away quickly and put his head down to his scattered books and pens, and he'd scribble in his copy book. He had a very young face. I considered him to be studying for his leaving cert or maybe even his inter cert, such students sometimes being permitted into the library to study.

John's fingers withered under my icy glare. His hand crawled back up its frayed sleeve. His head retracted into the collars once more like a gopher in a tunnel who spots danger on the horizon.

But ultimately the penetration through his brain was ineffective. My pleas hit bone and snapped as arrows would do on the wall of a castle. His eyes widened with the mischief and rebellion of a cunning child. "Say you had a state of the art gold watch, right?", John said, justifying the Taytos. A few weeks earlier he robbed a sausage roll I'd left on the countertop and we were both remembering it now. "Well if you kept taking it off your wrist 'n' shit and leaving it in the open, sooner or later it'll get robbed 'n' shit, right? It's a lesson to you. You'll pay more attention to the bigger things in life, like your top of the range sports car, or whatever. You are doing them a favour. No pain, no gain. Likewise, I am doing this person a favour, by eating his crisps. If you leave shit lying around, Kev, it gets robbed. He will learn to take care of the bigger things in life."

The yellow head rose higher and tilted an ear to catch what was being said. He scribbled furiously in his notepad. I had no doubt he was documenting the affair.

"So the bloke gets his gold watch stolen, right?" I flashed Yellow Head a smile. "Then what? He learns to take better care of his car keys. They get stolen. Then what? He learns to watch his house keys. They get stolen. Then what? He learns to watch his mansion. That gets robbed. Then what? He learns to watch his castle. That gets robbed –

"What the hell have castles and mansions got to do with anything? You're always speakin' feckin' gibberish 'n' shit."

"You're the one speaking feckin' gibberish 'n' shit. At every stage you'll be there – the house, the mansion, the castle – and you'll justify it by saying, 'I did that person a favour'. That's bollox. Crime is like fat people. You get into a cycle of stuffing your face with crap and the more you eat the more miserable you get and you can't help it and the fatter you get the less inclined you are to do exercise because it's too much effort. Before you know it you're a beached whale incapable of anything. It begins with Taytos and before you know it you're robbing banks -

He picked up the Taytos and ripped them open and scoffed the whole pack in three noisy mouthfuls and poured the remnants down his throat. He threw the empty pack on the desk and brushed off his hands.

"You happy now?" If I was expecting his reaction to be anything remotely like contrition, I was disappointed. A victorious, condescending grunt of air escaped his nostrils - reserved for those who had so chastised him, ridiculed him, and for those students around us now. He considered the pack of Taytos on the desk as only a tiny fraction of his due; it was something so trivial, so irrelevant, so low, compared to the summit on which he now stood, the all-pervasive view of love it gave from the top, and the steppes he braved to get there. Yes, he knew things were different now; in the course of his life he had fumbled along with awkward, ungainly steps, and then, today, his path had intercepted with Rebecca's, and now great things lay ahead. She had beckoned him to take her hand, to leave his defences, his snug exile. He had listened! The girl of his dreams!, wanting him alone, for who he was, his personality, his good looks and his intellect... all this while Dave, his nemesis and chider, had failed miserably. As he saw it, his encounter with Rebecca was nothing less than a rosebud thrown from heaven. Where most perish along the way, landing on barren ground unnoticed by the world, he and Rebecca had caught their rosebud with arm outstretched, palm upheld.

Suddenly, a sigh of pity, and relief, whistled through his lips. For didn't he have so much to be grateful for? He knew their encounter was a rarity that transcended mere coincidence. Two shooting stars can collide but trajectory provided only the bed sheet of John and Rebecca's enduring magic. The ebb and flow of their words, the glances into each others' eyes, the kiss - all these ingredients slotted perfectly into place; the likelihood that lobster and caviar on silver platters and Champagne in crystal glasses can manifest from thin air rather than being the intended outcome of a chef's pursuits was just as feasible as their acquaintance being some whimsical, haphazard matter. Their union was an act directed by the hand of Mother Nature herself, encapsulating his past, present and future, culminating in the fusion of their souls. Had they shown him the respect he deserved, the possessions and gifts being bestowed upon him now may have come sooner, but he would hold no bitterness towards them. He would seek the betterment of his fellow compatriots. It was as if he was grateful for the hardships he had had to endure, that had they not happened at all, the point he was at now might never have arisen.

 I walked over to Yellow Head's side of the desk and said, with as friendly a smile I could muster, "Excuse me, do you happen to know where we could find the photography section please?" I'd been in the library a million times yet right now I didn't know where it was. John came over beside me. "The photography section? What about the feckin' herons 'n' shit?"

 "There's something I want to show you, first."

 For a second Yellow Head bowed his head to his books, like he was hoping we'd disappear, but then, as if his yellow head were a buoy with a cord attached, being pulled and submerged deeper and deeper into the water, then released, he sprang out of his seat to lead us to the section we were looking for. He told us his name was Keith. He was doing engineering.

 "Thanks Keith. We really appreciate this. We're lost. I'm Kevin, and this is John."

He marched on through the Gs, the Hs and Is, through alleyways and gullies I'd never seen before. I told John that even if he could cook lasagna, was he going to make it for breakfast? Myles said he'd be over at 1. John said, "Slow down, Keith, there's no rush." He was marching on at a fierce pace. Me and John were getting out of breath, with all the talking we were doing. "Do you have a girlfriend, Keith?" Keith mumbled he didn't have a girlfriend. "You have it all ahead of you, man. The secret is... not to look for it. Just let it find you, naturally." He cracked me up. You'd have sworn his entire life was a saga of amorous losses and conquests.

I couldn't resist saying, "John's girlfriend is an astrophysicist who can make square circles."

We arrived at the photo section. Keith helped me carry the ladder to the middle of the aisle and I climbed up.

"She knows what she's talking about, Kev. Mathematics is her field. Her niche 'n' shit." I reached for the album and opened it on that photo of the actual size of Muhammad Ali's fist and passed it down to John to compare his own fist against.

"What do you think Keith? You're an engineer. Are square circles your field?" He shrugged his shoulders, giving no definitive answer one way or the other. "It's like apples and oranges, John. Two completely different things."

"That's exactly my point, Kev." He passed the photo album to Keith. 'Tell him, Keith. You can get green oranges and I'm sure there's orange apples in some parts of the world. It's not a black and white issue. Jesus, Keith... your hands are shaking more than mine."

Suddenly I was getting a strange feeling... like we were being *watched* or something.

"What's wrong, Kev?" I was smelling the air like a bloodhound. "Do you ever get a feeling something's not right? Like... you're being watched or something?" Then I remembered. My heart sank. I jumped the last two steps off the ladder. How stupid I was! How could I have forgotten it!

"Fuck."

"What's wrong?"

I rushed for the first row of shelves I could find on the aisle we were standing in and peered through the gap as far as the eye could see, towards the exit, or where I thought the exit would be. I could see nothing. The view was obscured by tall shelves of library books and students and beyond them more students standing and leafing through books and a librarian pushing a trolley full of books to be placed back on shelves... I couldn't see as far as the lobby at all. I didn't even know which direction the lobby was in.

But I knew he would be there: Mickey Moustache, the security guard, standing there at his station, at the exit, and there was no way to get out but past him.

"Jesus, John, how did we get ourselves in this mess?" I was still peering through the shelf at alternate angles, grappling for books and shifting them aside to hopefully see the exit, but it was in vain. I could see nothing.

"What?", John was saying, alarmingly. "What are you looking at?"

"The security guard, Mickey Moustache. I can't see him from here but he's definitely there... did you see him on the way in? He definitely wasn't there on the way in, was he? We'd definitely have noticed him." I put my hands to my forehead, wondering what to do. "Most likely he was on a break, which means he'd be back now. Fuck. Fuck. Fuck. I'd *never* have come in if he was there. What are we going to do? Seriously, there's no way we can get by him in our current state, tripping out of our heads. And... where the hell is Keith?"

Sure enough, he was gone. No sign of him anywhere.

"You go that way and I'll go this way.", said John, in an impressively leader-like, confidence inspiring way, and we started off in opposite directions. At the last second I said, "John!" Two students shot a glance at me. I smiled and nodded apologetically and jogged leisurely across the floor to John, who was already in the aisle across from me. "We meet back here in five minutes, ok? If we don't find Keith in five minutes, he's a goner. We just have to focus and look out for ourselves. Back here in five minutes, ok?"

"Why are you smiling like that?"

"Shh. I'm not smiling. Nothing's wrong." I was smiling so people would think we were the model of two level headed students going about our studies, tying up a few loose ends before exams the next day.

"You are smiling. You've got a big smile 'n' shit on your face."

"It's a *fake* smile.", I hissed through the smile. "Just don't let people know there's something wrong. They could call Mickey Moustache over in a flash. You get me? He'd kill us. You go that way, I'll go this way. If we don't find him, there's no point. Back here in five minutes." He gave me a thumbs up to indicate he got my drift and hurried off. "And John." He turned around for a second. "Walk slowly, like there's nothing wrong. Ok?" He gave me another thumbs up.

The backs of my eyes strained for the owner of that conspicuous pompadour of yellow hair, or even the rows of desks we'd pulled him away from in the hope he'd managed to return to them, but deep down I knew the chance of him finding umbrage, alone out there in the wilderness, was slim. I felt personally responsible, like a babysitter who'd let a toddler out into the busy street. I realised I had no idea where I was, let alone where Keith was. Not only that, I had no idea of the point we'd started out from. I was wandering aimlessly around a vast swamp of confusion. I peeped through gaps in shelves here and there, hoping to see John, or Keith - either of them would have done. If I had a map... no, that would have been a terrible idea. The thought of reading a map made me dizzy. I thought of goldfish and what it must be like to have a three second memory. I thought of everything except what truly mattered – finding John. I ventured into new territory, keeping an eye out for him. Practically tiptoeing with the vigilance of a trooper in a Vietnamese rain forest. Students cast discreet, suspicious glances at the huddled, incompetent wreck of bones trudging, uninvited, through their territory. Enemies peeping through leaves. I slowed my pace to a horrible self-conscious stroll. At a corner I took a book off a shelf and tried to read it to distract myself but nothing would sink in because all I could do was wonder where the hell John had disappeared to in this hostile jungle.

Chapter 11

The Business Idea

Finally, I saw him in one of the aisles. I ran over and threw my arms around him and hugged him, my long lost brother. I didn't care if anyone saw. "John, there you are!" Man, was I happy to be reunited. He could eat as many Taytos as he wanted, I didn't care. I hugged him tightly and pulled him deeper into the aisle, out of sight.

"We just *can't* let that happen again.", I said now, seriously, with anger seeping through, not at him, but at how close we had come to being truly lost, and annoyed at how an idea I was having now hadn't come to me sooner.

"But we were looking for Keith 'n' shit. Two eyes is better than one."

"No eyes is worse. It's like a warzone in here 'n' shit. I mean it's not like a *war* warzone but... you know what I mean."

"It kind of is like a warzone."

"It is, isn't it?", I said, happy we were on the same wavelength. Hearing private thoughts spoken by another had a consolidating, sobering effect. "It is like a warzone. I mean in the sense we have to stay together. If we get lost, we're fucked. Two people in a war always survive better than one. We need a code or something. Something we can shout out if we get lost so we can know where we are, like a team would do."

"'Help! Help!'?"

"Shh. Too obvious. We need something that won't get people's attention. Uno. Nice and simple. If you hear 'Uno!', or I hear it - obviously louder than that, you run for your life. Ok?" He nodded in approval. "Are you alright?", I said.

He seemed in good form, but there was something funny about him. He was walking funny, in a stiff-jointed way.

"What do you mean?", he asked.

"I don't know. You look like you're doing a C-3PO impression or something. Are you cold or... sick? You're not looking too well." Beads of perspiration populated his forehead like he had a fever. His arms were wrapped around his belly like he had chronic stomach cramps, like he could lose control of his bodily functions at any instant. He looked up and down the aisle. "I'm ok, I'm ok", he said. "A bit nervous about this security guard 'n' shit." And then quieter, and looking up and down the aisle one more time, "I've come up with a business idea." To a casual, unseasoned observer he had the corpse-like visage of a body stretched out in a coffin, but to me, his destined soulmate on this journey through space and time, who knew him better than his own mother right now, I could sense nerveways tickling with excitement in the brain behind those lively eyes that looked at me. To a regular joe soap he looked like he'd been pulled from a vat of formaldehyde, which was still dripping freshly off him, but to me I could see little incipient pin pricks of pink trying to burst out on his gaunt face, thwarted though before they could make any lasting impression, reined in by the reality of the path ahead, fraught with danger.

He motioned down with those eyes at something between his fingers, the fingers of the arm that was more free and not holding his belly as intensely as the other arm. I saw he was holding a copy of *The Art of War* in his hand, by Sun Tzu.

"What's this?"

"It's a book. I want you to take it out for me. On the back it says he's been read by business people for centuries and it got me to thinking you could make a fortune by -

"You could make a fortune by what?"

He looked about the room, worried someone might hear. "Can't talk about it here, Kev. You never know who's listening 'n' shit. We'll wait til we're outside."

"Look here..." I was peeping through one of the aisles again. We could see him now. John leaned over and squinted his eyes to look through the gap in the shelf at what I was looking at.

Out past the desks in the library, to the right of the librarians in the lobby who were positioned behind the big black leather kidney shaped desk and who scanned books handed to them for loan by students, my eyes settled upon the only thing that eyes could settle upon – to the right, the figure of the security guard, Mickey Moustache, standing there at his spot by the barrier, at the exit. He was wearing his green V neck jumper, a green tie, a white shirt and a pair of grey slacks, all immaculately pressed as usual.

He seemed to be there for 12 to 14 hours a day, his posture varying from standing there with arms folded, observing diligently people walking in, people walking out, to leaning slightly forward with arms by his side and fists clenched, ready to charge into battle. I'd say he was six foot five or six. He was in his late 30s or early 40s. He was part of library lore, the one person you didn't mess with in this neck of the woods.

"What are you looking at?", John said, squinting his eyes through the gap in the shelf, in the direction of Mickey Moustache, exactly where he was supposed to be looking.

"What do you think I'm looking at? I'm looking at that massive bloke at the barrier there, in the green uniform."

"That massive dude with the big fat moustache?"

"Yes, of course. Mickey Moustache. How could you miss him?" I couldn't believe John didn't notice him straight away. He stood out like a sore thumb. "He's like, ten foot tall. What the hell are we going to do? There's no way we can get by him in our current state."

There was obviously the big moustache that stood out, hence the name, but there were other things about him too that propelled students' imaginations, giving weight to the stories we'd heard. He had a scar on his face running down from the corner of his right eye to the side of his mouth. I could picture him in the mornings preparing for his day's work, the ideal employee - ironing his uniform, combing his hair, priming his moustache, then tending to his post, his feet rooted to the ground like a giant tree trunk, the sharp eyes in that head high above everybody else's in the library peering upon all and sundry with the vigilance of a lighthouse, like he was a patient, silent hound at the gates, ready to deal swiftly and efficiently with disorder. But there was that one percent of the time when he was far removed from the alert, conscientious gatekeeper that he was known to be. I remember one day when we were leaving the library me and Ciaran both remarked on the stink of tobacco that hit us as we walked through the barrier. His sleeves were rolled up, shirt cuffs unbuttoned, hanging sloppily about his elbows. His top button was undone, the knot loose on his tie. His hair was messy. He hadn't shaved in days. It was appearances like these, a break from the otherwise stellar record of upholding library decorum, that accelerated rumours and gave him a sinister reputation.

And the tattoo on his arm; a sword with a snake coiled around it. All I knew about tattoos back then is they're painful. They've better technology now and they're certainly more common nowadays; all you saw back in the day practically was a blotchy navy line on a person's arm or back of the hand like it was drawn by a child, or unfinished, like the person getting the tattoo didn't have the stamina to go through with the pain of it. The sword and snake on his arm was so ornate compared to all the others I'd seen back then with so much detail and colour and I was thinking it must have been so painful for him but pain was nothing to Mickey Moustache; whatever horror he had been through in his life was etched in his eyes if you looked closely enough, all would recoil and quieten as they approached the vicinity of his fiery gaze, a volcano like ten Krakatoas about to erupt, when you ventured by him you'd hold your breath, your heart would skip a beat, you'd hunker down to avoid his baleful eye -

"We're going to have to sleep the night here, John.", I said at last. He shook his head incredulously. "Seriously. They open at 8 in the morning. We can sneak out when people are coming in tomorrow morning." The pace of his shaking head accelerated.

"Yes, John, I'm serious, we've no choice. There's rumours that he killed someone. Killed someone!"

"Kev, Kev, Kev... ", John said, assuringly. He removed both his arms from his belly for a moment and stooped forwards uncomfortably and placed each of his hands on my shoulders, in the way of a person about to impart advice that would be the antidote to my tattered nerves. "I'll tell you what we're going to do. We're going to walk out of this library, nice and calmly, go back to the house, and chill out, ok? There's nothing to worry about. You just follow me. We're going to go home... and we're gonna watch Jean Claude Van Damme movies all night long."

It certainly was an enticing prospect, but there was the little issue of Mickey Moustache at the exit, whom we would have to pass were we to go back to the house and watch videos. "People say he was in jail. No, we can't go out. We just... *can't*. It's impossible. We'll go out tomorrow. I'm pretty sure there's none of those red laser beam alarms that go off automatically if you hop around and -

"We're not staying the night in no feckin' library, man. It's like you said Kev, we're the only ones who know we're tripping out of our heads 'n' shit. Nobody else knows. They don't have a clue what's going on. Even if this Mickey what's his face looks into our eyes and knows we're tripping... who cares as long as we don't do anything wrong? Is it illegal to be tripping in a library? Is it? No, it's not. I don't think so. LSD is a naturally occurring substance. As long as we're not doing harm to anyone else. We're gonna walk out that exit, we're gonna go home, we're gonna chill out and watch Jean Claude Van Damme videos, ok? Big fire, big cups of tea, crisps and bikies. There's nothing to worry about, Kev. Just relax. Let me do the talking, if we need to."

I was stupefied by his composure and his wisdom. Nothing like he normally was: quick tempered and jumpy. Whatever it was, he had changed. He was consumed with a desire for learning, for love. Where once he was content to spend his days reacting to obstacles that life threw in his path, now he proactively fought them head on, jumping into the fray to challenge his demons, rather than being their servant. Because of Rebecca, success had triumphed forever over failure's watery grave. Because of Rebecca, the future was imperceptible, but he knew the promise of beauty would be guaranteed somewhere along the line, as certain as the sun behind golden clouds, as treasure on the bed of turbid oceans. Initially he had judged the merits of meeting her, and the benefits that would arise thereof, as his own private, selfish cauldron of joys, to be hoarded and enjoyed as he saw fit, but now, Rebecca having set a flame of generosity alight in his heart, he would share it with the world. With her guidance he would attain the pinnacle of emotional and spiritual contentment that every individual strives to achieve. He would relish the journey, wherever it would lead him. The insecurities that plagued him were being smoothed and ironed out, the disappointments of his past life were being turned upside down. And his good qualities - his noble heart, the regular acts of generosity and compassion, she would further polish and galvanise. She would harvest the hay, put the poor grass out to dry for as long as it took, then harvest that too. And this voyage to distillation of spirit would be accompanied by her charms, her kisses, her whispers of sweet nothings. What bliss!

In the Kremlin earlier, with Dave, he was baying for blood, his eyes were full of malice and anger, hard as rivets, sharp as knives, but now they were anything but; rather, a kind empathy, a sort of all-knowing wisdom, shone on those in their wake; the generous, compassionate look one might reserve for a wounded, famished animal spotted from a hill top, limping along - oblivious to the watering hole on the left, the plentiful meadow over the hill on the right... and he was willing to climb down off his perch and guide the way, with nothing to gain for himself. He really was a leader, so selfless and considerate and resolute, and right now, he, more than anybody on earth, is the person I wanted to lead us through this quagmire from A to B. We were brothers, bonded into the same consciousness, fully comprehending each others' struggles, the only two people who fully understood each other, and the way he was looking at me and the way he was talking made me confident he'd lead me through swamps and fire pits to a destination far beyond that exit gate.

He was looking at me. "What are you looking at, man?"

At first I didn't answer. I was too busy looking at him and thinking about him. There was something so... humble about him. In spite of the physical torment he was going through to contain the crippling aches in his belly, and the droplets of condensation on his forehead and his eyes and lips that twitched and grimaced, he was prepared to persevere, to lead... he was prepared to fight through the pain and bring me home.

"Eh... I don't know. I'm just looking at you." His question caught me off guard, to be honest.

"Yeah I know. But why?"

"I'm just... I'm just in awe of you, man. You're like a philosopher. You're good natured, you're relaxed... a natural leader, I don't know. Whatever this acid is doing to you, man, or me for that matter... I mean... you're just so fucking intelligent. You're a genius. A genius."

He was genuinely chuffed, embarrassed even. "Gee, thanks, Kev. I sometimes think I'm stupid."

"No, no, you're not stupid John. You definitely got something. You're definitely not stupid. Genius, that's the only way I can describe it. I always knew you were intelligent but I'm just seeing a whole new side to you, I'm seeing the bigger picture. You know what I mean? And... it's just... brilliant. It's incredible. You have so much... potential. You're a genius."

"Yeah, you're right. It's a different kind of intelligence, isn't it?" He nodded, his eyes lighting like lanterns switched on at this new recognition of self-worth, riding on the growing wave my praises had sent in his favour. "You know what the best university is, Kev? The best university that money can buy 'n' shit, the best university that *no* money can buy?"

"What?"

"It's the university of life. Yeah, I'm serious. That's the university I went to. Can't learn that shit in here. No matter how many books you read, you can't learn that in here. You either have it or you don't. This library, you only have it for a while. Three days or some shit." A student perusing the spines of books on a shelf was nearby so I gave John's arm a tug to move along, which caused him to hobble along in pursuit of me, hunched over, his legs shifting awkwardly forwards like they were two vertical poles, not bending at the knees, and his hands around his belly like they were stuck with cement, like his guts would spill on the floor if he removed them.

"John, seriously, you are saying some amazing, far out shit, but we need to get you to a toilet. Big time." He looked at me with patient, querying eyes, his chin raised and practically looking down his nose at me. "What do you mean?", he said. Who was I to challenge his confidence?

"You've had it for three days, you said. You're obviously talking about some tummy bug or something, yeah? Sorry, I just can't stop thinking of Mickey Moustache. My head's all over the place. I don't know what I'm saying. What were you saying?"

"Ha, Kev, you're nuts, man!", he said, starting this sentence with a hearty laugh, but which quickly turned fragile with the risk of Mickey Moustache hearing us and catching his attention. "Three days... I said that's how long you can take a *book* out for from this place, this feckin' library. You can take it out for only three days. Everybody fighting to study. Or so Edward said. Used to drive him mad. That's the funny thing about it Kev, that's what's so feckin'... I don't know... *ironic* 'n' shit. This is just the warm up act. The university of life. You get me? *That's* the business idea. Wash, rinse, repeat 'n' shit. It's the equivalent of having an endless supply of oxygen when everybody is living in the moon. You know what I'm saying?"

"Sort of."

"I ever tell you about Patsy Burke?"

"No."

We walked nowhere in particular, mostly just because we felt like moving, doing our best to avoid the prospect of facing Mickey Moustache. "He was a friend of the family down the road. Back in the day asked me and the auld lad to build him a new roof. Took weeks. Burke said it was giving off funny vibrations 'n' shit. Never paid us. Now if he had been a *stranger*, we would have got money out of him quick smart, before we'd even started the work, but when it's a friend of the family 'n' shit... it's different... Basically, don't do business with friends 'n' shit, that's what I'm saying. That's what I've learnt. Keep your friends close and your enemies closer. Can't learn that shit in here. Now let's make a plan 'n' shit and get out of here. I need a drink. Mouth feels like feckin' sand paper. Yes, there's lots of different intelligences. You're right. And mine is just... business. Simple. It's just business. That's it. So many people don't have it. That's what amazes me, so many people in here reading books 'n' shit and they don't have it. It's being street-wise 'n' shit. That's my intelligence, being street-wise 'n' shit."

Chapter 12
The Mouse

On our meanderings, I related to John the dreaded story of Mickey Moustache, or at least the one of quite a few that had left the biggest impression in my mind, anyway. We didn't know where the exit was but some part of my brain subconsciously figured if we veered continuously leftwards along the wide swathe of floor we'd get there eventually.

"Two friends of mine... Martin Quinn and Philip Keogh. Philip was a joker, great sense of humour... His mate, Martin, was terrified of mice. And Philip took advantage of his fear. He had the whole thing planned to a tee. It was wintertime. One evening before Martin got home from lectures Philip cut a finger off an unused glove and stuck a piece of shoelace through it, so it looked like a mouse. Then he locked the kitchen door that led out to the back garden. The lengths he went to! There was a spare key to the door hanging on the nail beside the sink and Philip even hid the key so Martin wouldn't find it. He unscrewed all the light bulbs downstairs so that if someone pressed a light switch it would look like there was a power cut. This turn here. Anyway, when Martin arrived home he asked, 'Why is everything so dark?' Philip explained there was a power cut. 'And worse', he said, 'There is a mouse in the house.' Martin froze. 'Where?' 'In your bedroom.' - which was the room right next to the kitchen. Martin was terrified. Philip told Martin not to worry, that he would capture the mouse. Martin peeped his head in the bedroom door occasionally to catch the sight of Philip in the dark on his knees, searching for the mouse. All of a sudden Philip rushed out of the bedroom! Towards Martin! It all happened so quickly and before Martin's brain could function as to what was happening Philip had the 'mouse' – the finger on the shoestring - dangling under Martin's nose in the dark and yelling, 'I CAUGHT HIM! I CAUGHT THE MOUSE! LOOK! I CAUGHT THE MOUSE!' The kitchen door was locked so he had to stand there, screaming, Philip dangling the 'mouse' in front of his face, and then he ran past him out of the house."

"That's a lovely story and all, Kev.", John said, "but what does it have to do with that big bastard at the barrier?"

"Good question. Right turn here... And let go of my hand, it looks gay. This story of Martin and the mouse spread like wildfire. The shy, reserved Martin, who had been little known throughout the college, was suddenly one of the most recognized people in its history. He'd be cycling down the road and a complete stranger would go 'Squeak!, squeak!' Or a person in the queue in the shop would go 'Squeak! Squeak!' *Everybody* would go 'Squeak! Squeak!' Martin couldn't deal with it anymore. He's quite shy. One day in the library he got Philip in a headlock and started punching him. All hell broke loose. According to eye witness accounts, Mickey Moustache darted through the library, grabbed the two of them by the ear, carried them across the room and the three of them disappeared into one of those little storage rooms behind the lobby."

"Rumour has it", I said, quieter, "that when Mickey Moustache returned to his spot at the entrance, there was the hint of a smile, his first expression ever, people say, beneath that enormous bushy moustache of his. And as for Philip and Martin, well, they were never the same again."

"What did he do to them?"

"Shhh. Keep your voice down.", I said, enjoying the hold my story had on him, wishing to expound on the rumours as it's satisfying to see someone so engrossed in your story. To express those stories vocally though meant mentally having to immerse myself in them, so I pulled back just when I was on the cusp of going into macabre and gratuitous scenes, for it would have made me more scared than I was already, propelling my fragile, scattered mind into an even sorrier state. I cut to the chase. "They said they were brought to a room, that's all. That's all they told us. A small room with only the 3 of them. Nobody knows what happened, but the rumours are terrifying. Damn it, it's not this aisle... come on, keep following me... they were different though after that, that's for sure. They always had this glazed over look in their eyes. It's hard to explain. It's like they were hypnotised or some shit, I don't know."

At last we arrived at our destination: the large automatic sliding door to the lobby, where the librarians scanned the books at the big desk in the shape of a kidney bean, and to the right of that, the exit, where Mickey Moustache was standing. "Ok, there it is, John. The exit. You ready to do this?"

We looked through the glass of the sliding door out onto the wide open plain of the lobby, not saying a word, just watching and listening to life around us. Fingertips tapped on keyboards. Scanners beeped over barcodes. Photocopiers hummed. And throughout it all Mickey Moustache stood at his spot at the exit, watching over it all, surveying people, ensuring the order of things was kept.

John took a deep breath and exhaled slowly, readying himself for the task at hand, as did I.

"Let's go."

"Are you sure?"

"We have nothing to worry about, Kev. We're the same as everybody else. It's the same with magic mushrooms. As long as they're naturally occurring substances then it's ok."

He spoke with such authority, I couldn't possibly disagree with him. It was like the old John had been razed to the ground.

"Ok, Kev. I'm ready... Let's do this shit."

Chapter 13

The Toilet

We stepped into the lobby and proceeded on our way, surrounded by clusters of students walking in and walking out around us, but suddenly I stopped like a horse whose reins are pulled back. "What's wrong?", John hissed through clenched teeth. Just the sight of Mickey Moustache ahead and the task we had to do. It was overwhelming. His stature reminded me of a North Korean border patrol man I'd seen on TV, twice the size, poised for war.

"What if he asks us a question?" I pulled John's arm. He was keen to keep going. I whispered, putting on that stupid grin again, just in case we stood out like a sore thumb, and saying through the grimace, "I can stomach if he says something like, 'Bye now, have a good summer.' A simple grunt or smile will suffice, and we just keep walking. But if he asks a question and I have to look him in the eye and think of an answer... I really don't know what I'll say. It mightn't sound like it John but I'm a babbling wreck." It was hard to see what he was looking at. He was quite a bit away. The last thing we wanted was to stare and get his attention so we turned in towards the wall by the photocopier and continued our conversation in whispers and hushes, with heads sunk into shoulders and collars up.

"What questions would he be asking us?"

"I don't know... even just something simple like, 'Did you find what you were looking for, lads?' Just a little thing like that, it would send me into spastic mode. I'd just stand there, like a tool. We shouldn't be having this conversation here, he's right in front of us."

He'd said earlier he was thirsty so mostly to assuage his thirst, but partly in an attempt to delay what was coming down the tracks, I pulled two paper conical cups from the Ballygowan water cistern besides us by the wall and I filled them and offered one to John. He gulped it back. "Need some beer 'n' shit."

"Well there's no beer so drink water. And keep your voice down." I filled him another and he gulped that back too, water dribbling down his throat like he'd spent days parched in the desert. Those cups were tiny.

"We're not even talking loud, Kev. He has no reason to suspect anything. Plan A is, we're going to keep our heads down, don't make eye contact, stay close behind me, and we'll just breeze by him like he's not there 'n' shit. Ok? You ready?"

"Of course I am, I was born ready." I gave a furtive glance towards the barrier. The prospect of approaching it was as attractive as walking barefoot across hot coals. "Are you sure you don't want to go to the toilet first? You're not looking too hot."

"I'm fine, Kev. I'm fine. In great form." He raised his chin and stuck his chest out and looked around imperiously, as if reminded of the responsibility he was carrying. He looked far from fine. He shivered. His thick brown hair was clotted and sweaty. His eyes were twitchy. His black eye glowed with a sickly sheen. Not the appearance of the person you're hoping to lead you through battle. His arms, wrapped tightly around his belly, only left it momentarily, like if he got jittery and needed to grab hold of my hand or arm to reassure himself I was still there, or to drink a cup of water.

"The last thing I want is you to have diarrhoea or some shit in the middle of the floor.", I said, regretting those words straight away. He looked in that fragile zone already. I didn't want to incite it with imagery. His wide eyes flitted between me and the view over my shoulder, which was Mickey Moustache standing at his post, solid and immobile like a warrior ready to rush forwards and crush the opposition. "That moral, grabbing a bull by the horns, is so true 'n' shit.", he said, in a whisper. "A bull can kill you, facing your fears, which is good, because of the adrenaline rush 'n' shit, but the other part is a bull won't stand too long in the same spot, waiting for you to grab its horns."

"I'm in no mood for running towards a bull right now. This is real life John, not an old fecking wives tale. The bull is real life. The bull is standing right there, at the fecking barrier, and we don't even have a cape."

"Is he looking at us, Kev? I'm sure he's feckin' lookin' at us."

"*You* look at him. You're facing that way." There was no way I was turning my head around. We'd already been looking at him too much, and the last thing we needed was both of us staring which would only have redoubled his suspicions.

I started for the toilet and John followed. He was all hunched over and holding his belly. He took his steps in sweeping, protracted arcs, hardly able to even bend his knees.

I pushed him hurriedly through the door into the little corridor and from there into the other door that lead into the toilet. I headed to the urinal for a whiz and John hobbled along more rapidly than normal for one of the two cubicles, spurred on by the relief that being inside the cubicle would provide to him, and he locked the door.

"Do you not think...", I said, standing outside his cubicle. There was a lot of shuffling around in there.

"Do I not think what?"

"Nothing." On second thoughts I reckoned there was no point saying it. He'd already discounted the idea.

"Jesus, John, would you look at the state of us.", I said. I was looking at myself in the mirror over the sink and throwing handfuls of water in my face to try sober up. I was flabbergasted at the size of my pupils. There were no blue irises, just big black holes, and those black holes were expanding into the whites of my eyes. The black holes were gateways into my soul. My body had definition, or structure, like a pink head, with messy hair on top, and shoulders, but my brain, or conscience, or soul, or whatever, somewhere behind my eyeballs, fascinated me. It was an empty, black void, judging by my eyes. My brain was a plate and my conscience was a marble rolling around on the plate. It threw out ideas and images out of nowhere from the void through my eyeballs into the mirror, reflecting them back like as at a stranger.

"I just feel so feckin' paranoid. With you and your... I don't know... your indigestion or whatever it is... and me with my eyeballs... I feel people can read my mind. Did you ever get that?" I was hoping the black holes would get smaller with the refreshing dollops thrown into my face but if anything they were getting bigger and the marble on the plate was rolling faster, causing the back of my skull to vibrate.

"Nobody can read anybody's mind, Kev. We'll be grand."

Whenever he spoke his voice was muffled, like talking from the bottom of a cave. I could hear clothes being unzipped.

"Are you ok in there?"

"I'm stressed, that's all."

"Stressed? Stressed about what?"

"Love, in a nutshell. Love."

"Are you talking about that Rebecca one again?"

A sigh from inside the door was noticeable amidst the shuffling and moving about. "Yes. And No. I'm more worried about my business idea, to be honest."

"Starting a new business is always tough, John.", I said through the door, adamant to revive his focus. There were a few 'ifs' and 'buts' there and if anything we needed bravery and valour and single-mindedness more than ever. "You need to have killer instinct, you need to have..." The passion I was trying to muster sounded hollow. "Jesus, listen to me." I threw dollops of water furiously into my face. I went out the main toilet door, the one leading into the corridor and into the lobby, and opened the lobby door slightly. I stuck my head out the gap, just as much as I needed to peer around the edge of the door.

He was looking straight at me! I pulled back quickly and hurtled back into the toilet and to John's cubicle and said through the cubicle door, "Do you not think we're better off staying the night in here, is what I'm saying? I mean not here here, in the jacks, but in the library? That way we wouldn't have to go past him. We could walk back in and hide down the back and walk out in the morning. He only starts his shift around 10 or so. It would be fun! There's a whole board game section -

"Being stuck in a library on acid all night... that would be my feckin' nightmare, man."

"How long are you going to take in there though? You've been in there for feckin' ages." I kept hearing noises like clothes being thrown onto the toilet seat and stuff being hung on the hook on the door.

"That's like asking, 'How long is a piece of string?'"

A thought occurred to me. "You didn't *shit* yourself, did you? If you shat yourself I can leg it back and get you... Jesus, no, I can't even do that. There's no way I'm going out there by myself. And saying, 'The answer to your question is like asking, 'How long is a piece of string?' doesn't make sense."

"It makes perfect sense. Great ideas start in the toilet 'n' shit. Like that bloke who shouted, 'Eureka!'"

"Yeah ok, great ideas happen in the toilet. But I'm talking about the string. Were I to ask you, say, 'What time is it please?', in the context of us talking about lengths of string, and your answer to that question being like, 'That's a bit like asking, "Is it 5 o' clock?"', makes no sense. I'm the one asking the bloody question. But anyway, who cares about pieces of string. What matters is you're ok in there and we're both safe. Where's the old John? We need him back."

At last the cubicle door opened. He was smiling, and there was a little blush of life in his gaunt yellow cheeks. He was still holding his belly, but he was smiling, and seemed relaxed, which I was glad to see.

"Are you not going to flush the toilet?"

"No need. I'll tell you one thing Kev, when I have money to invest 'n' shit... a good investment is shoe laces. People will always need shoelaces. So... where were we... head down, no eye contact -"

"Head down, no eye contact, don't say a word, follow close behind you... I got it. But first I want to show you something."

"Show me what?" He was less than enthusiastic to hear a potential new hurdle thrown in our wake.

"It's hard to say. Come here." He didn't budge. "Follow me." His eyes followed anxiously behind me as I walked through the toilet entrance door once more and his body followed, hobbling along behind me into the lobby, all hunched over, but his legs had more movement than previously. I walked right up to the lobby door and waited for him to stick his head out and tell me what he saw but he just stood there.

"Well? Open the bloody *door*.", I said, like it was the most obvious thing in the world. As soon as I said it, it hit me - how *could* he know what I was expecting of him? The words, "Open the door and poke your head out." had never left my mouth. I consciously tried to engrain it in my head that people couldn't read my thoughts unless I said them. He swiftly put his hand on the handle and tugged it but only a tiny bit before I jammed it with my foot and said, "Stop!". I closed the door fully again. He looked like he was expecting a grizzly bear or something to snatch him if he opened the door.

"What's so funny?", he said. I was laughing. Just the surreal yelp of my voice, and the vision I had if he had yanked that door open - Mickey Moustache standing there, just staring at us.

"We're supposed to be in a serious situation, Kev."

"I know, I know. It's nervous laughter."

"No, seriously, we're in a matter of life and death 'n' shit and you're going on like it's feckin' hilarious."

"I never feel more alive than when confronted by death. I know, John, I know. Nothing's funny. Or at least it's not funny funny." I leaned over with my hands on my knees to take a few deep breaths. "It is fucked up funny though. You have to admit it. The two of us in here on a Friday night, in the library." I raised my fists to him and nudged him on the shoulder. "We're just two lost souls swimming in a fish bowl." He wasn't amused.

"Seriously, we need to focus 'n' shit."

"I'm sorry, I'm sorry." I stood up straight and put a serious expression on my face. "Open the door. Slowly. Very slowly. And look out. Tell me what you see." A different reflex to twitching commenced in his eye; the eyelid of his black eye fluttered; just undulating or flickering rapidly above his iris, yet the eye staying open as he absorbed my words. His lips, a pale grey, quivered slightly. It was the way I was looking at him intensely and focusing on my words as I had newly resolved to do, with gravitas, like taking a deep breath and waiting five seconds before saying anything in public to make sure I was about to say it and then saying each word very slowly as I said it, to be sure I was actually saying it, that worried him. "It's not something that's going to jump on top of you or anything.", I explained. "You're not going to die. I just want to be sure you're seeing the same thing I'm seeing. I just want to be sure it's right, that I'm not seeing things. I'm not going to tell you what it is. Go on, have a peep out, and tell me what you see, and we'll see if it's the same thing I see. If we both see the same thing then more than likely it's the real thing."

He started to pull the door handle, slowly this time, his gaze fixed on me, like he was hoping for me to break into a smile and say it was a joke. He opened the door and poked his head slowly around the edge as I had done a few minutes earlier. How he reacted stressed me out more than what he said: "That dude, with the big fat moustache, is halfway across the bloody room!"

He ventured back along the corridor and tried to open other doors but they were locked. He hobbled quickly back into the heart of the jacks, with me on his tail. "What are you doing now?", I said, exasperated. He ventured straight into the cubicle he'd just left. "You've been in there for like half an hour, what the hell is going to change this time round?" It was like that old adage, stupidity is repeating the same thing and expecting a different result the second time. Dread washed over me. It occurred to me we could be trapped in the toilet forever.

This time though he left the door open so I could see what he was doing. He looked ridiculous. He closed the lid of the toilet. He seemed to be trying to kick or scrape his shoes on the rim of the toilet bowl, while hopping up and down. He did this with both feet. His arms around his belly the whole time. An outside observer would have pitied him as a man plighted with severe polio, trying to scrape chewing gum or dog crap off the soles of his hiking boots on the rim of the toilet. "You look like you're doing the Can Can... a solo version." He gave up his attempts and he stared at me.

"Stand on that." he said, panting now, out of breath. He was talking about the toilet seat but he was looking up at the ceiling like something of great importance was going on up there. He couldn't get up on the toilet seat, as he couldn't bend his legs. I looked up at the rectangles on the ceiling. "Those slates on the ceiling are made of foam.", he said. "Get up on that, push up one of the tiles, and we might be able to go out that way."

"You mean crawl along the feckin' ceiling? To where? We don't even know where it leads to." I was disappointed. Mickey Moustache was about to charge through the door, John was our only hope in coming up with a scheme better than anything I could do myself, and the best he comes up with is climbing on top of the bloody ceiling.

"There's no alternative 'n' shit, Kev.", he said. He was adamant. "We can't walk out there past him, there's no alternative."

"But sure we could be crawling along the ceiling the whole length of the bloody college and we wouldn't know where we're going. What if we fell through the foam tiles and landed in the middle of the bloody lobby in front of him?" But on reflection the prospect of having to crawl around earth was indeed preferable right now to having to cross the lobby and face Mickey Moustache so I jumped on the toilet as he suggested and stood on my tippie-toes and pushed a foam tile with my fingers, which moved, as they were light as he had said, not fixed in place, which encouraged me to keep going, as theoretically an adult figure could indeed crawl through the hole and find an alternative route out. John pushed my ass up further, so my elbows and arms got to be resting on one of the metal grids that supported the foam tiles, and the foam tile was resting on my head as I peered around in the darkness above the ceiling.

"What do you see?", I heard from below.

"Not much. Lots of pipes, like air filters or insulation. To be honest John I don't think this is a very good idea." I could feel my ass wobbling in the hands that were holding me up. "John? John?" Suddenly I didn't feel his hands supporting my ass at all. The metal grid was bending with the weight of my elbows and arms and chest.

Far away I heard his voice say, "I'm thinking. Catching my breath 'n' shit."

Leaning on that bar with my head stuck in the ceiling where it was hot and hard to breath felt ten times longer owing to the precarious state I was in, bars bending underneath me, one of which might have snapped and cut my face with a sharp piece of metal. "You're thinking? What the hell are you thinking about?" I could picture him relaxing down there against the wall, 'thinking'. "Get me down, John! This was your fecking idea!"

There was the sound of renewed vigour of rubber soles squelching quickly on tiles to confront an urgent task. Once again I felt his support. The rate at which the tiles and interconnected bars were sagging with my weight visibly reduced. I remember noticing how odd it was that I was begging him to hold my ass in his hands.

"Use both your hands, I'm going to fall!"

"Jesus Kev, I never knew you were so fat." My feet kicked like a fish on a line flailing about in the empty air. His hands guided me down. At last my feet reached the lid of the toilet. After having been up so high, it felt more like a minor step off a kerb, like a few inches in height, rather than the actual height from the toilet to the floor that it was; sort of like walking the horizontal escalator in the airport, and when you get off, you feel like you're walking very slowly.

We both rested there in the cubicle for a while, John sitting against the wall and me sitting on the toilet, catching our breath. The foam tile I'd removed to get into the ceiling had been discarded somewhere above. Even if John guided my ass back up and I found it, there was no way it would slot into place. It looked like someone had come through the ceiling at huge speed with a dodgy parachute that only half opened and couldn't fit directly through the irregular shaped hole the person had made and the wallop it made on the top of the ceiling had brought a big part of the celing closer to the floor. It was a ragged, sagging, glaring hole. The edges were nearly touching the tops of the cubicle partition .

"It looks like we're going to have to resort to plan B.", John said.

"What's plan B? Please tell me it's better than plan A."

"You'd probably just insult me if I told you. Like you did earlier."

"Why would I insult you? Were it not for you John, I'd be lost. Even after what's just happened. You're our key out of here. You're my rock. Seriously, if you weren't here, I'd just be rocking back and forwards in the corner of the room like a vegetable. But let's do it quick. The longer we wait in here the bigger the chance Mickey Moustache is going to mozy on in and when he sees the state of the roof, we're fucked. This is a nightmare, John! I'm fucked anyway. He'll remember my face. You're ok - you're gone. I have to come back in September. If we're still alive by that stage."

Chapter 14

John's dilemma

Riding the wave of John's confidence in bringing a hasty resolution to the matter, I followed him with gusto into the corridor. He paused at the lobby door and closed his eyes and took a deep breath before opening it. He withdrew an arm slowly from his belly and slid the hand into his pocket. He looked furtively over his shoulders to the left and to the right, as if to conceal what he was about to show me from spies or eavesdroppers wandering about our vicinity which, of course, there was no chance of happening, as we were the only two people in the corridor.

He slid his hand back out from his pocket and took something out which I saw was the strip of acid tabs from earlier. He proceeded to tear two squares from the strip of acid; as painful to watch as it was for him to do. When he at last tore the first square off he held it snuggly between his thumb and index finger and started to tear the second square from the strip. He applied a little more pressure than necessary to the first tab between his fingers, lest it fall on the ground. As he tore the second tab he observed it like he was trying to thread a line through the eye of a fish hook, concentrating, knowing his hands were shaky and there was sweat in his eyes. All this, too, without removing his arms from his belly; shielding it like outside forces were actively trying to liquify it.

At last he presented the first tab to me on the tip of his finger. "This will help us be more relaxed.", he said, and swallowed the other one. I did likewise, both of us looking into each other's eyes like we were making a pact as we did so. Swallowing that acid and looking into his eyes I couldn't help but be reminded of a documentary I saw about a Croatian soldier's personal account of the war in Yugoslavia. He had seen his friends decide to blow themselves up in a forest with a grenade rather than face the wrath of the approaching Serb army. With John by my side I felt he was the stalwart between us and the barbarian hordes, and I was hopeful that with his bravery such a harrowing, desperate act of suicide would not be necessary.

Looking over his shoulder one more time he put his hand in his pocket again and handed me something wrapped in cling film. I thought it was hash but I saw it was a dried, crumpled pink flower. "They were getting withered and Edward would have thrown them out soon enough so I kept this one as a souvenir."

"A flower? Why did you keep it as a souvenir?"

John always struck me as a person for whom deep worries didn't occur, but now I was seeing a new side to him. I had considered him a man who worried only about what was going on around him at that particular time. He was sensitive and self-conscious, like I said; like if the girls were in the house his eyes would dart about the room at their faces as surreptitiously as possible, gaging if they considered what he'd said as smart as he thought it was, but that was the extent of his anxieties. He came home from his day's work and put his feet up. When something was done, he didn't dwell on it. If life was a canvas, he painted with broad brush strokes, rather than worrying about the nitty gritty with a fine brush. In fact I was seeing he was a tortured artist, not some stoic, detached observer. Silently and humbly, he had in fact been lumbering on, longterm, against his urges and passions, pedantically, in pursuit of perfect craftsmanship - in this case, all along forging the cornerstone in preparation for the relationship with his soulmate, Rebecca. The hotheadedness I had known in preceding months masked a deep well of perspicacity, commitment and loyalty - a loyalty that can be fatal. I was seeing that far from the couch potato I believed him to be, he was a visionary and a man of letters, on a level which now astounded me.

He sighed and closed his eyes in preparation for what he was about to say, as if it were a cause of some embarrassment. I thought it was the prelude to a joke but I soon realised he was deadly serious. Little pin pricks of pink swept outwards in his cheeks, suggesting life in his corpse-like visage. A glow came into his damp sweaty face.

"Before today, I loved Vanessa.", he said. "She's so kind and pretty. The way she'd give us flowers 'n' shit. I knew there would never be a chance of anything happening between us. We come from very different backgrounds. But there was always something to look forward to. That flower in your hand kept the dream alive."

"What the fuck! You're talking about Edward's Vanessa?"

"Yes. I've fancied her ever since I first set eyes on her. I couldn't get her out of my head. Until today. Until I met Becs 'n' shit. I always felt, with Vanessa, starting a relationship was like pushing a JCB up a hill 'n' shit. Edward was in the way. Not that he was in the way, if you know what I mean, but Vanessa and Edward are so happy together. That's just not my style, breaking up a relationship between two people 'n' shit. If I see a good thing I don't want to break it up. With Becs, there's no pushing any JCBs up any hills. It's all downhill. I mean it's all *uphill* but it's like the JCB is rolling downhill, if you know what I mean. I feel like I've met the one. When you've met the one, you know you've met, 'the One'. That's the way me and Becs feel about each other 'n' shit, Kev. Today I discovered that Becs is the one for me and she discovered I'm the one for her. The stuff she was saying to me in the Kremlin, Kev! It's never happened to me before, someone being so nuts about me. She's good looking, she's smart, she's intelligent -

"Holy shit John! What the hell has happened to you!" I started to crack up laughing and stopped immediately and checked my surroundings to make sure I wasn't in the library by the water unit with Mickey Moustache looking over. Confident I was where I thought I was, and the door between the library and where we were was closed shut, I started to let rip the laughter I'd been holding onto but then thought better of it in case he might still hear and laughed only a moderate amount. I couldn't resist the temptation to tease him a bit. "That Stephanie one. Wow. What a cracker she was."

"Stephanie wasn't a patch on Becs. Becs is a cracker *and* she has an amazing personality."

"I wonder how Dave's getting on with her. She seemed like she really liked him. Wow, she was hot."

"Becs is way more than Stephanie. That's what I'm worried about. With these elite crackers you only get one chance 'n' shit. We've hardly started dating and already I'm considering breaking the promise I made to her only this evening 'n' shit. I want us to be one hundred percent on the level. I mean this plan B will definitely work, if we did it, it will get us out of here, but ethically and morally 'n' shit, I'm worried it could cause trust issues down the line 'n' shit. I don't want one of these relationships based on lies. They never work. Maybe I'm overthinking it with the drugs 'n' shit."

"I think you're definitely overthinking it 'n' shit."

"My question, Kev, is this: if you've promised the person you love to keep a secret, is it ok to break that secret if it's a matter of life and death?"

"What secret are you talking about? Life and death! Oh my God, when you describe it in such stark terms it makes me realise the situation we're in! This is our charging at the trenches, our pact in the forest when we tell each other we'll see each other in the next life and hold hands and pull the grenade together. You don't even have to ask, John! It's a rhetorical question. What matters is getting out of here alive, end of story. She's your muse, right?" He nodded. "What's the purpose of a muse? To bring out the *best* in you. To *inspire* you. If she's in love with you as much as you say she is, she'll understand." He was mulling over my words enthusiastically so I kept talking, tilting the balance towards enactment of this great plan, as I was naturally keen on getting out alive, regardless of what the hell Rebecca thought. "I mean what's the bloody alternative? Think about it. If you come out of this maimed, or injured, or worse, *dead*, you really think she's going to say, 'oh John I'm so upset you didn't keep our secret.' No way. If she loves you she wants you in tiptop condition no matter what the cost.

Personally, if you have something that's going to get us out alive I would pay you like, a million quid, if I had a million quid."

"Exactly." He nodded to himself, getting more reassured with what he was hearing and what he had to do. "She'll understand. When I explain the situation we were in - if we need to even *go* that far Kev, because I don't think we will - when I explain it to her 'n' shit, she'll understand. Because I don't think we'll even have to do it 'n' shit. If I have to let the cat out of the bag, so be it, but if I don't have to, I won't. He'll just let us walk out 'n' shit. We look just like anybody else in here, Kev. It's all in our heads. We're wearing hoodies, coats... nothing different... But if I *did* have to do it, she'd understand."

"Yes, definitely. But what cat out of what bag are you talking about?"

"You'll see, Kev. It would be disrespectful of me to say anything. It's on a need to know basis only." A sad, compassionate sparkle came into his eyes, the look you'd reserve for a friend who'd seen better days, a friend you'd give your life for. "He won't figure it out. He's smart, but not that smart. The hash doesn't help. He smokes too much hash. It's something that comes to you in a flash, she said. Dave was into it big time in the Kremlin. He's never going to figure it out. He's too involved."

"Are you talking about square fecking circles again?"

"I am, Kev." He nodded with the enthusiasm of a kid being asked if he'd like to start the Easter egg hunt. "That's what I'm going to do 'n' shit, if he wants me to help him, I'm gonna make him give me a foot massage. Can you imagine Dave giving me a fucking foot massage? Ha!"

"Let's keep our voices down." We were becoming quite noisy, the pamperings John would be having at Dave's expense causing his voice to rise with glee. I pulled him into the toilet where two doors separating us from Mickey Moustache was more comforting than just the one door of the lobby. He turned serious, contemplating the enormous day ahead. "To be honest, I'm nervous about meeting up with her alone. The brains on that girl. Opposites attract, alright. I'll help Dave with the riddle, so hopefully he can come along too. That's the deal we made. I'm meeting her anyway but if he wants to come along too that's the deal we made, he has to solve it himself."

"It's so far-fetched."

"What is?"

"Square circles. There's no conceivable way it's a valid shape." I went to the mirror over the sink and licked the tip of my index finger and drew a circle on the glass and looked at John like I was giving a maths lesson. "Look. That's a circle, right? Agreed? How is it possible to draw a square one of those?" I folded my arms and looked at him, awaiting concession on his part. A firm rebuff of the craziness he was talking about wasn't evident. I turned to the mirror and with a wet index finger I drew a square inside the circle. "That's the closest you can possibly get to a square circle, and that's only a square *in* a circle. You could draw the square outside too, but other than that it's not possible. It's not a de facto square circle. Even something like this..." I drew a squarish shape with curved corners. "Jesus, John!" He was looking at me with his chin raised in a haughty way, like there was something I couldn't possibly comprehend, which I knew wasn't the case, and it infuriated me. "It's an oxymoron and shit! One is diametrically opposed to the other. I don't know how you could fecking fathom for a quarter of a second that a square circle is fecking possible to draw."

"I thought you said I was a genius."

"You are a genius, John. The way you're as cool as a cucumber and coming up with all these cool ideas like setting up businesses and stuff. But you're blinded by love, as all geniuses are. You're so in love with your one Becs you hardly know what you're saying. And even if it was possible, what are you expecting? Do you really think Mickey Moustache is going to care about a square circle? This guy is a bloodthirsty Rottweiler. He doesn't care about square circles."

"If someone showed you a square circle, Kev, wouldn't you let whoever it was mozy on past you?"

"Yeah, I would let whoever it was mozy on past me, but Mickey Moustache doesn't strike me as the mozying on past you kind of guy. Anyway, let's not go down that rabbit hole. Basically, what I'm saying is, making a square circle isn't a trivial thing John, that's what I'm saying. That's my opinion anyway."

He stared at me with eyebrows raised high in supercilious arches like I was a mere plebeian mortal unworthy of his full open gaze. "I'm on your *side* here, John. I'm agreeing with you." I felt he was being condescending or something, or teasing me about something I couldn't understand.

"When Rebecca says it's possible to do something, believe me, it's possible. Trust me."

"Unless we're missing something and she's figured out a dimension we don't know about. They do say there are lots of dimensions. You'd have to get her to call in."

"Rebecca call in here? Why?"

"To see it in advance. If it's even possible, which it probably isn't. You'd have to call her and tell her to come in with it and we'll meet her in here. Something of that magnitude over the phone wouldn't work. It's something you have to see drawn out for you, in advance. She'd be like, 'What you do is John you join dot A to dot B.' You'll be like, 'Just one minute, Mickey Moustache, I'll be with you shortly, I'm just getting instructions over the phone on how to draw a square circle.' We'd be dead by that stage. Mickey Moustache won't hang around. You want to have the solution in your hand, ready to go. Maybe he would go for it, I don't know. It would be a pretty messed up thing to see, I suppose."

"I'm smiling because I have the square circle right here in my pocket." He patted his pocket and he smiled triumphantly.

"Fuck off."

"When seagulls follow the boat it's because they think sardines will be thrown into the sea."

"Seriously, this is a matter of life and death 'n' shit. Don't be laughing about it."

But he wasn't laughing. It was more like his eyes were smiling at being one of the chosen few made privy to such an astounding revelation. There was a brash serenity about him. His irises, normally brown, became less brown, their dark hue perishing the way a receding tide rushes from the sand. A softening filled their place. The significance of the juncture he was at was dawning on him once again; the pitfalls that could have arisen, the obstacles that could have torn it asunder, and his arrival in spite of these turmoils. His reward had come late in life, but wasn't it better it had come belatedly than not at all? Wouldn't Mother Nature want him to look favourably upon those poor minions who were denied the love and great gifts that lay in his possession? Wasn't it his duty to share his wisdom and knowledge with others less fortunate than himself?

"Let me get this straight.", I said, and closed my eyes and took a breath, for what I was saying sounded ridiculous. "You're telling me you have a square circle in your pocket?" I was saying it slowly, to let the words sink in, so there'd be no confusion.

"Yes." Seeing the gobsmacked look on my face caused his shoulders to vibrate up and down with little giggles.

"I don't believe you. Show me."

"Oh I will show it to you Kev, believe me. And when you see it, it will blow your mind. It's like looking into the eyes of God. It is unreal. Un. Fucking. Real." Every fibre of his being radiated with a divine certainty that the piece of paper his muse had given him in the Kremlin and stashed now in his army jacket was indeed the mathematical colossus he said it was, the real deal. A little smile dripping with self-assuredness on his lips planted the seed in my mind which tilted me towards believing that this girl Rebecca had indeed broken through the rubicon of mathematical understanding. She had discovered a miracle that could get us out alive, and it was in John's pocket.

"It is some trippy shit man, when you see it. I couldn't believe it myself Kev when she gave it to me. It's nuts. Nuts!"

"Show it to me!" I lunged forwards to reach into the pocket to grab it but he recoiled quickly; there was no way he was letting me near it.

"No." The tide of euphoria receded and the giggles stopped abruptly and the joyful eyes turned solemn and serious. His inviolate, stern gaze that burnt through me nearly made my heart stop. I was no match for his strength of character and unswerving loyalty. "Not now, Kev. Don't get me wrong 'n' shit Kev, I will show you, but not now. It would be just plain wrong for me to show you now. She tells me not to flash it around to everybody 'n' shit and I go showing it off to half the world 'n' shit. I mean a matter of life and death, yes, I can explain that one, but it has to be on a need to know basis only, like if he threatens to kill us 'n' shit. Otherwise, it's top secret, like I promised, and I'm showing it off to no one now, only tomorrow, like I said, not before. It would be a massive breach of trust 'n' shit."

I was disturbed for a while how this man I'd known for months was in fact a stranger to me, but that uneasiness turned to a great appreciation for being exactly where I was, with who I was; I was witnessing an important piece of history, the night when John Daly's boundless potential had been ignited. He would set up many businesses. He would be a Tipperary hero. His influence would spread far and wide throughout the country after this day. I could not have wished for more than the brave, wise chieftain alongside me, to escort me through the predicament we were in.

"I'm so happy for you, John!"

"I told you she was an astrophysicist!"

"Holy shit John! Show it to me!" I lunged forward to try grab it once again and then remembered I couldn't. "Ok, you can't... but... really... just so we're on the same page... you're saying in your pocket you have a square circle? Like the shape of a square and also the shape of a circle at the same time? I mean not two different shapes just one fecking shape? As in... a *square fecking circle*!?" It was more to confirm my ears were functioning properly rather than mocking the insanity coming from his mouth.

"Yes!"

"Holy Shit John! Do you know what this means? Do you know what this means!?" Seeing his ecstasy and hearing his wild guffaws, and he seeing and hearing mine, elevated us to a shrill pitch and a state of momentary rapture where for a while we forgot about Mickey Moustache completely and couldn't care if he could hear us through the door or even came barging in, broken ceiling or no broken ceiling. The solid beams shining from his bloodshot eyes into mine thawed any doubts I had as to the veracity of his claim. I believed he was in possession of something incredible which Newton, Einstein and Archimedes were turning in their graves to catch a glimpse of.

"This is huge! This is... bigger than a cure for cancer. *This...* John... *this* is the business idea! This is fecking titanic! Ha! Who cares about Mickey Moustache anymore! I mean... obviously we have to care about him and getting out of here alive but... really? A square fecking circle? Holy shit. I can't fit it inside my head John, I can't even imagine it."

"I know!" He beamed a proud smile. "It's fucking mad! Now, you ready to do this?"

"Yes, I'm ready." We headed back out into the corridor, that would take us into the lobby, ready for war.

Chapter 15

Roscrea Meats

While my brain cells bounced about my skull to try picture the conundrum in his pocket, with limited success, John pushed down on the handle to open the door that would take us into the lobby and then onwards out the exit past Mickey Moustache, but at the last second I said, "Wait!" and he stopped and looked at me, an inch before opening the door fully.

"What is it now?"

"I don't know. I'm just wondering. Let's think this through. Don't open the door just yet. We're going to have to walk quick. The last thing we want is for him to come over this way and peer in the door and see the fecking hole in the roof. He'll eat us alive if we give him half the chance. He doesn't care about small talk. I mean... what, exactly, is the plan? Holy shit. A square circle. I just can't believe it."

"The plan is, we walk out, like I said, and if Mickey monster gets stroppy with us 'n' shit, we try to reason with him and if he's still stroppy I tell him if he lets us live and go peacefully I'll show him the most amazing thing he's ever seen and when he sees it obviously he'll let us go and we go back to the house and chill out and watch Van Damme videos 'n' shit. And then you make lasagna or help me make it because I've never made it before. You should join us, Kev. You and... whatever her name is. Hello? Earth calling Kev?"

"I'm listening... I'm listening... I'm just thinking. Wow. I just can't get over what you have in your pocket. Are you... crying?"

"I'm crying because Da would be so proud if he could see me now. These are tears of joy." Listening to him now, seeing how he was crippled by tummy cramps or whatever, doubled over, practically limping, and how every once in a while a painful wince stretched across his face and the sweat poured down his collars and his hair stood on end like a hedgehog's, I was reminded how ailments of the body are no detriment to an amazing mind. His eyes burned with a sharpness and confidence through the tears and I was humbled to realise how sometimes the mind even works better in defiance of those ailments.

"You know who you remind me of right now?"

"Who?"

"René Descartes. He's a philosopher. He went through the same shit you're going through right now, all this mental turmoil and anguish and agitation and shit for a few hours. You're exactly like him. He's the 'I think therefore I am' fella. He locked himself in a room one night, having cold sweats and dreams and mad ideas and probably couldn't even walk himself, wrapped up in a blanket, in a fireplace I think, and when he went out of the room the next day or after the weekend, he wrote it all down on paper. Half the world's philosophy today is based on what he says. You could be the next René Descartes, John. I'm not messing. He lit the world on fire with his ideas, like you're doing now."

"He sounds like a freak."

"Well, I don't know, maybe freaks have the best ideas. If it's not freaky, chances are it's not a new idea.

Let me just say, man to man, that whatever happens out of this John, whether we make it out in one piece or not, whether we live or die, you're an amazing individual. You're a great guy. I love you."

"Gee, thanks Kev.", he said, abashed. "I love you too. You're a cool guy too." We gave each other a hug on what we knew might well be our last sally together.

He pushed his hand down on the handle of the door that would take us from the corridor into the lobby. "Wait now.", I said, one more time. "Before you even reach into your pocket, before you even have the time to take it out to show him, boom, we're dead. My suggestion is you take it out now and hold it in front of you while we're walking towards the exit so he'll see it straight away, knowing you have something important in your hand."

"What good will that do?"

"Eh, so he'll see it.", I said, in a tone denoting something so obvious it hardly needed explanation. "If he grabs us in a headlock or something, he'd snap our necks, quick smart. It would be over before it's even started. At least if you have it in front of you it will startle him. It will be like one of those hypnotised hens when you hold their head down and draw a line with a piece of chalk in front of them. He'll be in shock, not able to do anything."

"I have my hand on it right now, Kev." He motioned with his head at the arm which was wrapped tightly around his belly and I saw the hand of that arm was indeed reaching into his pocket, ready to be withdrawn. "If I take it out of my pocket in advance there's a chance I'd see it by accident. As soon as there's the slightest hint we're in danger, out it comes. 'Call me when you figure it out, John, or just give it your best shot.'. 'Leave a voicemail if I don't answer.' That's the way I want to keep our relationship from the get go 'n' shit, honest like an open book." He pulled open the door into the lobby and before I knew it, the two of us were in the lobby, marching towards the exit.

"What do you mean there's a chance you'd see it by accident?"

"I promised I'd try figure it out myself first."

"Have you not seen the square circle yet?"

"No, not yet. But when I imagine it I can both imagine it and not imagine it at the same time, you ever get that? And when I imagine it I picture something that... *blows my mind.* Shhh. Voices down. Here we go."

He was holding my hand again and I tried to pull him back and stall for time but he was a man on a mission, his eyes torpedoes on a sea of white, ploughing towards the exit. It was like rigour mortis had set into his vice-like grip.

"Everything ok lads?", he said, when we were right up to him.

"Everything is ok.", John said, one hand on mine, the other on his belly. "We were reading books. We have exams. Don't we, Kev? We were studying." He lowered his head like a bull focused on the red cape and walked swiftly for the electronic barrier that opens automatically when you approach it and, with him tugging me along, I had no option but to follow suit, my head bobbing about on my shoulders, not knowing what to do or say, just looking at everybody standing around us with that silly grin on my face.

Except... the electronic barrier didn't open automatically. It stayed closed. And alarm bells started ringing.

"Step back into the lobby please.", Mickey Moustache said. Oh yes, they were all looking now! Electrodes of stress ricocheted down my spine. The old ladies behind the desk were aghast with mouths ajar, the clusters of gobsmacked students in the lobby shuffled from foot to foot and looked on with bags dropped to the floor, too scared to stay yet too nosey to depart. Finally I disentangled John's sweaty palm from my own and jumped back into the lobby, doing as I was instructed. John had other plans. He crashed into the barrier like a stubborn ox. It wouldn't budge. Mickey Moustache took two steps and tossed him into the lobby beside me like he was a rag doll rather than a fully grown 21 year old. He ran again and this time Mickey Moustache let him past. The barrier stayed shut, the alarm bells ringing.

If he'd looked me in the eye he'd have seen the leadership skills I'd entrusted him with quickly evaporate but he was too busy pushing and pulling on the barrier, like a broken wind up toy. John wasn't to know but the barrier moved up and down, not back and forth. If he'd tried to lift the bar, maybe, or even just duck under it...

Throughout this ordeal Mickey Moustache watched him in a leisurely, composed way. He had his hands on his hips. The thick bushy eyebrow of his right eye, as I was standing to the right, watching his sidelong profile, arched upwards in a satisfied way. You couldn't see his upper lip, with his moustache over it, but he looked to me like he was smiling. He didn't know I was watching. If I suspected he could see me I wouldn't have dared look into his face at all. John rattled frantically on the gate back and forth. He reminded me of a rabbit shaking his foot in a snare. Mickey Moustache watched him with that raised, curious eyebrow and under that sweeping moustache over his mouth - I'm sure I saw it... a laugh!

John's eyes were not totally forlorn of hope throughout this pointless escapade, for the shore of paradise ahead on which his eyes were fastened, the elevator down the corridor which would take us outside, the path to freedom, was so close and tangible and within reach, he was sure he would reach it.

Suddenly he stood totally erect, his back straight, like he'd been tied to a plank. A patchy, blotchy hue, like a purple liquid quickly filling a white transparent bucket, flowed upwards from his neck into his cheeks. Something was happening between his legs. A whine that would have startled a banshee came out his mouth. His guts were falling onto the floor! The alien was bursting out his belly!

"Uno! Uno! Uno!", I yelled. I jumped back into the corner by the photocopier, hoping the wall would swallow me.

What was in fact happening was that, with his hands and arms applied to pushing the gate and no longer shielding his belly, all the stuff in his bulging jacket, buttoned up to his neck, which any fool could tell contained library property he had been at pains to conceal, started to fall from his coat onto the floor.

Mickey Moustache had had his fun - for the time being anyway. He approached like a wolf, probably licking his lips under that moustache, John's squeals and grunts whetting his appetite all the more, and he grabbed John by the arm and tossed him into the lobby beside me. The trickle of stuff from John's coat onto the floor became a deluge.

"I brought those in with me. Isn't that right, Kev?"

"Huh?" That's all I could say. I was bamboozled by it all; the beeping alarm, the onlookers... and Mickey Moustache actually talking to us.

"Open your jackets. Pull up your trousers."

I did exactly what I was told, lest my servility be in question, and pulled up my hoodie. John, on the contrary, seemed to be giving him a challenging look. What the hell was he doing? He had his hands in his pockets, still holding video tapes in place under his jacket, I was sure. I felt like kicking him. Mickey Moustache bent over and analysed the items that had been tumbling from John's coat onto the floor, yet never seeming to take his eyes off us - like the cop on TV with the gun pointed at the villain, not taking any chances. VHS tapes, tons of them, scattered on the floor.

"'Blood Sport', 'Kick Boxer', 'No Retreat, No Surrender'", Mickey Moustache said, perusing the titles on each box in his large paw before laying the box on the growing mountain of boxes and books besides him and taking another box. "You brought these in with you, eh?"

"Yes.", John said. I could feel his fingers reaching for mine. He shuffled from foot to foot. "I brought them in with me. I'm just bringing them back out. Isn't that right, Kev?"

I nodded. I kept wishing he'd stop getting me involved. The librarian with big red buttons on her cardigan was tempted to pounce on the phone and make a call but instead she just stood there with her mouth open, grateful the large kidney shaped desk on which the phone was placed divided her from the madness, I'm sure.

"But, why did the alarm go off? The alarm only goes off when library property hasn't been scanned for rental."

We would have expected a swift and clinical dispatch of John for what he'd tried to do, certainly no conciliatory tone, no attempts to understand John's side of the story. I'm sure I heard sighs and gasps of surprise from those remaining students who hadn't scurried through the gates when the trouble started with the alarm bells. John saw it too. He shot me a quick sideways dart like he couldn't believe his luck. He had never met or seen Mickey Moustache before. I had described him as a velociraptor who'd tear him to shreds. Instead he was more like a friendly uncle, genuinely inquisitive about alarm bells and how they functioned.

"I worked in Roscrea Meats one summer. If the weight coming in isn't the same as the weight going out it goes off."

"Roscrea Meats? The meat plant?"

"Yes.", John said, delighted a common theme had been struck between them. At the beginning I sensed panic at a situation unfolding grossly at odds to how he'd envisioned, but he quickly recovered and pulled up his socks. His eyes rose to those of Mickey Moustache who had been glowering down on him. John's approach had disarmed him. The ceiling of my happiness and relief got higher and higher as I realised that among the many nuggets of wisdom bestowed on him on this special day was that honesty is the best weapon to deal with potent evil. He had learnt that no matter how ruthless the enemy, that enemy had a tender side, and when confronted with relentless honesty, that tender side would inevitably show itself, because we're all human, even the most despicable of us. The result was that Mickey Moustache's eyes did indeed appear to get kinder, his innate human emotions being stirred and starting to flower as John had planned, recognising John's persistence and sincerity and frank and candid charm as laudable qualities rather than vile ones. He was keen to hear what this brave student, half his size, who knew he could be crushed with a stamp of his foot, yet who was so open and approachable, had to say about Roscrea Meats. "First job I ever had. I live nearby. It's the weight of the meat sensor that does it." A smile replaced his trembling lips. He stepped forwards. He really did work in that meat plant one summer. Happy memories of days of yore flooded in. "Some of the lads there, ha! Great craic. It works the same way. All this shit on me, all my video tapes, which I came in with, they were probably falling out my coat on the way out, so the weight doesn't match up because it's different to the weight I was coming in with. You see?"

"I do, yes." He eyed John suspiciously, but still with that little smile on his eyebrows, I was glad to see. "What are you? An engineer?"

"No, I'm not an engineer. That's just how they do these things. If the weight of the meat sensor is wrong the alarm won't go off. Your weight is the fingerprint 'n' shit. If the weight of the cow isn't right the gate doesn't open." I think John had actually convinced himself they were his own video tapes. He reached out his hand. "I'll have that back now please, and we'll be on our way.", he said, referring to the copy of "Double Impact", John's favourite film, which Mickey Moustache had picked off the ground and was still holding.

Astonishingly, Mickey Moustache handed it to him! He believed the tapes were John's! Students inched in closer, keen to catch every electrifying next word. The two librarians perked up their heads, observing astutely lest they miss a beat. To all those who knew the rumours of Mickey Moustache, it looked like what was transpiring would be a valuable piece of library lore into the future, the day Mickey Moustache was stood down and brought to heel by some strange student called "John".

Mickey Moustache pinched his nose and closed his eyes like genuinely trying to understand the situation. "These video tapes are yours, that's what you're saying? You came in with them. You think there's something wrong with the weight sensor? Or the meat sensor?"

"Yes, yes! The weight sensor! That's what we're trying to say!" A huge stress was lifting from my chest. It was hard to grasp what was happening. He'd seen them fall on the floor with his own eyes, the video tapes John was trying to steal from him. Somehow John had made him believe the VHS tapes were his. I was in awe of his audacity and his cunning. I wondered if there was any limit to the depths of his newfound gifts.

Despite the relief I was conscious we had to make hay while the sun shined and talk our way to freedom and get out as quick as possible. The spontaneous mood could disappear as suddenly as it had arrived.

"If it's ok we better be on our way to study for exams.", I said.

"Just a second, just a second. Yes, I understand it now. The meat sensor. How silly of me. It's not the books or the video tapes. It's the weight that sets off the calibration chip. Well of course! You're free to go. I'm sorry for the inconvenience. This must have been terribly embarrassing for you. Look at you, such a lovely couple. And such commitment. Coming in to study on a Friday night. Well, if you brought them in with you, if they're yours, my apologies. You're free to go." He stood aside and ushered us to leave, his hand and arm trailing like he was giving us a big welcome.

Naturally, you can imagine not a few gasps of stunned disbelief were released on the part of the crowd, so at odds was this pacifist tone with what we had known and heard about the violent, unforgiving Mickey Moustache. John looked at me and smiled. My unbounded confidence in him had returned. He brushed or dusted off each of his arms with the opposing hand and arranged the collars on his coat and rolled his head on his shoulders and started for the barrier like a guy walking out of a shop, proud of the new fancy suit he'd just purchased. He started for the barrier with a light and breezy gait and I followed, responding with a smile of my own, believing wholeheartedly we were now walking the path to freedom.

Chapter 16

Stefan

We walked by Mickey Moustache and just as we approached the barrier he called out behind us. "Just a second.", he said. My bones shuddered and my heart jumped. "Aren't you forgetting something?", he said, pointing generally at the floor. He was talking about the VHS tapes and books that had fallen out of John's coat. "Are you not going to take them with you? They're yours." It would have looked obvious, if we'd left them. We scurried about the room, picking up items. By the end of it John's jacket was bloated like a scarecrow full of straw. There was still so much on the floor. I was tempted to ask how the hell he'd managed to fit everything in the first time round.

"Has anyone got a spare plastic bag?", John said.

"We don't need a bag, John." Talk about making it obvious - requesting a bag to carry all the stuff out when we hadn't needed one to carry it in in the first place. "We didn't need one coming in, we certainly don't need one now." The alarm bell whirred and whined. The coterie of observing students were too astounded by what was going on to be able to move.

There was a pocket in the front of my hoodie, the one where you can join your hands together, but just "Blood Sport" and "Kick Boxer" was a squeeze to get in. Much to my chagrin, Mickey Moustache continued to surprise us with his benevolence. He offered to help me by constructing a tower of items in my outstretched, cradled arms, an offer I could hardly refuse. He laid the hard video cases as a base layer. He added other items on top with the precision and delicacy of a person building a house of cards. He smiled at me, and I smiled back, like two kids enjoying a particularly thrilling game of Jenga, always pleasantly surprised at managing to add yet another item to the construction. For a while I was afraid I wouldn't be able to see, it was getting so high. I was terrified, knowing stuff would fall as soon as I moved. A little book fell off the top. He cursed under his breath at what I prayed was the house of cards he was building rather than the foundation holding it. He placed it back on top of the pile. I found it ironic how it was my life in their hands rather than theirs in mine.

"There you are. I told you we'd do it." He gave me a playful slap on the shoulder; a bit too hard, I thought. I followed John like a person balancing a bowl of fruit on their head towards the exit.

"Would you like me to accompany you down on the elevator?" We told him we'd be ok. "Off you go then. Walk around here, look, the exit side." He raised the bar for us to walk through. I left the items that fell on the floor, pretending I didn't see them. "You're going through the entrance. Forgive me for bothering you. Bye bye now."

We'd only taken about two steps though when again he interrupted us and shut down the bar he'd been holding up for us to walk through and he straightened up and blocked our path outright, before we'd had the chance to go through it. "One moment." I knew it was too good to be true. You just didn't *do* this with Mickey Moustache.

He was analysing, or pretending to analyse, one of the videos he had in his hand. The finger of the other hand was raised in the air, as if something had just dawned on him. "Look here, this is very bizarre. The back of the corner of this video you brought in happens to have our distinctive microchip on the cover. What a coincidence. And look, that video there is the same. Tell me, did they have microchips on the sausages in the meat plant too?" The jig was up. "Open your jacket! Pull up your trousers!", he said, for as well as the video tapes and books John had picked off the floor and put in his coat, he still had some items tucked in his socks he hadn't revealed, which was obvious by the bulges in his trousers, below his knees.

"Roscrea meats.", Mickely Moustache sneered. We ran back into the heart of the lobby. His hands and fingers were gnarled like the claws of a ferocious, hungry lion pouncing on its prey. We scurried backwards to the wall, where we could flee no further. I teetered forwards, aiming to shoot out of the library like a human cannonball, but his arm span encompassed all angles the projectile might shoot.

"We know all about you, Mickey Moustache."

"John... please stop.", I said, hardly able to watch, shivering like a bucket of ice cold water had been thrown on me, trying to slink in behind the photocopier. A communal holding of breath was palpable amongst the remaining students, their confused eyes bouncing about from one to the other. I tugged on his sleeve to hopefully shut him up, my knees quaking, but instead he stepped closer to Mickey Moustache, his chin raised, his hands curled into balls, more emboldened than ever. The younger blonde librarian was frozen on the spot. She had the scanner in her hand ready to scan the book of the next person in the queue but she had completely forgotten he was there, so sucked in she was by the debacle in the lobby, and the student had forgotten about the book too, being equally stunned. The queue at the desk had disintegrated, people more concerned with finding a suitable spot from where to observe the spectacle than rent books.

"Say what you did, Mickey Moustache. The truth will set you free."

"What are you talking about, you idiot."

"I know robbing a few books and videos is bad, but it is nothing, *nothing*... compared to what you did."

A shrewd bookie would have eschewed the possibility that anything could surpass the bounds of insanity that had been reached with John's talk of meat plants, but Mickey Moustache surpassed it by throwing a VHS tape box at John; I mean *really* throwing it, like he wanted to decapitate John's head off his shoulders. Luckily John was in close proximity. If he'd been a bit further away, the box picking up speed, and he'd hit him in the eye or something, it could have done serious damage. It hit him in the mouth. "What the fuck!", he said, as shocked as everybody else in the room. "Did you see that? Did you see that!?", he asked of the befuddled students. "He threw a fucking box at me!" Some students near the exit sneaked out as discreetly as possible. "I will tell you one more time. Pull up your trousers. You have three seconds."

John looked at me, his eyes shrunken and wet, the look of a man on the cusp of imminent defeat, about to confess all and beg for clemency from a higher power.

The glimmer in his eye I had mistaken for contrition was in fact stupidity. "Yeah, it's you alright, coming back to haunt me. Mean and cruel one minute then guilty the next, is that right?" Mickey Moustache stood there, looking at him. "And then the next day all nice and cheerful 'n' shit, like nothing's wrong. You tell yourself, 'All is good now.' But it doesn't go away, does it? It gets worse." There was a bit of blood on his lip. He wiped the blood off his lip and with defiance in his eyes he continued to look at Mickey Moustache, whose eyes were glaring down on him. "Wake up for a few whiskies in the middle of the night, yeah? Prick. You think you can hit people across the head and chew up their feelings and spit them out and get away with it? That's not the way the world works, Mickey Moustache. I know your type. Me and Kev know your dirty, sordid little secret. Don't we, Kev.", he said.

"What dirty little secret do you know about me?", Mickey Moustache asked, with a sardonic smile on his face, waiting for John to make a fool of himself further and say something stupid like the video tapes were his, that he'd come in with them.

Even at that stage though, with the blatherings coming from John's mouth and myself huddling against the wall, was there not a tinge of nervousness in Mickey Moustache's expression? Wasn't the wicked, sneering smile, conveying delight at the ridicule he was shovelling onto another, really a veneer to cover some untapped reservoir of emotion which John was prodding at? When Mickey Moustache turned to the gobsmacked students, wasn't he praying for a concurring chuckle to affirm that the noises from John's mouth were the ramblings of a madman, for deep down he suspected there was indeed some degree of sanity and logic to his words?

"You know the secret, Mickey Moustache. You pushed it out of your mind like I did, but I know you know I know."

"Sherlock Holmes says I've committed a crime, eh? Sherlock Holmes would be wearing a suit and a hat, not a bunch of rags." He laughed in a way that was supposed to be mocking but it lacked weight alongside John, who was the new cynosure in the room. Students dared to raise their nosey-parker heads from their shoulders like turtles sticking their necks out from their shells, keen to get a closer look. They could not know fully of his leadership and oratorical skills I knew of, having been privy to the transition from silent watcher on the sofa to poetic visionary with amazing business acumen, but they knew they were seeing something impressive. Whatever he was doing it was apparent his words were somehow sowing a rare seed of introspective doubt in Mickey Moustache's head like we'd never witnessed, making him act in ways we could not have imagined. John should have been dead by this stage. And yet here he was, penetrating deep into Mickey Moustache's psyche, bringing out responses in him that were almost human.

"What's Watson got to say about all this?", he said, looking at me. "Is this man telling the truth?" I shrugged indecisively like I didn't know what was going on - which, to be fair, I didn't. All I knew was I was in awe of John. He reached deep into the valley of his repertoire of dormant talents. The new one he pulled out impressed me as much as the others. Judging by Mickey Moustache's increasingly confounded face, John had found something he was quite a master of - the art of psychological warfare.

The more he continued to speak, the more Mickey Moustache reached closer to the stage where he closed his eyes and lowered his head and nodded to himself, John's pithy words travelling into his ears and filling his mind. Every pregnant pause between his carefully chosen words, every peak and trough of his intonation, was part of a well thought out strategy. He really was a genius. While I was losing my mind, John had never let go of that central thread all along; as he had promised when he looked me in the eye in the library - trust him, and we would get out alive. Everything I was witnessing now was part of an incisive, well thought out master plan. It hurt my head to think of the foresight and courage it took to implement such a scheme, and the precision with which he did so; every syllable tapped home perfectly like little stamps on the edge of the shovel deeper into the recesses of Mickey Moustache's subconscious, causing thoughts and memories to be tossed and turned.

"Both of you in the backroom, NOW!" He resumed his advance, his fingers bent aggressively like a man who's used to catching rattlesnakes with bare fingers.

John stood up to him, brimming with that battle hardened spirit I was now used to seeing. "When I look at you now, I don't see a brave, tough security guard. I see a coward. I see a man full of regret. I see a loser." People craned their heads out, so keen they were to catch every word and to observe every piece of the colloquy that was transpiring.

"You come in here and try to walk out that door and lie to my face and then talk like this to me? Who are you? What is your name?"

"My name doesn't matter, Mickey Moustache. What matters is that I know your name, and I know what you did." Balls of steel. My position migrated from the wall to standing over the shoulder of my shepherd and guardian, egging on his every word, my knees trembling now in awe of what he said and how he was so brave rather than through terror and stress at the havoc Mickey Moustache would wreak on us. "You can make jokes about me Mickey Moustache but I don't care. A few hours ago, maybe, but things have changed. When someone tells me to keep my mouth shut I keep my mouth shut. You might feel like you're stuck in a hole like you'll never come out the other side, like I did, but you can. Where there's a will there's a way 'n' shit. I've only just met you Mickey Moustache and I feel I know you better than anybody. Every day I think of Da and every day I get up in the morning thinking about the day he'd like me to have and I try to live that day exactly the way he'd like me to. 'Today I am going to be me, and if the world doesn't like it, well then to hell with 'em.' There's so much shit going on you can't control. You just have to let the storm blow on. That's what it is 'n' shit, a storm. A big windy storm trying to blow you over 'n' shit."

"How did you find me? Tell me your name. I need to hear you say it. I remember everybody that comes through these gates and I know I've never seen you before."

"You haven't seen me before. Not in this life, anyway. It's not the faces we have in common. It's the scars it left us with. Me and Kev went through the rabbit hole together. Danced at the foot of rainbows 'n' shit. I have been at the long end of the stick myself, Mickey Moustache. I was one of the lucky ones 'n' shit.

People live, people die. And when they're gone, they're gone. Sink or swim. I've been where you are now. And I swam. I managed to beat it. Most people don't beat it. Most people sink. I treat people like crap myself sometimes. But deep down I know I'm not a bad person 'n' shit."

Mickey Moustache raised his hand to his face and pinched his nose, reflecting deeply on what he was hearing.

"You have brought to my mind so many things I have chosen to forget", Mickey Moustache said, "and now, listening to you say these words, I see instantly what a fool I am." He was on the verge of tears – yes, I swear to God – tears! The dreaded Mickey Moustache, subjecting himself, ingratiating himself in such a manner! I had to pinch myself to be sure it was real. "Compared to you, coming all this way to find me, I am nothing. It is clear that you have spent endless days preparing for this rendezvous, rehearsing in front of the mirror. Fidelity is a friend I have wilfully rejected. Justice a brother to be embraced with open arms. Mercy a loving sister who always waits for us. In you, all three of these virtues are enshrined."

"You're welcome. I'm only doing what I can to help 'n' shit."

"You haven't changed one bit, you know. A bit older, yes, but still so stubborn. You have your father's eyes. How true it is that the truth will set me free! When I called into you and your family on that fateful day in your native Germany, I detected you alone were aware there was more to it than meets the eye. Your mother and brothers suspected nothing, but you... yes, you knew... didn't you, you knew! You will go back before me and tell them to be expecting me shortly. I will seek their forgiveness, which I do not deserve. Oh, Stefan! Your father would be so proud if he could see you now... emulating him, no doubt, dressed like a soldier as you are!"

John was suddenly as confused as the rest of us. "Who the hell is Stefan 'n' shit? Stop changing the subject. Say what you did to Philip 'n' Martin 'n' shit."

"Philip and who? Ah, your brothers! Your father told me everything, Stefan. You were such a little boy back then. So innocent. How much you have grown, and so quickly. Please, come into the backroom with me, Stefan, let me hear all the words you have longed to say for so long and you will hear mine. Gertrude, Marion, please hold the fort for a while." – they were the librarians behind the desk. "We've had our share of anger and fighting for one day. No more! Your friend can join us, if you wish. We have much to share. Come. Away from this melee. I will reveal everything to you. Your father talked so much about you. All of you. Your mother and your brothers. Let me feel that selfless nature that has urged you to come looking for me, let me touch once more, through the progeny he has left behind -

With an agility and speed I could only have expected to see in a panther, John lept at Mickey Moustache. Mickey Moustache grabbed his throat with fingers bent and curled with the hardness of an eagle's talons and lifted him off the ground and forced him back to the wall. John threw punches but couldn't reach, his arms flailing about, inches from Mickey Moustache's face. Students in the lobby, recognising the brewing cataclysm, moved towards the exit in growing numbers.

"This is an emotional time for me too, Stefan." He peered into that reddening head enclosed in his tight grip.

John had his hands on Mickey Moustache's hand, trying to prise his fingers open to no avail, spluttering and stammering. "Who are you!? How do you know Dad?!", he managed to say.

"You're killing him! He wants to talk but can't!"

Mickey Moustache let go. John fell to the ground and held his throat and swallowed air with the intensity of a man just smashed through the surface of an ice sheet. Cherishing our dwindling humanity and lamenting our sealed fate, I crumbled like a leaf onto the floor beside him. A shroud of silence, a sort of fatalistic bond, descended upon us; no words, actions or flight to higher ground could change its course. Armageddon was neigh, Krakatoa was about to erupt.

"My name is John from Borrisokane... never been out of Ireland in my feckin' life... "

The thunderous sound that emerged wasn't the sky collapsing on our heads, thank God, it was Mickey Moustache roaring out in a big laugh. "Get up.", he said. He hunched down on the ground like a giant leaning into Lilliputians and offered his hand to me to stand up which I took and he did the same with John and he stood up too. "At ease, soldier, at ease." He slapped John on the shoulder like a father proud of his son. "When you can confess openly to people you don't know, that is when the healing process can begin." He rubbed his hands together the way an ambitious person might relish a new project, keen to get their teeth into it. "Yes, it is best to talk. Please, don't be afraid. I know your name but you again, sorry' – he nodded at me – "What did you say your name was, young man?" I told him my name was Kevin. His eyes were kind. "Please, come with me, John and Kevin. Normally I tell nobody about my affairs, but the genie is out of the bottle now. Life is too short to spend it fighting. If there's one thing I've learnt, it's that. Oh, Walter! Only in the coalface of battle can such a rare friendship be forged, durable and precious as a diamond. Walter was the red diamond amongst them all. The memories and feelings which I will confess have always been there, dull and tarnished as they have become, but because of you, they are vivid once again. Pain is weakness leaving the body. Come with me, John and Kevin, and I will tell you my secret, as you call it, and you can judge for yourselves whether my conscience should be clean, or not." He started leading us out of the lobby and into the corridor we'd been in earlier and where one of the doors would lead us into the "back room", I presumed. Great. The library looked deserted. I couldn't see any librarians or students. "Up to a short time ago I had forecast the remainder of my days in this library. You are right, there needs to be change. With wrongs unreckoned, with recourse to justice not pursued to the bitter end, old age and happiness cannot grow in unison. I know that with public disclosure of what I have done will come repercussions. I'll recount my story with relief now, to you, for the first and last time, before reporting that same story with grief to the authorities."

Chapter 17

The Giant Dildo

As soon as Mickey Moustache started to lead us through the corridor towards the back room, a hand at each of our backs and telling us how happy he was to meet us, to be able to share whatever it was he wanted to talk about, John had started these retching movements, or spasms, like he was about to vomit. Luckily nothing was coming up, yet, only blasts of air with hints of beans and beer, but his look said it all: the explosion he'd been suppressing in his belly he could suppress no longer, and unless I had a bright idea, it would soon be unleashed upon the room.

At the end of the corridor Mickey Moustache swiped a security pass or something at one of the doors and the three of us went into a room: the backroom; a kitchenette, with a white microwave, kettle, toaster and so on along a white countertop. John and me went instantly to the wall and stood with our backs pressed against it. He was all zipped up, still with video tapes and books sticking out of his pockets. Mickey Moustache sat in one of the chrome stools. There were three chrome stools with white padded seats in the eating area. The glare of the chrome on the legs of the stools and the shiny toaster and the aluminium pieces on the white countertop reflected on the white walls I'm sure added to the nausea John was feeling with his retching and Mickey Moustache leaned forwards in the stool with his elbows on his knees and his feet on the chrome rung of the stool and he nodded his head looking at me and John against the wall and said, "This is funny, isn't it? Who'd have believed something like this would happen, eh? You look so like him, John, his son. He had big brown eyes, just like you. Just like his father." His gaze lingered on John like he really was this boy from the past. "Sophie, his wife, was every bit as beautiful as Walter had described her. She had the dignified pose of an Egyptian statue. Curls of jet-black hair rolled onto her shoulders. He wrote letters to them, about me, and it felt like we knew each other even though we'd never met. That's who I thought you were out there. His eldest son. Out there in the lobby, when you approached me the way you did, with your obstreperous defiance, I had fixed in my mind that today was indeed our day of reckoning, that you were he, that you had crossed the seas to tell me you knew of what I had been afraid to say. I thought we finally had the chance to put things right between us at last.

"They trusted me and believed me that day. Yet I sensed that Stefan knew there was more to my story than meets the eye. I had full intentions of revealing everything. Knowledge that their version of events could remain a falsehood was too much for me. As Sophie and two of her boys sat on the edge of the settee, listening to me, keen for me to continue bedecking their minds with glories of how Walter lit up the regiment, their chins raised high, I noticed the eldest of the three boys, Stefan, looked at me differently. He appeared to be unimpressed by his father's legendary antics, unlike the others, their eyes blotched with proud tears on hearing of the tributes I paid to their father, and husband. His eyes seemed to burn right through me as I spoke, analysing my every fidget, my every word. Nothing was said on the matter, on his part or mine, but he was looking at me like he knew my secret.

"When I departed without saying what I had crossed the seas to say, I always sensed that someday we would meet again. I thought it was you, John. What were you thinking, trying to get away with hiding so many videos and books in your coat? I understand the pressures of cramming for exams, maybe trying to get away with one or two extra books, but in all my years as security guard what you attempted was the stupidest thing I've ever seen. Come on, both of you, sit down here, and tell me a bit about yourselves." He patted one of the white padded chrome stools beside him with his big hand.

I'd sooner have sat next to a Bengal tiger than sit on that stool. "Let's talk about you. Your story sounds interesting." The thought of the tongue-tied gibberish that would pour out my mouth were I to talk at length was petrifying. A table between us would have been nice, like a buffer or something.

"But... where should I start? There is so much to tell."

"Start at the beginning."

"Earlier if you want."

"Well, ok, then. I won't bore you with the facts of my earlier life. Suffice to say, as a child, somewhere between the budding of youth and the ripening of adolescence, in no small part due to the impression made on me as a boy by stories of faraway lands and adventures, I was encouraged to follow the routes of those heroes and villains I'd read about, of pirates with their treasures hidden in creeks and coves, of princes on a mission to rescue some fair lady. You probably don't remember this, but the eighties were a tough time in Ireland. On top of having to scrimp and save every penny, there was Sandra, there was my gambling, there was the death of my father in the spring of '86. After years of trying to wash the cracked, brittle slate of painful memories and unsubstantiated dreams, of trying new beginnings which constantly resulted in disaffection, I knew the time was coming to quit it all, all I had known, and make the quantum leap to an entirely new domain. I crossed the seas to join the French Foreign Legion. Look at you, holding hands. You guys are funny." He sat back and slapped his legs with the palms of his hands and roared out in a deep laugh that shook the room. "You should have seen your face, John, out there, when I pointed out the microchips. 'My name is John from Borrisokane.'" He burst out laughing again.

John looked straight ahead to avoid eye contact and squinted to avoid the light, trying not to retch. "Who's Sandra?", he said, through grimaces.

"Who? Oh, Sandra! She's nothing. Nothing compared to what happened after, anyway. She is partly the reason I joined the Legion though. We met each other in primary school. From the first day I saw her, I was crazy about her. I used to cycle my bike in the estates, calling out her name. Were she ever to have answered, I'd have withered on the spot. There were four of us, best of friends; me, Sandra, Ed the numbers man, and Paul. My father used to tease me back then, considering me a youngster swept under by a lovestruck crush. How wrong he was. In '85 I asked Sandra's father the long awaited question, if he would oblige me by giving me his daughter's hand in marriage. We were set to be married in 1987 in a small church at the foot of the Dublin mountains, one we frequently passed on our hikes. How quickly things can change. I succumbed to the allure of glitz and glamour that my father had so frequently indulged in - gambling, and drink. Sandra ended it then. For a few months my job at the garage and everything else was consigned to the most shadowy edges of my ambition to make room for winning her back. I thought no amount of unanswered phone calls would deter me. Once I stood in her garden and threw rose petals at her window. It all ended that day when her father walked the driveway to where I stood at the garden gates, forlorn with a sad glint in his eye as we had always respected and liked each other, a letter in his hand. On reading that letter I knew our zenith had been climbed. I fancied I saw her petite figure behind the voile curtain of her bedroom looking at me as I read it, turning from me for the last time, dabbing tears from her eyes, heavy as my own."

"The memories! You bring them all back! A sigh would whistle by the children's lips when I told them about Ireland, a green country like Rwanda, but where sometimes there was snow, with waves crashing into cliffs. Forgive the digression, but I wonder now at what might have been, had things gone differently, had I continued to serve in the Legion. She is not just tattooed on my arms. She flows through my blood and is in my heart. Walter would have returned to his family, but I would have chosen to stay, renewing my contract ad infinitum. When vigour was depleted, when old age slowed my bones, bringing responses to orders a deadly second too late, I would retire, becoming a Legionnaire emeritus, in the chateau of Puyloubier. We would grow wine in the sun, play petanque in the evenings. Perhaps in the future I would be summoned to Aubagne, as 'les Anciennes' had done for us; old soldiers so bronzed by years of hot African sunshine and cold desert winds that race and nationality could only be guessed at. In rooms at the end of long corridors of marble floors, echoing with antiquity, their walls laden with portraits whispering of heroes and valiant deeds, I might have brought something myself to the yolk of Legion lore. Upon the assembled room I might have showered my own tales, my own drops atop its rich history, of Walter, of our experiences in Rwanda, and for some young, disillusioned man – just one!, the mirror of life might have shifted a new direction, his soul being set ablaze with purpose."

He clapped his hands with a suddenness that made us jump and he got out of his stool. He turned around and walked briskly to the kitchen door and stood in front of it and looked at it, threatening or daring it to open, which it didn't.

He opened the door, nice and slowly, like I had done earlier with the lobby door, peeped his head out and looked left and right diligently down the corridor, like a sailor on the bow of a ship scouring the horizon.

"If they knew what I'm about to do, they'd fire me. You can never be too careful in this place." John and I looked at each other. I could tell the same thing was going through his head: making a run for it when he had his back towards us and barging past him for the lobby and then on and on, but every fraction of a second longer by our comfort zone at the wall, which was the least comfortable comfort zone I've ever been in, made it harder to shift, knowing Mickey Moustache would turn around any time soon.

He closed the door and approached us so closely I was afraid he'd crush us with his chest. "Do you mind me asking, what do you fellas think of homosexuality?" The pungent odour of cardigan infused with cigarette smoke lingered before my nose. "As long as it's the legal age and there's consent I'm all for it.", I said, wishing I'd kept my mouth shut.

He walked by us and rounded the countertop into the kitchen area and bent down and rooted in the white press. "What are you looking for?" We didn't know whether to run or stay.

"Just something from a while back." He had his head stuck in the press. "Where is it... Where is it... The last time I tried this particular one was in Rwanda, with Walter, but I promised myself, when the time was right, that I'd try it again." A thud came from the press. We jumped back to the wall. "Aha!" He stood up and came over to us, a small black backpack he'd retrieved from the press in his hand, and a devious, cunning smile on his face, his nostrils flaring with excitement or lust.

"Personally I have nothing against homosexuality, as long as it's kept outside the Legion.", he said. "A lot of the others considered it a problem. Listen to me. Les Anciennes, Legionnaire emeritus... You must think I'm a madman. Would you believe this is the first time I've actually sat down and collected my thoughts in this way, about what I'm telling you now?" He seemed to consider the spasmic muscle contractions on John's face with his black eye twitching and his retching and the rocking back and forth with his hands around his belly to be fits of laughter, like John was partaking in the hysterical serendipity of the whole vile affair. "I know, it is hilarious, isn't it, how you can be talking about one thing, me another, and then all of a sudden we end up in here, talking about this? What had you so incensed out there in the lobby, John? You were furious. It's a long time since anybody stood up to me like that."

"What's in the bag?"

"I think it will be right up your alley. It will set your belly on fire. Have you ever been blindfolded? Have you ever walked blindfolded? It's impossible to know where you're going."

"He's going to get sick!", I rushed towards the door, tugging John by the arm that wasn't on his tummy, it having made a sudden rumbling noise. Mickey Moustache tugged John's other arm, following my lead. We hurtled through the corridor for the door closest to us and Mickey Moustache kicked it open.

"Quick! Get in!"

At the very last second I remembered the sign saying "Gents" on the door, with the broken ceiling!

I pushed both my feet against the door jambs, lying almost horizontally, pulling John's arm with all my force, while Mickey Moustache pulled in the other direction, trying to drag him into the toilet. He hadn't seen the ceiling, behind him. If he turned around, he would have. "What are you doing!? He needs to go to the toilet!" I was surprised he was so adamant to get John to the toilet but then I thought: who wants the last chore of their long shift to be cleaning up someone else's vomit, or worse? Unless he made us clean it up.

"The hole in your belly, John, the hole in your belly!". My cryptic clues were flops. His face squeaked like a piece of sticky rubber against the vacillating door in accordance with the tugs me and Mickey

Moustache applied to his arms. His lips twitched with a dwarf's passion. By the look in his eye that wasn't squashed against the door I could see he was asking the same question Mickey Moustache was asking - could I not see he clearly needed to go to the bloody toilet?

"The disabled toilet!", I said, delighted. I remembered a disabled toilet further down the corridor. Mickey Moustache let go. John ran in and locked the door. With only silence between us except for John's intestinal ruckus through the door I rambled on about anything at all to cover it up as I was terrified there'd be a space of silence when he'd ask a question I wouldn't be able to answer. I could feel him burrowing into my brain with his eyes like he was catching on to my grand scheme and stroking his chin with his index finger, trying to figure me out. I didn't dare look directly at him. I'd have degenerated into a babbling wreck but I knew he was watching me. He'd have seen instantly the lies and secrets behind my pupils if I looked into his eyes. I looked everywhere but into his face. I was fascinated how his moustache was overwhelmingly filled with black bristles but there were also brown bristles, grey bristles and even blonde ones.

Sounds from inside the toilet filled the void making my train of thought untenable. His laser vision burrowed into my head like a drill which was getting closer to my brittle secrets of broken ceilings and I worried about the ceiling crashing down around my lies and I worried about the black backpack on his shoulder. I worried about homosexuality and I could feel his curious eyes watch me under his furrowed eyebrow and his lips pinched under his multicoloured moustache and wondering at my fixation with toilets. How could I sincerely believe John didn't need to go to the toilet, he was thinking, while he, only having just met John, could see instantly how badly he needed to go to the toilet. If this dude is so eager to use that toilet, just let him use it, perhaps there's something I'm missing, I hoped he was thinking; a toilet is a toilet is a toilet and it doesn't matter which one you use as long as you use it. Or maybe he was contemplating the punishment it warranted. Some people take disabled toilets very seriously. I remembered once in the crowded canteen I squirted a bit of milk into my cup. The girl at the counter shouted, "You have to pay for that!". That was like being caught sneaking out of a disabled toilet but on this occasion John's desperation clearly justified using that toilet - he was at least *partly* disabled. Technically he wasn't disabled so technically we were breaking the rules but there was no queue and given the circumstances it was acceptable.

"Sometimes he gets so nervous it makes him sick. In lectures he comes in the backdoor instead of the main one. Jesus. It's hard to say something straight. About that homosexuality thing... no offence, what you do in your own time is your business but me and John just aren't into it. I've got nothing against it and neither does John but me and John aren't into it. I mean I'm all for the freedom to do it if that's what you're into but that's just not me and John's cup of tea."

"Homosexuality?"

"Did I say that out loud? What you have in the bag. I've got nothing against it. John either. It's just not our cup of tea. Apologies for my behaviour, Mickey... " I stopped. I didn't even know if he knew people called him by that name. "What I'm trying to say is... He doesn't like being seen. He just freezes. Sorry about this."

"What has him so nervous?"

"Exams. It's like literally, nonstop. You know some exam halls are literally just across the way from the Kremlin? You're doing an exam and you can hear people singing, having pints. On a Friday night too."

"Come on, let's go for a piss ourselves, like men, like we used to do in the bushes." He put his arm around my shoulder and turned on his heel, leading me down the corridor, for the door labelled, "Gents". I politely shrugged his arm away.

"What about John?"

"What about him?"

"We can't just disappear. He'll have a nervous breakdown."

"That's the second time he's flushed. It doesn't sound like it will stop anytime soon. He'll be fine. Go on. You go on in there." He pointed at the door of the canteen. "What I have in here will lighten your load. You'll be refreshed like you can't imagine. I'll be back in a jiffy." He slapped me on the shoulder and then started down the corridor. "I'm going for a quick piss first." At first I thought this was a good thing. I'd bang the door for John and we run. But the time frame wouldn't allow for all this activity. He'd see the pit of carnage on the ceiling and be straight back out. "Stop!", I shrieked.

"What are you doing?"

I sat on the ground, to indicate I wasn't moving.

"He has a condition. Paraplexism, it's called."

"*What's* it called?"

"Paraplexism. It's like a very serious form of stage fright. I have the condition too. If he thinks he's with people like a bunch of friends and then he finds those people gone like if he walked out the toilet and saw no one here his legs and brain just, like, stop working. He freezes."

He laughed. "And you? Are you ok?" He stood over me, leaning down, seemingly compassionate, but unable to hide how amusing he found the whole affair.

"Me? I'm fine. Why?", I said, before realising what a pathetic sight I must have made. "Three days you can take a book out for. Sometimes it's like a room full of food in a famine, everyone clamouring over each other to get the books." Suddenly I was overcome by a burst of hysteria. I sat more firmly against the wall and pulled my legs into my chest and tucked my chin into my chest and leaned against the wall and buried my face in my forearms on my knees because I was shivering with a fit of nervous giggles which I didn't want him to see. I was terrified but it made me giddy to think how in the face of imminent death I was fascinated by what his reaction might have been had I reached for and clutched his hand when I was begging him to please stay with me, like I nearly did; how getting on my supplicant knees is the last position I wanted to be in, with what the black bag in his hand might contain.

"What's wrong with you now?"

"My tummy is sore. Nothing makes me happier than being here with you, listening to your story, the one you were telling us. So please stay here with me and we'll wait for John to come out."

Incoherent praises and requests in this vein went on for what felt like the length of the Byzantine empire and at last the toilet flushed for the last time and John sauntered out, more refreshed looking than I'd seen him in hours, his jacket opened casually for the first time, the books and videos he'd removed left in the toilet, and his face wet and cool like he'd been splashing water into it.

"You hear that, John? This man is looking out for you. We were just about to walk away. You could have died. With your condition." I pushed John aside, in case he asked questions about this "condition".

"Do you want to go to the toilet now? We'll wait for you." The disabled toilet being vacant, I thought we could bolt for the exit if he fell for the bait.

"No, no, I won't keep you waiting. I know you are busy and have notes to look over. We'll give the whiskey a miss. Exams are the priority. Off you go."

"Whiskey?", John said.

"What I have here." He patted the bag with his hand. "What did you think it was? Bushmills, aged 12 years." He took the bottle out and held it by the neck and looked at it adoringly. Sparkles of light hit all its corners and edges, like a big jewel. It looked like a copper coloured stream rolling over pebbles in the summertime. "Beautiful, isn't it? I knew if I kept it in my flat I'd just drink it. Look at that colour. Isn't it beautiful?" It certainly was a pretty bottle, with its auburn hues and glistening corners. The thought of whiskey tingling on my lips made me slightly euphoric. "I bought it in the duty free when I was coming back from France. I told myself I would open it on some special day in the future, one which I was sure would happen at some time or other, and today is that day, or as close as I will ever get to it. But if you have to study, you have to study."

"What happened in the French Foreign Legion 'n' shit?", John said. I wished he felt sick again. He was full of life. He didn't stop talking. I was keen to get going but John said he wanted to hear Mickey Moustache's story. I was going to be more forceful but he had that calm, commanding look in his eye. He was still my commander in chief, a paragon of worldly advice and a warrior. Mickey Moustache was nodding eagerly too, wanting to say whatever it was he wanted to say. I had no choice. I thought it was the whiskey John wanted most, but when Mickey Moustache handed him the porcelain cup with whiskey - he'd taken 3 glasses from the shelf but changed his mind for 3 cups, it was a while before he even took a swig, which made me know for sure he was engrossed in what Mickey Moustache was saying rather than it being purely the whiskey that enticed him. I have to admit, I was curious to hear it myself. He sat on the stool facing us. We returned to the wall, our backs against it. The more he spoke and the more we listened, I saw he was no monster at all, but a kind person, unworthy of the guilt on his shoulders. He'd been dealt a bad hand and tried to make the most of it rather than throwing in the towel.

Chapter 18

Mickey Moustache's story

"It was in the free time we had before the bus arrived at St Michael's cathedral, a bulwark of a monument that couldn't be missed which le Sergeant had picked out especially for that reason, when me and Walter drank this whiskey.", he said, after taking and savouring his first sip. "There were about 50 of us, just arrived in Kigali, waiting to be taken to our base. We split up into our friendly little groups, meandering here and there around the town. Part of the adventure me and Walter went on that day, along with meeting the locals who were as fascinated by us as we were with them, our white kepis attracting compliments and well wishes from the local folk, was to a small bar off a side street. It was crowded with people in colourful clothes. It reminded me of the bar in Star Wars. What made it all the more joyful - how we ushered in this new adventure to Rwanda! It heralded a new dawn! - was to see this bottle there on the shelf. So far from home, yet so close. I don't know if it was aged 12 years, but it was Bushmills. The whole time we sat there getting it into our bellies, Walter's face rosy with excitement as stories poured from his lips, I wondered at this man who at one time I thought I could never know, so taciturn in temperament he had been, and I was reminded how wrong I had been about him.

"The first time I saw him was on the first day in France, while sitting on the wall across the road from the registration office. I was rolling a cigarette watching the cars go by. Walter was sitting on the kerb, across the road. It was a hot, sweltery day, the cars on the streets of Marseilles beeping their horns like crazy, as they always do. I noticed him because he seemed nervous, and uptight. He fidgeted with his hands. I knew he was there to enrol. He was sitting right in front of the registration office. Most prospective recruits had jagged, dishevelled mats on their heads, which would quickly be reduced to piles on the lavatory floor. Walter already had his cropped in a tight crew cut.

"In those first weeks in Castelnaudary, he seemed close to the stage where he'd desert us for his beloved Germany, even at that early stage. He never socialised with us. Where the rest of us would be polishing our boots together in the mornings, or getting some R & R after a hard day's work if we got the green light from le Caporal in the evenings, Walter would be nowhere to be seen. We would be singing, deepening our bonds as members of the 'Family', happy to give our service in whatever part of the five continents we would have the honour of being stationed, while Walter was in his dorm, writing to his wife and children. Was he even married?, we asked. Why come to an organisation surrounded by men? Surely he was a repressed homosexual. Personally, I didn't care; the content of his character is what mattered to me, but in an institution where manhood is extolled, where fists are turned into iron, it was a slur of the most defamatory kind.

"All of this changed one evening when we were in the canteen watching a game of poker. Three players remained in the hand – a south american who often got angry when he lost, Carlos Rodriguez, le Caporal, as usual screwing new recruits of their meagre earnings, and Walter, which made the game all the more fascinating, as normally he didn't fraternise with us, like I said. Le Cap is someone who should have had more sense, instead of adding fuel to the flames. He was the person entrusted to prepare us for the field of battle. He improved over time, like a block of Camembert, but at the start he was a nasty little man to us new recruits. Apparently he joined the Legion because his wife ran off with another soldier. Most of us come to the Legion to forget our baggage; he brought his with him and piled more on top. Every morning he would walk the yard and slap us with his stick. 'I need someone to demonstrate this. You, the German.', he'd say. Walter was the smallest of all the Legionnaires. He'd punch him in the ribs, or kick the back of his leg. It infuriated us how he'd never retaliate. He just took it, and did nothing.

"In that game of poker, Carlos folded. Le Cap folded too. 'What did you have?', le Cap asked. 'That's a secret you will never know.', Walter said. Le Cap said, 'Are there any other secrets you want to tell us? Pauvre pédé!' That was the last straw. Walter jumped up and grabbed the two front legs of le Cap's chair and pulled it from under him. 'Do you really think I don't know what you are saying about me behind my back, eh?!', he yelled. How we laughed! He was standing over le Cap, waving his fist. Le Cap was curled into a ball, mumbling things we couldn't hear but along the lines of, 'Please don't hurt me.' Walter was smaller than the rest of us, but he was the toughest. Endurance wise. 20 miles he could run, through rocky desert. In full kit, too.

"From that point on, not only was he respected highly throughout the regiment, he joined our happy little ensemble of me and two or three others. Me, Carlos, Bungo from Bulgaria, we had always stuck up for him. I asked him about the first day, when he was sitting on the kerb. Why did he look so serious? He told me he was afraid there'd be a queue, that he wanted to be first in. I knew it! That happened sometimes. You're told to come back another day. From that moment on, I can clearly say we bonded. In the Legion we are taught that we are never strangers, only brothers who have not yet met. I felt Walter was a friend waiting to be discovered. We treated him as our own. Legio Patria Nostra. We were determined to bring him into our fold, to instil him with some 'joie de vivre'.

"He told us that the morning of the poker game he was called into le Sergeant's office. Le Sergeant told him that unfortunately he didn't fit in as a legionnaire, that it would be best if he returned home to Germany, to his wife and children, where he belonged. If only le Sergeant knew. Getting away from his wife and children is exactly what he *had* to do. He was mixed up in some bootlegging business in Berlin. He got some guy sent to jail. When Communism collapsed, it was like the wild west. The people who were in jail were getting out and running the show. So he came here, the Legion. In exchange for a new identity, for being able to start afresh and wipe the slate clean, all that is asked of Her indebted subjects is loyalty; to the Legion, first – all comrades stand or fall as one, and to the weak and trampled upon, second. Mercenaries, thieves, killers... you get us all there. On arrival we are a disparate bunch. The solid thread running between us is one that turns us into honourable people, should we stay the course. La Légion étrangère. That saving knight of the estranged and revered alike.

"We went to Rwanda after three years of service, two of which were spent in France, one in Corsica. We had every intention of delivering justice and mercy to those who had been denied it, as we had been trained to do, and dealing swiftly with those who show none. How disappointed we were. Every day, every hour, it was pumped into us that we were strictly a peacekeeping mission. Things could have sparked up again at any time. How could we sing our songs of bravery, knowing what was going on around us, not being able to retaliate? And this was when the war was over. The punctilios of legionnaire life we had once fulfilled with vigour and dedication petered out. Slowly but surely our days' labour in Rwanda stopped being bookended by our runs at dawn and push-ups and pull-ups and climbing ropes at dusk. It annoys me to think about what a charade it was. Medecins Sans Frontieres, UNAMIR... Everybody was leaving when we should have been staying! Our strict routines gave way to idleness. We should have been ready for what happened.

"We worked in the refugee camp, mostly with food deployments and construction work. In a few months I would spend the better part of my day in the local village, rather than the camp. La Colline Magaba. My happiest memories are of my time there. It really opened my eyes, how lucky we are here. Their boats were still docked on the little beach on the lake which la Colline Magaba overlooked, but there were very few men left in the village. One of the pro bono duties me and the other legionnaires were only too happy to fulfil was to walk the 50 metres or so to the lake and fetch them pails of fresh water. In the evenings after a hard day's work, or the afternoons if we were lucky, we would go there, to visit them. They became our friends. They were always so happy to light a campfire for us in the evenings, to sit around and talk and sing, despite all they had on their hands. It was a welcome break from the company of men, which we did cherish and enjoy, but after spending a whole day working together, it was nice to see new faces and to unwind.

"It was on one of those afternoons when I was walking up the hill after fetching a pail of water that I saw Habimana for the first time; the sweetest flower from the prettiest of villages. Habimana. God exists. She was wearing a pink dress and a purple shawl. She carried a weaver basket of oranges. So commonplace, yet so magic. I would learn later that her parents and brother were dead. Such sadness, and she was always smiling. She lived with her grandmother; Granny, as she was known throughout the village; a sixty year old tobacco-chewing, obdurate, unyielding guardian who put shivers into a legionnaire three times her size.

"That first day I saw her I almost dropped the bucket from my hand. I remember a painting I saw in the Louvre in Paris - the subjects are trembling with awe on the portico, their heads pointed skywards at something we cannot see in the golden clouds; that afternoon on the hill, Habimana was to me that illustrious thing in the clouds. I was standing with those figures in the painting. The birds, those majesties of refulgent plumage perched on the branches above, their chorus on many a day keeping a smile on worn-out legionnaire faces, seemed to be singing louder in the trees around her than anywhere else. It was like the clouds opened to reveal the sky's azure blue and the sun scudded in, laying a golden carpet to illuminate the gentle trod of her feet. Something from somewhere gave me a shove to overcome my natural shyness. I went over to her, knowing going to say hello was the right thing to do. Her eyes were green. Around the campfire they were brown with glitterings of orange, but on sunny days they were green.

"Two months after first meeting her I got a job teaching english in the primary school. Or, the class, rather. It was one class for all ages. Habimana is the one who suggested I do that. She was their teacher for all the subjects. She said it would be a novelty for them, a big tall white guy with a hat on his head, speaking funny english. Throughout the day I would manage to get quite a few jobs done around the village. On the school break Habimana and I went for walks in the forest and talked. Other times we walked in silence, only the birds singing overhead.

"I knew straight away that this was the girl I wanted to spend my life with. At work le Cap would shout humorously, 'Work harder, that way you won't have time to think!' They could see firsthand the pep in my stride. A comrade would clasp a palm to his chest, impersonating a man ravaged by love. I had a smile which lasted from morning to bedtime, and I'd say ear to ear in my sleep. Three months after teaching in the school, I asked Granny if she would give me permission for her granddaughter's hand in marriage. She glared at me with eyes hot enough to melt metal, turning my proposal to halts and stammers. But soon tears welled in her eyes; a bittersweet sensation, perhaps, seeing how the object of so many compliments from my mouth had blossomed under her stewardship, yet remembering her own daughter, her first departing flower, who flew to heaven on angels' wings in the dreadful summer of '94.

"Walter organised our wedding day in the village, and the reception back at base camp. Le Sergeant gave the wedding his permission, but even he wasn't sure what would happen when it was time to go back to France. It's ridiculous how irresponsible you can be when you're in love. Father Sentwali did the ceremony. All my comrades were there, as well as 3 UN soldiers, good friends I had made. 2 were leaving Rwanda the next day.

"On our walks in the forest preceding the wedding day we often talked about where our adventure as partners in life should take us, be it abroad or in Rwanda, but deep down I knew that as long as we were together, it didn't matter. New axes would constantly be drawn for us to spin to new heights. Tales of Paris and the Eiffel tower made her eyes grow wide with wonder, but her allegiance was to the people of la Colline Magaba. A flurry of butterflies would launch in her chest, but ultimately in the middle of my most ardent attempts at wooing her these would rise only briefly, like burning paper; her excitement would fall, knowing she could never leave that village. That is what made her beautiful - her selflessness, and the sacrifices she made for others. She raised a village's beleaguered brows the way a rising tide lifts all boats. As her husband I would be honoured and only too happy to stand by her side and help her.

"On the way back to base camp for the reception, Walter made Habimana and me get out of the jeep, and blindfolded us. He made us walk a hundred yards or so. I couldn't believe my eyes, when he took off the blindfold. Everybody was standing in a semicircle around us, applauding. There were flowers and bottles of wine on so many tables, covered with white table clothes. Every other day it was plates on a weather beaten plastic table, which was dirty no matter how much you scrubbed it. Lambs on spits were being cooked by Christian and Battista, who I now realised I hadn't seen at the ceremony. Actually, this is funny. Walter and I got quite a laugh out of it afterwards. While we were performing our wedding vows, all I could think about was pumpkin soup. That's what I was led to believe we'd be having. I'm in the middle of my wedding vows and I'm thinking of pumpkin soup! I didn't think we'd have enough spoons. I was very nervous. I hoped no one noticed how giddy I was. With each 'I do' that passed her lips, my heart thumped faster. The sound of the stream rushed in my ears like the hooves of a hundred unicorns."

He stopped talking, reflecting on what he'd said, or thinking about what to say next. "All this talk is beating around the bush, really." He took a swig of whiskey and didn't say anything for a while, like pondering those days in Africa. "I'm still playing the same old tricks on myself. The truth is that life since leaving the Legion has been nothing but a series of diversions and distractions. There's nothing to be gained by telling you the flowery details of my life. I killed him. I killed my best friend. There. I've said it."

Chapter 19

Mickey Moustache's story continued

We were still in the flow of picturing soldiers in short sleeve shirts drinking wine with flowers on tables and unicorns in verdant pastures when he said that last part so it took a few seconds for the words to sink in, but when they did, John's eyes met my own. For a while I had actually considered myself grateful for being stuck in a room with Mickey Moustache. Mickey Moustache actually telling us this! It was a fortuitous encounter that would grace the ears of Limerick students for generations like Mickey Moustache's paintings in marble archways. Wait til the lads heard it. But when we heard the words, "I killed a man", those happy rosey feelings and that hazy stupor of joyful numbness swiftly evaporated.

Nothing would have pleased me more than to move on from the topic currently under discussion but John clung to it tenaciously like a dog to a bone. "You killed him 'n' shit? You really killed him?",

"Yes."

"How did you kill him?"

"I stabbed him in the heart with my bayonet."

"Stop, stop, stop.", I said. I'd heard enough. I was reminded that being stuck here in the backroom, with no witnesses or anyone to intervene, was a terrible situation to be in.

"What's wrong with you, Kev?"

"Eh, hello?" I gave him a dirty look. "What do you think is wrong with me? What's wrong with you for not noticing?" He was so short term. Just because Mickey Moustache was all rosy now, he thought it would last forever. "You remember the way we were in the library, right? Let's not totally forget that. Ah! Ah!", I said, for he was about to protest with something I wasn't interested in hearing. "Like the girl was saying to you in the Kremlin, John. Ah! Ah!". I raised my finger in the air, like scolding a puppy.

I smiled at Mickey Moustache. I turned to John again and looked him deep in the eye and spoke in coded language. I spoke in a low voice through clenched teeth with a smile on my face, to convince Mickey Moustache I wasn't talking about him.

"Let's just not forget what we were talking about in the library, ok?"

"The roof?"

"No. Shh. Keep your voice down. The warzone. The jungle. People can go home, have dinner, reflect on things, follow through on things later. You know what I'm saying? We have to be wary of what's going on around us." Judging by the ghoulish green that flooded his cheeks which made clear to me his tummy was on the brink of tossing and turning yet again, he got the gist of what I was saying; not knowing what exactly, just that it was something gravely portentous. I stepped forwards from the wall, determined to be John's defender, to reward him for the relentless bravery he'd shown earlier. "I think we better go, Mickey Moustache. We have to study."

"Sit down and relax. I know you don't have to study. You can hardly even walk."

"Ok maybe not study but yes it is Friday night and we said we'd meet people. People are waiting for us." I remembered a film where a captive English man pretends to cannibals that his army is looking for him. They were going to eat him but now they decide it's wiser to let him live. "We said we'd meet Keith and Bobby and Myles and the lads at nine, John, right?" I looked at my watch. "It's half nine! They'll be looking for us." I felt my acting was terrible. "No offence Mr..."

"Michael is good."

"I've never met someone who killed someone before, or even someone who knows someone who killed someone before, or at least I don't think I do. It's a lot to take in. We've only just met you and you're telling us all this. I thought you were just the regular security guard." His legs were so big and knees so high on the stool. "And now we're stuck in the back room with you. Fantastic. Why would we want to hear that kind of information? Anywhere we go, John, he can track us down, with the skills he acquired in the Foreign Legion."

"You're afraid I'll kill you?"

"Yes... I mean no... I mean it crossed my mind but I don't think you would. It's more for your own peace of mind I'm saying it. I've done a few things in my time I'd never tell anybody about. Maybe this is one of those times."

Suddenly he got up from his stool and came straight for us. John and I huddled closer together. He continued on past us, going behind the counter. He looked towards the door to make sure it was closed shut and opened the press and topped up his cup with whiskey. He raised the bottle to John and me, gesturing would we like a top up, and laughed at us.

"Look at the three of us like cornered, terrified animals. Here, have some more." Before I could think of an adequate excuse to hasten our departure he said, "One more won't kill you." He topped us up and put the bottle back in the press. He walked around and sat back down again, and then stood up again. He took a box of John Player from his trousers pocket. "Would any of you care for a cigarette?" What I would have loved was indeed a cigarette, and a cold pint, but it didn't seem appropriate, especially from the security guard. It was strictly a no smoking policy in the campus buildings. As if he could read my mind he put the cigarettes away and sat down and said, "You're right. I should know better. About what you were saying, Kevin, about the books, about how long you can take them out for, I will talk to Dr Walsh about it. He sometimes passes by and asks how everything is getting on. Although I think he's just being polite." He patted the white padding of the stools on each side of him. "Come on, for God's sake, take a seat. Both of you, stiff as broom handles." We left our not very comfortable comfort zones by the wall and sat on a stool on each side of him like docile little kids sitting on each side of Santa, cups of whiskey in hand, as the alternative to what might happen if we didn't was unpalatable to think about.

"Nobody is going to hurt you. I am in the zone now. I have to tell someone. The library will be closing soon anyway. You won't be here for much longer." He took a swig of whiskey. "I killed him. I killed Walter." An expression on his face transitioned from revulsion to joy. "Do you know how good it makes me feel to say that? I killed Walter, my best friend! The truth really does set you free. I wonder what they are doing now, my comrades. Some might have left, some would still be there, scattered around the four corners of the globe. Stop worrying, I am not going to do anything to you, I just want you to listen to me. When I am done here, as soon as I can, I will go to Germany and say properly those words that couldn't cross my lips the first time. Then I will call to the brotherhood I shared with Walter and tell them what happened, too. They will disavow the honours and accolades they once showered upon me, and I will be sad and ashamed, but it will be worth it. The Legion has taught me that only by feeling sorrow in equal measure to the joy I stole can my soul be saved."

"Most of us worked during the day but we would do night shifts in rotation with the UN soldiers, staying guard at the refugee camp and some of us also staying at la Coline Magaba. There were supplies kept at various depots in the camp. We'd keep vigil til morning time, when everyone else arrived on the scene. In la Coline Magaba we'd typically have 3 or 4 of us staying in the village on a given night. That night, there were 3 of us; me, Walter and Giles. It was a usual, typical evening. A lot of my comrades came to join us at the campfire. When the red sun dipped behind the hill, a soft orange sheen being bestowed upon their charming faces, they returned to base camp. Habimana was wearing a necklace given to her by her parents on her 18th birthday. Her hair was plaited in that style that awed me - so many individual, intricate strands, each one itself being a work of art.

"That night, I woke with a start. Walter was already in my room. He stayed in the house across. This was different to everything that happened before.

On occasion when le Cap got word of a skirmish or something he'd get three or four of us to grudgingly leave our breakfast and go off in the jeep to investigate. In the vast majority of cases we'd return home unfrazzled to our tartines and coffee, but this was different. There were the deep voices of men, and screams. Several of them were going from house to house.

"Luckily, we both took our FAMAS with us, but how we would grit our teeth later and swear at ourselves, firing bursts of our FAMAS into the mob through the bars, for not taking our Walkie Talkies. On our way I fired a burst of my FAMAS in the air, to slow and scatter the mob, which is something I regret, for it only caused more upheaval. I couldn't see clearly who was who. The sole source of light was the orange flickering from the fire torches they guided themselves through the village with. I could see teeth and whites of eyes and glints of swiping machetes. I was carrying a 3 year old boy, Alexis, in my arms, and the 5 year old boy who Habimana was tugging along got startled by the gunfire, or everything going on, and he ran. Habimana and Granny ran after him. Eric. Such a sweet little boy, but for years later I would be angry at him. Eric picked flowers for the coronation we put on the bonnet of the jeep on our wedding day. He made a string with coke cans which clattered on the road all the way to base camp.

"I should have fought them. Just fired and fired and screamed like a crazy wild animal and advanced and stabbed with my bayonet and killed as many of the bad guys as I could and saved as many of the good guys as I could. Had I done that, I might have found Habimana and Granny and Eric, and saved more people. I called her name in the forest but there was no sound. The forest was probably the wisest thing to do. Walter screamed at me, saying we had to go to the school, which is where in the frenzied few seconds before we all separated we said we'd meet. 'The school!', we said, 'The school!', hoping to sweep up whatever wandering lost souls we could take under our wing. With the pandemonium it was fewer than I would have liked. We walked backwards, threatening with our FAMAS and shooting occasionally to offset their advance, trying to keep cool heads and underplaying the significance of the moment. Walter had told me he'd never killed anyone before and neither had I. I shot one man who swiped with a machete. I shot another who ran towards us.

"The school had a heavy steel door. It suddenly occurred to me it was probably made for occasions like this. I ran around the back of it to have a look in case they couldn't open it and were hiding. When I was coming back around I had an altercation with a lone scumbag who'd ventured ahead of the rabble. He gave me this scar you see here. I shot him in the throat. He did us no favours when Walter pulled me in the door after getting the others into the school. In his dying gurgling gasps he pointed at us, inciting the pursuing mob to advance towards the windows where me and Walter had taken positions.

"They were two windows without any glass panes, just empty rectangles about waist height. They had heavy metal vertical bars bolted into the wall, which no man would have been able to rip off. We ushered the children into the classroom at the end of the corridor and locked the heavy metal door and stood with our backs to the wall of the corridor in front of the windows, wishing we could go back further. The spaces between the bars were narrow enough so no man could squeeze through but we had to be on high alert for a machete or rock that might come in. Sometimes when necessary we fired a sparing burst of our FAMAS, careful not to hit the bars themselves, for they ricocheted wildly, and we certainly didn't want a bullet to knock a bar loose. Most of the time we'd rush forwards and stick them with our bayonets. The kicks and pounds on the heavy steel door and the shouts through its gridded window subsided, no doubt those making and ceasing those sounds coming to join the mob at the windows, whose bared teeth looked like those of wild dogs. We were up close and personal with them, baring our own teeth back to show we would fight to the bitter end. A clever bastard had the idea of breaking furniture and sticking it between the bars and lighting the place on fire, so we had to be right up to the window with our bayonets to keep them away. We wanted to keep our ammo, having no idea how long we might be trapped there for.

"As if someone clicked a finger, the foreheads of the angry rabble pressed against the metal bars and the blades of the outstretched weapons retracted and pulled away. The growing drum of engines and doors slamming at the far end of the village was capturing everybody's attention and they turned their heads towards it.

"At first I thought it was more Interahamwe arriving to replenish the mob, as if any such thing was necessary. What a tide of relief I felt when behind the flashing stars and bursts of gunfire my eyes could discern the concerted movements of my comrades in the dark, and my ears their commands to surrender and shouts of encouragement to us.

"'Cover for me, I am going to get Habimana. I know where they are.', I said, at the first sign of the mob dissipating. The next thing I knew Walter was standing in front of the door, blocking me. 'If they are in one of the houses nearest us, they are safe.', he said. 'If they are in one of the houses further away, they are dead already.' He was right. They were dead already, as would 22 other villagers die that night, 2 legionnaires and 1 UN soldier. Through the window in the door I saw a cluster detach from the main mob and make a spot check into one of the houses near the school Walter had been talking about, saying they were safe. 'Get out of my way Walter.' 'Look at what's going on out there! Are you mad? We have so many children in that room.' 'Look at what is going on out there is right!' I loved him more than life itself but at that point in time I hated him. We had a fully fledged fist fight. I couldn't get past him, no matter how much I tried. He broke a chair and took one of the legs. He was like a rock. I cannot blame my impetuous nature for what happened. In that split second I was totally cognisant of what I was doing, no matter what excuses I make for myself. I remember the weight of the FAMAS and the intense clutch my fingers made on its cold metal casing. I remember the force of my clenched teeth. I remember the loss of Habimana turned to hate that wilfully guided the bayonet into Walter's heart and I remember holding him as he lay there in blood. But... I did not mean to do it. Do you understand me? It was a moment of... of madness.

"You've endured me long enough. I've said what I have to say. You can go now, back to your Friday night. Why did he have to die the way he did though? You know what his last words were, as I comforted him in my arms? 'Next time make your own fucking pumpkin soup.' He was laughing! Such good cheer, at the moment of death! He knew it was an accident. He knew I was full of remorse. Bastard though! I sometimes think he laughs at how that adieu to our friendship torments me. He found it hilarious I had no comeback, that he would be the one with the last laugh. Despite what happened, we preserved our friendship to the bitter end. We both knew that. Maybe he was so close to death he didn't realise what he was saying but from what I've read truth is at the top of a person's mind in those instances.

"The strange thing is, nobody ever asked me what happened, and I never told anyone, which means I wasn't really that full of remorse. I never lied. Not once. I didn't have to lie. In the minds of my comrades, it would have been insane to think that something even more nefarious than what they believed had happened to Walter had actually happened. They had no reason to suspect anything, but perhaps had it been a different bunch of people, the unvarnished truth would have come out. Whenever things got close to the gravitational pull of what actually happened that night, the arc of our conversation would tilt boisterously upwards; there were no awkward attempts at incisions behind the facade, no discussion of the minutiae within the timeframe of the dreadful deed; before things got heavy, we'd revert to slapping each other on shoulders, reliving past events, telling stories about Walter and Giles, believing that fraternal good cheer is the solution to all our woes, as we had been trained to believe. A whole narrative can be created without you actually saying anything. If Walter was there, he'd have asked me. If someone had come straight out and asked the question I'd have told them the truth.

"I left, then, after my five year tenure, not renewing my contract. How could I continue to listen on cigarette breaks to my comrades making encomiums in Walter's honour? They worshipped me for what they believed I did that night, saving children and trying to save Walter, which made the fall from grace all the more painful. Walter was awarded posthumously with France's highest accolade, le Legion d'Honneur, as was Giles. And you know how they award me for my lies and treachery? They bestow the honour on me too!

"No, I could not continue to have my presence stain that paradigm of beauty. I made a speech at the funerals. My close comrades insisted on it, saying it would be a rallying call to the troops. I commended Walter's bravery. I said how thankful I was to him, for having saved my life. The bravery part is true, but in the second part I remember thinking it was another lie on top of so many lies already told, for in truth I wished I had died instead of him, or with him.

"I commended Giles for his bravery, too. From the testimonies of those who saw it and lived to tell the tale, he was a hero. He was at the top of the village, where the thugs had first arrived. He managed to contact base camp. The legionnaires who got the call said he was literally fighting while he was talking. I can picture him, his head full of stories of our ancestors who'd made similar sacrifices to the one he was making now, his bayonet cocked when the bullets ran out, determined to take as many with him as he could. He was always the one on Camerone day marching with his chest out and his kepi nearly falling off his head with his chin raised so high.

"Leaving the Legion, then, was the only option. I wanted to cry out and say it. It got harder to do with every passing day. The shame of publicly admitting betrayal of the Legion, to the Legion. She - my tutor, my guardian, who clothed me, who housed me, who held my hand when I needed Her most, having to hear now of my lies. I couldn't. For two years I wandered in the wilderness, an opportunity arose, this job, here, as security guard, and I took it.

"They believed Walter had saved my life. He had fought them off, single-handed. Who am I to shatter this heroic image? What good would I be, languishing in some cell? No, I will not go to Germany. I will leave them with those happy thoughts. Walter. I like saying his name. When my comrades think of that game of poker a smile surely lights up on their faces. The stories of Walter resonate in their minds, wherever they are now."

Chapter 20

Chez Bobby's

After our conversation with Mickey Moustache, John and me at long last gladly crossed the rubicon that was the library exit, got outside, and went our separate ways. We smoked a cigarette together, gave each other a hug, one that communicated all the throes and pains of having been in a war together and the joy of having emerged on the other side, then he departed to find Dave. I went to the nightclub where I said I'd meet Edward. He gave me a handful of cigarettes before we split up. What must've been a good forty-minute walk - I smoked all of them - felt more like five minutes.

I'd never been to Chez Bobby's. I'd heard about it. I had a fair idea where it was, a bit past the Dunnes Stores roundabout. There wasn't much happening on that stretch of road, just what looked like warehouse after warehouse. It was all dark. If you didn't know where you were going you'd have thought you were going the wrong way. It was well away from everything else. But soon you'd come across one warehouse different to the others. There were techno beats pumping out of it. Lights flashed from around the edges of blacked out windows. Crowds gathered in the car park. I knew that's the spot I was looking for.

There were crowds gathered on the portico before the door which you got to after mounting some steps with flickering orange lanterns on each side of the steps, all the way to two white marble columns on each side of the doorway. They vibrated with the music inside. Most likely fibreglass, those columns, but to me I felt like I was entering a palace. Scantily clad princesses reclined on chaises longues awaited me on the inside, I imagined, with extended arms offering cornucopias of grapes and alcohol. I floated up the steps towards the music. The fresh air on the walk did me good. The acid in the library did me good.

At the top of the steps was a bouncer. He moved to block my entrance when he saw me coming. Even he couldn't thwart my enthusiasm. I was in the zone. More bouncers, more security... no security could frazzle me now, after what I'd been through with Mickey Moustache. "How are we feeling tonight?", the bouncer asked, the standard bouncer question, studying me from toe to head. Lights from the ceiling in the doorway behind glistened and flashed on his bald skull.

"Great!", I said, smiling. Which was so true. I felt I was wired into the universe and the universe was wired into me. I could understand everything; whatever I didn't understand, it didn't matter. And that's why I understood it all. Because everything isn't important. All that mattered was that I was here, and now, and I was happy, and I knew that.

To highlight my sobriety I asked some questions of my own. "I don't suppose you saw a bloke come in here tonight, cream silk shirt, pair of jeans, brown leather jacket?" I looked up for a neon sign or something. "This is Chez Bobby's, right?"

"Small fella? Bald?"

"He's actually quite tall. Big head of fair hair."

"Sounds familiar. You're looking very casual tonight, eh?"

"It's a casual sort of night", I said, and walked around him. He didn't even come after me.

As soon as I saw how packed the place was inside, I thought it best to give Edward a call. There was no way we were just going to randomly bump into each other. You hardly had to walk. Everybody walked for you. If I'd lifted my feet off the ground I'd still have moved forwards. The morass of bodies would have carried me like a surfer riding a wave. I grappled for my phone in my pocket. They shouted and smoked in my face. I loved it. The beautiful relentless barrage of noise pounded in my ears. Heavy techno bass mingled with the baritone roar of a thousand souls. They banged pints off my chest. They were my family, my brethren. In the same way a person gets tired of his siblings' quirks and ramblings at Christmas dinner, only pulses of gratitude for their bad habits coursed in my veins, I loved them all the more because of those very faults.

One girl I squeezed by was standing by the wall, smoking a cigarette, talking to no-one. There was a nice gleam of sweat on the bare balls of her shoulders. She took drags of her cigarette with her head raised towards the ceiling. She looked like she was breathing underwater with a straw, there was so little space. It seemed like a ripe opportunity to ask, or shout, rather, "Do you know where's the bar!?" She indicated with her head and there I saw it: some way in the distance, conspicuous amongst the pulsating bursts of greens and purples and yellows from the roving disco lights overhead, a steady beam of white light on the ceiling... I couldn't properly see what was underneath with all the writhing silhouettes and bodies but no doubt it was the bar.

Edward wasn't answering, which wasn't surprising. Likely he couldn't hear his phone. I don't think they even had vibrate mode in those days. I didn't let it ring for too long. If he answered it would be pointless. We wouldn't have been able to hear each other. I was going to send a text saying, "Where are you?", but with people shoving you, and predictive text in those days, it was a hassle. He'd see my missed call and ring me back. So onwards through the dense mosh towards the bar it was, wondering about my next steps to find him. I wasn't certain he'd still be here, or even if he'd come here at all, but I didn't mind, happy as I was to be ensconced on all sides by this festival of love and youth. Some danced with elbows flailing, which you really had to be vigilant of to avoid, some sat and chatted – or, rather, shouted into each other's faces to be above the noise. How I loved them all! I wanted to throw my arms around my brothers and sisters and embrace them, to celebrate forever in the glare of their drunken ineptitude! Their whoops and cheers contained a passion that no call to nationhood could ever match, an eloquence that no poem could surpass.

To my right, above, at the end of a long, wide sea of heads, was what looked like a mezzanine, or balcony area, which would provide a good view. It was higher up than the rest of the place. I could see people leaning on the balustrade and looking down on us. It didn't look so packed up there, or at least not as packed as down here. They could move their elbows, at least. The problem was getting there; that vast sea of heads dividing us, with bodies attached which you'd have to fight through, made it feel like a thousand miles away.

I thought a drink at the bar would prepare me for the long journey ahead, like a warm bowl of soup for the long climb up a mountain, but there were so many people on the long squeeze to the bar I wondered if skipping the soup would have been easier. Luckily, I was in a content, thoughtful, analysing mood, happy to sit back and observe, but had I been stone cold sober, catching the barman's eye would have driven me crazy, especially after the trouble to get there. Even though I was chilled out with the patience of a saint, I could feel the incipient tingle on the tips of my ears of that patience getting frayed at the edges. The bar was a sprawling, shapeless blob. I'd done everything right. I'd joined the blob and squeezed in between those on swivel stools at the counter with my ten quid displayed bullishly between my fingers, edging closer and closer to my destination, my chin up, my eyes trying to lock onto his to entice him over... but it was a futile exercise. He just wasn't looking up. There was another barman further down the bar, not too far away in real life but in terms of squeezing through the blob at the bar life it was light years away and even *that* would have been quicker than waiting for a pint from this dude, so I had no choice but to start edging towards this new top class barman, miles away. There were three barmen. They could have done with one more. He was a few years older than me, in his mid-twenties I'd say, the really good barman, tall with a lean face whose chin and nose and forehead resembled something out of an ancient Greek masculinity study, with lots of pleasant angles. He had thick curly brown hair, black trousers and a white shirt, with his dickie-bow buttoned all the way up. I could go on about my admiration and awe for good barmen, how their job is on a par with fire fighters and bomb disposal experts, but I'd need a book bigger than this to tell you about it. A bad barman can ruin a good night. A good barman makes you believe you're the only person in the room. This new barman was doing that part impeccably. He was constantly on the go, pulling pints and looking up, and even smiling back at you. Queuing at the bar, too, in a crowded pub, is an art in its own right. It's not like queuing in the supermarket. The supermarket is like live-baiting, while queuing at the bar is like fly fishing. In the supermarket, you cast out and catch something straight away. In a crowded nightclub, you really have to *sell* yourself to get a drink. There's technique involved. If you just stand there, you're not going to get anywhere. The blob will walk all over you. If you're too aggressive, or rude, you'll get nowhere either. The barman will ignore you. You have to walk a fine line. Like with the wind that can mess up your cast or a bad flick of the wrist that puts your lure in the wrong spot the blob is cruel and fickle, people will emerge through the blob and get in before you, the barman will skip you and serve others before your rightful place in the queue. You have to be strong and remember that only one in 20 casts results in a bite and that's on a good day and even then the elusive fish can escape. You have to fight with dignity with head and money high but not so high to be rude or obnoxious. You have to remember it's a subtle dance between barman and hunter, between man and fish; you have to strike that perfect medium between patience and persistence, politeness and aggression, humility and brashness, that only with that approach is catching the fish going to happen. The story of the humble barman is one that should be recorded in the annals of great patriotic deeds, like a soldier's commitment to his country, a point of posterity for future generations to look up to.

In the long trudge to my new barman's territory, shuffle by painful shuffle, I contemplated these barman wisdoms. He was lonely with his talents in that crowded room. To cut a long story short, my eager tenner was raised with confidence without being rude, like waving it arrogantly about in the air and yelling, and my efforts were paid almost instantly. With a sweaty sheen on his sculpted face he leapt through the order of the blob and lifted his head above the zoo-full of thirsty beasts and locked his eyes onto my own. Our collective conscience merged. He nodded his assent. "Pint of Stella!", I yelled. He arrived with my pint surprisingly swiftly. He handed me my change with a gracious smile, with the patience of a saint. I said, "Sorry I know you're extremely busy and I don't mean to intrude but I don't suppose there's a job as barman going over the summer?"

With all the time in the world he pointed a finger further down the counter towards the end where the bar started to curve. "See that bloke there? That's the bloke you should be asking for a job."

"Who?" There were so many people. I scanned the faces in the general area of where his finger pointed... the guy in the Aran sweater. No, couldn't have been him, he was too young and baby-faced – he must've been boiling!... the bloke in the red checked shirt nodding and frowning in such a way at something the girl beside him had said that you could be sure he hadn't heard a word she'd said but had guessed that's the reaction she wanted to see... no, not him... the fella who was locked – *really* locked - further on who suddenly recognised the latest song playing and who'd risen from his slumber, who I was afraid would stand and dance on his stool, suddenly stamping his feet now and clapping his hands like he had time for just one more celebration before the world ended... no, definitely not the kind of person you'd be asking for a job...

Then I saw who I was sure he must've been talking about. He was an old man sitting by himself.

"Who's he?"

"That's Bobby. He's the owner."

Bobby. The nightclub owner. I pictured a Ferrari outside. It used to be my dream to own a nightclub. On a beach. Marius, a play I read in college, gave me that little pub dream. Thank God it never happened. I'd hate beaches. I'd have nowhere to go on holiday. He was wearing what looked like an expensive white suit. A skinny black tie cut the suit into perfect symmetry. The tie was buttoned all the way to his collar. He looked elegant and suave, alongside everybody else. It wasn't hard to look elegant and suave surrounded by us ramshackle students, with our hoodies and baggy jeans and runners, but this guy would have looked elegant and suave alongside the best. He was old, at least his seventies, which together with his attire, gave him an air of authority, the sort that makes you nervous to approach him, like he was a mafioso or something. The fingers of his right hand were on the counter tapping nervously on the rim of a hat, a white hat like the one the man from Del Monte used to wear, and in his left hand, also on the counter, between stubby wrinkled yellow tips for fingers, was a cigarette billowing over an ashtray. There was a spotlight over his stool, shining on him, giving the impression of a magic, unpierceable halo around him. The smoke traversed through rays and beams in thick shimmering gold and green tranches, disappearing and reappearing, up towards the spotlight. His face glowed with a lemony hue. Maybe it was his suit was so white. Where normally the two empty stools on each side of him would've been nicked in a shot, the crowds of bodies now meekly stuck their heads out of their hoodies, keeping ample distance, deeming themselves unworthy of his presence. Inaudible murmurings, no doubt of healthy envy, came with the glances of admiration that landed on him.

Actually, no. I realised he wasn't alone. The stools were empty on each side of him but two girls were standing on each side of him, by the stools. Stunning, gorgeous girls, a blonde and a brunette who, like Bobby, were dressed for a place more extravagant than the one they were currently in, with long dresses and shiny necklaces and high heels. They were older, too, in their 30s or even 40s, which was about half the age of Bobby. They were standing from their stools, caressing and manhandling him to no end. Hookers. I think when I reach that age, seventy-five or whatever, I'd rather be married or something rather than sleeping around with everybody.

One of the girls, the blonde, stunning looking, with a glittery turquoise dress, which fitted tightly and made her figure impressively like an hourglass, turned Bobby's swivel stool to the side. She pouted her juicy red lips and rubbed his face and looked him alluringly in the eyes. She kissed his forehead and arranged his hair; thin wisps of hair the colour of thick yellow smoke, strategically placing them on his pate in an attempt to reconstruct a longgone hairline and conceal his baldness. I don't know why people do that. I'd rather be bald. It's so graceless. The brunette on the other side of the stool, behind him, massaged his shoulders and whispered in his ear. I could just imagine the filth coming out her mouth. The shape of her lips made words like 'suck' and ones that rhyme with it. When she spat out the words her wide eyes under giant mascara covered eyelashes turned into vicious slits, and her nose wrinkled and she bit her lip like she really wanted to inflict damage in the bedroom. I envied and pitied what Bobby had ahead of him. Sometimes spray or spittle came out her mouth. Bobby was literally sweating, eager to get going. He kept trying to pull himself up. The brunette pulled him back, continuing her filthy sweet nothings in his ear. The blonde licked her fingers and pasted his fringe into shape. It's like they were competing for his charms. All the while, the students ogled at this old man with two girls insanely in love with him, aspiring to be this legend who still had the magic long into the future.

 Yet there was something sad about him, all the same. I waved in his direction. At first he didn't see me. Then we locked eyes through the smoke. In that instant all his secrets were revealed to me. There was no music or even people in the room, it was just me and him, a sort of squaring off of manhood. The immediate vicinity behind him crackled with energy, sidelong glances of awe were shown his way by those who felt unworthy of being in his presence, the two girls competed for frantic little activities to be applied to his clothes and face, like he was the most important man in the world, and through all that chaos and movement and false promise he revealed to me how at the end of the day they use you for status, they use you for money, they use you for glamour. He raised a little glass of brandy or whiskey to his lips. His eyes were like black pebbles in deep sullen pockets. He knocked it back in one swift gulp before he got off his stool and led the girls away. His eyes didn't meet mine again but I had seen enough in that glance to know the "dream" he was living was insatiable, and that he knew it too; deep down he knew there was more to life than hookers and rock 'n' roll and fancy cars and despite this here he was, reduced to this pitiful charade, walking slowly like the old man he was, surrounded by as of yet uncorrupted youth who cherished the dream he knew to be a lie and who he would knowingly lead to ruination by his false acts and his shallow glitz and glamour, all this torturing him all the more by the fact birds used him only for money and fame with no interest in him personally, and probably despised him more than anything.

"Sorry, *who* is he?" I hadn't heard him the first time. I was looking at barman 1 down the length of the bar, thankful to have escaped. Torsos were splayed over the counter in front of him, baying like walruses in a zoo at feeding time. Someone else would go 'Arf! Arf!' and he'd rush that direction instead. No wonder he wasn't looking up. He was afraid of being eaten alive.

"That's Bobby. He's the owner. Oh I know what you're thinking! Your eyes will be as sad as they are sore if you keep lookin' like that fella. They're hotties alright. We call 'em the cat and the scarecrow. Well you're two years too late man, and the scarecrow, Jane... Bobby's not letting her out of his sight, that's for sure. She's his little flower. He'd poke you in the eye with a cigarette if you tried it on with her, especially it being another Dub after Jim." He sounded like he had a Kildare accent. I was wondering if he was from Kildare or Limerick. I'm always getting those accents mixed up.

"Who's Jim?"

"He's the other fella."

"Do you think he'd mind if I ask him for a job?" He was getting up from his stool and walking away with the girls. A premonition of a Rottweiler being torn from a sumptuous bone flitted through my head.

"You can try it. Although he does have a lot on his mind, as you can see."

"Off to his threesome." I muttered.

"He has the stamina of a stallion, that fella. No rest for the wicked, eh? He'd go all night if you let him." Suddenly, he looked sad. "But it is time to hang up the boots. Sure he's only just out of hospital with a heart attack. This will be one of the last times now, to be sure. You could be witnessing a bit of history here. His wife says it's time to put the feet up and enjoy the tea."

"His wife!?"

But he was already gone. He, the zookeeper, who could put a spring in the step of the crankiest of customers, with his loquacious, friendly nature, had already departed, continuing his battle to the next hungry sea lion, who he'd no doubt make feel like his guest, as I had felt. There's good leaving cert results, being good at crosswords, whatever... for me the ultimate form of intelligence is being able to keep persevering and staying calm and level headed and circumspect in spite of the frenzy of animals and insults that might be thrown your way. Moreover, being able to come through the other side with a cheerful disposition and a smile on your face, and putting one on the customer's face, too.

Pint in hand, taking care to not get it knocked and spilt, I made the long, arduous route to the balcony area, where I would have a better view from above and hopefully be able to spot Edward. I could picture him saying "goodbye!" to everybody, all teary eyed and giving them a big hug. He genuinely was going to miss Ireland. I couldn't wait to see his expression when he saw me here. I'd say he thought I'd forget to turn up at all.

Chapter 21

Dance Competition

When I finally got to the top I managed to carve out a niche for myself in the middle of the balustrade, people leaning on either side of me, and set about the seemingly impossible task of trying to pick Edward out from among the throng of figures below. With elbow space more permissible from my vantage point on the ledge I sent him a text saying, "At chez bobby. On balcony section." The fields of heads below me were dancing in what looked like a meteorite crater. The dance floor. Steps descended to the crater on all sides. There were steps all over this nightclub - on the way in, leading up to balconies... I eliminated subjects on the basis of height, hair colour, dance technique... Hair colour was hard to tell. There was so much of it. It kept changing with the light. And it was smoky down there, with the dry ice on top of the cigarettes. It was like a thick fog. There was frenetic, mosh-like activity at the centre, a knot that tightened and thickened rapidly like a giant peristaltic muscle. That wasn't Edward's cup of tea at all. He was far too civilised for that. I looked for him on the perimeters, where it wasn't so packed. That's where he'd be, with more room to flaunt his wares, his twists and mashed potatoes and whatever else he was into. Yes, dance technique - that was the main, distinguishing factor. For the most part people were stooped over, ungainly, awkward, with lolling heads and thrashing arms.

Edward had style. He once told me he got dance lessons.

Three Japanese blokes were standing in the area just below my section of the balustrade, on the edge of the dancefloor. I was looking right over them. They were drinking cocktails and looking at the people on the dance floor strutting their stuff, as was I. They were fascinating to watch. They were all wearing suits. I'd never seen a Japanese person *not* wearing a suit. They're very businessy. I read somewhere they spend a lot of their time at school. They've got something like five days summer holidays, something crazy like that. Two of them had hair you don't normally see on Japanese people. They had hair like *my* hair - this tangled brown, wiry crap, growing all over the place and in knots. I'd never seen Japanese people with hair like that.

Running along the wall of the balcony area, behind the balustrade on which I was leaning, was a crimson coloured, velvety sofa. It was one big sofa that swept all the way along the wall of the nightclub. In front of the long sofa were several modern round frosted glass tables fixed to the ground, spaced at intervals. At each table were two or three crimson coloured poofs, matching the sofa, or sort of cushion stools. They weren't fixed to the ground. A bunch of people – must've been ten or fifteen of them – were seeking out and asking if they were available and pulling spare poofs to two or three of the tables grouped in proximity so they could be seated closer together. They all had vodkas and whiskies and cokes. They were making a hell of a racket. One bloke had a big huge horsey laugh. People at the balustrade were turning around to see what he was laughing at.

All of a sudden I felt a light tapping on my elbow and when I turned a girl in a belly top was standing next to me.

"Are you here all alone?", she said. She was from that group, the one behind me. She had to shout it out because of the music and she had this pitiful, sorrowful expression on her face, like I had no friends.

"No, I'm waiting for a friend to turn up", I said. I didn't feel like telling her I was all alone. "He's not here yet." I asked her where she was from. She had an English accent.

"England", she told me. She had a nice smile. She told me the name of the town she came from but I can't remember. She told me her name was Juliana and I told her my name.

"Are those all your friends? How come there's so many of you?"

"We've just finished our exams. A lot of us are going to Africa in a few weeks." They were studying medicine. They were going as volunteers to do charity work, I gathered. "Come on, sit over with us!", she said.

So I did. She didn't introduce me to every single one of them because there were so many, but she introduced me to a few – just the ones sitting on the sofa and the cushions and poofs nearest us. The first bloke I talked to was Daniel, from France. He loved Ireland. Quite a lot of them were foreign students, over on Erasmus. Daniel said he didn't travel as much as he would have liked in the year he'd been here. He was particularly interested in the Giant's Causeway. I talked to this American dude, Ben. He had on this white T-shirt that said 'I ♥ Ireland'. He helped me carry the drinks. I told him on the way the I.R.A wasn't the cause of the Troubles, it was a *symptom* of them.

The whole time I was talking to everybody, though, I had Juliana on the brain. What a girl. Fair balls to her for coming over to me in the first place. As soon as a slow set came on I said, "Juliana, do you wanna dance!?", just in case one of the others beat me to it.

We walked hand in hand down the stairs and into the centre of the dance floor, which had emptied out now, becoming orderly, leaving it to the slow dancing couples. There was a beautiful scent of perfume on her neck. I shut my eyes and tried to dispel mouthwatering fantasies. The sway of her hips and the faint twitch of muscle under her jeans enflamed the fantasies. In the dark of my eyelids I counteracted them by picturing china dolls that could shatter under roving fingers or rice paper that could evaporate under hot tips. I found a natural resting place for my thumbs just below the small of her back which I presumed was her belt, but in fact was the elastic of her knickers. I started the slippy face job - my cheek sliding against her cheek the whole way until I got to her mouth. I was doing it very slowly - it took me about fifteen minutes to reach her mouth, and when at last I did, she pulled her head back. I hate that. Just that second. She didn't walk off on me or anything, like I thought she might - I'd've hated that - she just explained to me about some bloke in England she was seeing. She was smiling while she was telling me. I like girls who smile when they tell you those sorts of things. Especially after the slippy face job. The ones I hate are the ones who just walk off. The head-ball she was going out with was a Rudolph or Randolph or something. I wasn't too interested, to tell you the truth.

As soon as we got back to the balcony, Juliana's friends said they had to leave. They said they had to get up early to visit a fish aquarium. "Go on, stay.", I insisted. Suddenly I remembered the pile of money Edward had given me. In the future was the fish aquarium, yes, but now, *right this second*, I pleaded, was an invitation to let the night live long. One guy, Eoin from Donegal, I think, was an obvious candidate for having his arm twisted. He looked at me with the doleful eyes of a dog tied to a lamppost, watching his owner walk away into the sunset. "A shot of tequila for old times' sake?" That clinched it; there were murmurings all-round of "Ok ok let's stay for one more."

Suddenly, the music stopped. All the lights dimmed. We ran to the balustrade. We had to fight for elbow space. There was only one light on. It was aimed directly over "Bobby", the old owner guy, and followed him, as he walked from the far edge of the dance floor to the middle of the dance floor, a microphone in his hand.

"Welcome, everybody. Welcome. Welcome." The dance floor was emptying fast, with no music playing. Bobby dominated the room, pacing calmly back and forth. A dedicated group of observers on the far side of the dancefloor hung on his every word. It was hard to tell the number of people he was talking to as there were students lingering around and it was hard to see in the dark but I'd say 40 or 50 core relatives and friends, sitting at tables and chairs on the edge of the dancefloor. They hushed for silence from students who were asking why the music had stopped.

"What an important night this is. A time to celebrate the future and reminisce over the past. Some of you I grew up with, some I've met more recently, but if you're here, you're supposed to be here. I'm a Kerry man, as you all well know, but I don't hold it against you if you're not." There was general laughter at his witticism. "So yes, as you all know, today is a big day. Where is she? Where is she, my little honey pot?" From my excellent spot overlooking all this on the balustrade I could see, in the darker recesses of the room, far away from the limelight, shifting, glittering movements, approaching the dancefloor. The chance to impress Juliana by being the first to notice what might be a decisive turn in a saga on which everyone was hooked was too much to resist, and I quickly pointed it out to her. The dark shifting forms ventured slowly through obstacles of family and friends sitting at groups of arranged tables and chairs in the dark and when they were on the edge of the limelight I could see the defined shapes of the two stunning girls in the sequin dresses emerge, the blonde and the brunette who'd been with Bobby at the bar. The blonde stayed behind while the brunette walked right into the centre beside Bobby into the limelight and put her arm around him. He looked longingly into her eyes. She was quite a bit taller.

"Look at you. What a beauty. You've been doing the gymnastics thing for years. A body to die for. Jane now, the accounting one... come here to me Janey." Jane, the blonde, who was standing a bit further out, walked into the limelight, joining the two of them. "Ever since I brought you out to buy that dress in O' Donnell's when you were barely a spring chicken I had no pre... pre... prete..." The sentence was interspersed with gasps for breath and tapered out into a high pitched sob before he could finish. The brunette pressed him into her bosom, comforting him like he was a little child himself. The blonde wrapped her arms around both of them so they were all cuddling in a happy threesome. He'd started with the valour of a lion and what seemed like effortless courage but now the mask was off. He dropped the microphone to his chest and his shoulders slumped and his head dropped, obviously overwhelmed with emotion. The friction of the mic on his suit made the sound of thunder on the horizon. The girls kissed him, and kissed each other, tears in all their eyes, and there were hugs and tears in his family and friends observing this.

The intimate gathering provided the invigorating jolt he needed. He made a sudden exhalation of air, a healthy burst like someone bracing themselves for some big feat. His shoulders rose. He separated himself from the huddling trio and dusted off his suit jacket. He held the microphone higher to his lips and looked longingly into the brunette's eyes, this time though like someone in full control of his emotional faculties.

"Isn't she gorgeous? Isn't she *gorgeous?*" He took a tender chunk of jowl between his forefinger and thumb and tugged it gently and affectionately. "Arlene and I have been blessed with 4 beautiful children, 6 grandchildren and... who knows, maybe more to come?" He winked at the brunette and slapped her on the bottom. The suggestive gestures caused general relief and mirth in his cohort of family and friends that he was back to his old self but it got a rise in particular from the more testosterone-charged, drink-fuelled members of the room, of which there were many. They made wolf whistles that died quickly. They got daggers from the more sober circles of Bobby's friends, who sat on the edge of the halo and flashed their heads at these young bulls showing they didn't appreciate the lewd commentary. The wolf whistles stopped, owing to the wrath they'd face later should they accidentally send Bobby into another spiral of emotional turbulence.

"You go and sit down now for a while honey pots.", Bobby said to the blonde and the brunette, and I thought he was going to smack the brunette's bum again, but he didn't. "I'll be a while here. Join the others and I'll call you up later." He kissed the brunette on the cheek. With the way it appeared to me she'd been uttering filth in his ear I'd expected her to be slutty and vulgar, like leaning in to chomp on his lower lip, but rather she seemed reserved and dignified; she giggled shyly, being the centre of attention in the limelight not something that came naturally to her, apparently.

She turned on her heel to skip back to the deep shadows, gladly, but before she'd even reached the outer part of the halo a friend from Bobby's inner circle pulled a chair for her to sit in, and one for the blonde too.

"Thanks Larry. The gentleman, as always.", Bobby said. "Yes, it is a special night tonight for the Kavanagh family. We've been here for decades, Arlene and I. We made the leap of faith from the Kingdom in our twenties to this beautiful part on the south side of Limerick city. What an adventure it's been. What. An. Adventure. It started off as a simple idea with humble origins. Everyone of you out there knows I have a story to tell with each and every one of you." There was a round of applause. "Now, we all know the obvious reason why it's a big day. And the other reason... well, it's true. Yes, it's true." There were grumblings of disappointment, like they'd been hoping the rumours weren't true. An elderly couple at a table on the edge of the limelight hugged each other. Bobby nodded regretfully, his lips pinched, like he'd given the matter some thought. "Yes, yes, it's best to quit when you're ahead. It's time to hang up the boots. Do you remember the way this place was, Larry? Back in the fifties?"

In the dim light there were mumbles of "I do, I do" from the guy who'd pulled the chairs out for the girls.

"This place was run down. Run down. There was nothing. Literally nothing. You younger fellas have no idea the way it was, with your computers and telephones." There was satirical laughter at having to listen to a story for the umpteenth time. "No, I'm serious, you don't. The Rooney brothers in Ballinorig, Larry, tell them about the Rooney brothers."

"Sleeping under a sheet of corrugated iron.", Larry said, in a muffled voice unlike that of Bobby's, as Larry didn't have a microphone to his mouth.

"Sleeping under a sheet of corrugated iron. That's right. Me and Arlene and Larry called into their house to bring them milk and they were sleeping under a sheet of corrugated iron. Their bedroom had a hole in the roof -

"The bedroom had *no* roof."

"That's right. No roof. Just a big hole. They couldn't afford blankets. Arlene was pregnant, we hardly had a quid to scrape between the two of us, me, Arlene and

Larry said to hell with it, let's go to Limerick. And here we are, 50 years later. When I see how much this place has progressed since those days, it makes me so proud."

"Stab city!", a Kerry relative interjected, to much teasing consternation from the crowd, like a line had been crossed, but it was all in good jest.

"Who said that?", Bobby said, his hand over his eye, spying for someone in the dark. "Is that Peter Fitzgerald? Someone give that bollox a thump." Chairs shifted and figures leaned over tables dutifully, doing as they'd been instructed. "Thanks to the goodness of God, Arlene and me took a punt, bought this run down warehouse and did it up, and voila, we haven't looked back since. Chez Bobby's was born. 45 years since we had our first wok 'n' woll competition right here in this room. Would you believe it? 45 years." There was applause from the crowd, and rumbles of "hear hear".

"Arlene bore me 4 fantastic children, all of you here tonight with your own husbands and wives and children of your own. Katey, Lorraine, Brendan, and now Jim... bloody Jim! A bloody Dub of all things!" A bunch of people shouted "Boo!" at a man in a white shirt sitting a bit away from the group by himself - Jim, I presumed. Someone threw a plastic cup at him. The brunette turned her head to smile at Jim and he reciprocated with a shrug of his shoulders saying, "What can I ever do to make these guys happy?"

"Yes, it's best to quit when you're ahead. Age, the great deceiver, catches us all, unfortunately. My legs are gone. My eyes are gone. How many years did I say? 45. I just had a heart attack. As someone once said, there can be no true beauty without decay."

"No! No!", people in his posse were saying, shaking their heads incredulously, like he would never get old, that he was still the same legend he always was and would always be.

"Yes, yes, it's time to put up the boots. The memories will live on, but physically, my knees are at me. I've enjoyed every minute of it. I took a gamble on you people and boy, did it pay off."

"Cute hoor!", someone yelled.

"I like to think I know a bargain when I see one. I hail from the Kingdom, after all. Laughing matters aside, there's no one sleeping under corrugated iron any more. As soon as I walked into Jimmy Clarke's office that day... is Jimmy here?" He put his hand over his eyes and peered into the dark. "I'm here, I'm here.", someone said, from the dark depths. "Good man Jimmy. That day we went into your office Arlene and I got the whiff of magic in the air. We've become a... what's the word... a *cosmopolitan* city." There was a round of applause from everybody, even the students, who recognised what they were seeing was a heartfelt spectacle that warranted recognition, even if they didn't have a clue what was going on. "Thank you, thank you." Bobby said. "It was fun while it lasted. So, that's the retirement thing out of the way. Now for the important stuff. Where is she? Where is my little flower?"

In the brief silence and in the dim light I noticed a turning of heads among Bobby's crowd from the edge of the limelight all the way into the depths of the dark bowels, to what I saw was illuminated with a little rectangle of light above a door, at which there were noises. Very quickly, the room seemed to spontaneously erupt into a giant game of musical chairs. Everyone from Bobby's entourage jumped up and shifted tables and chairs to different positions. I smacked my forehead repeatedly with the palm of my hand, which made Juliana laugh.

It soon became apparent they were making a pathway from the back of the room all the way to the dancefloor. A vehicle, with big wheels, was coming into the light from the far end of the room. I could discern a woman's head at the front of the vehicle. I could discern the heads and arms of two burly figures in dark shirts directly behind her. By the way the metal corners and curves on the vehicle glistened wildly in the engulfing light and by the way the people on the sidelines applauded and cheered and laughed at how they had to dodge their feet in case of being hit by the vehicle I was sure what was coming was a Harley Davidson with Arlene riding in front and the two burly men sitting on the saddle behind her, a retirement gift from all his friends gathered around him now.

"Oh Arlene.", Bobby said. His voice crackled with emotion. As the old lady with white hair was being wheeled into the centre of the dancefloor to Bobby, a burly Limerick or Kerry man guiding each handle, the brunette returned to the limelight also. "To celebrate all that has passed, and all that is to come, I ask you for this dance.", Bobby said. He kissed and embraced the lady in the wheelchair. A slow song came on. I thought he was going to take her out of the wheelchair and dance with her but instead he danced with the brunette while the old lady stayed in the wheelchair, looking on and smiling. Throughout, not a few more eyes were dabbed with handkerchiefs. What might have been an intimate moment between me and

Juliana, thanks to the romantic sweetness of the occasion, was hindered by the guy behind us trying to squeeze in between us. When he laughed, warm beery breath wafted across my face. I pressed my arm into Juliana's, creating a seal. There were people barging on all sides to get a better view. There's no way I was letting him in.

When they'd finished dancing Bobby held the microphone to his mouth and said, "I ask all my family and friends to join us shortly for the reception upstairs... but first... but first... Bernard?" An instrumental version of *Do you love me* began playing on low. A roar of excitement emerged from his posse. The merriment was contagious. Students joined in the cheering, happy to be part of the excitement, whatever it was about. Arlene scowled at him. He pretended he didn't see. "Now one more time, it's Wok 'n' Woll time! Who is in? Who is in!? Turn it up, Bernard!" Couples from his gang went quickly to the middle of the dance floor like it was a great honour to be first there. Others started joining - just regular student couples, when they saw members of Bobby's cohort joining.

Edward was one of the couples. Which wasn't surprising. I could see him from the balustrade. He was a rock 'n' roll freak. "I know that guy! He's my housemate!", I yelled to Juliana and André and whoever else would listen. "Which one?", said Juliana, her arm pressing against mine, our faces close. "The one there! In the middle! With the jacket on." He was wearing his brown leather jacket, but it didn't impede him. Wow, he was good. It was like spotting your regular Joe Soap buddy on TV. His head seemed to float, remaining stationary, like it was being held from above by an invisible wire. Meanwhile, his arms and legs and hips were a flurry of movement. The way he maintained equilibrium was impressive.

Bobby weaved with surprising nimbleness and deftness among the contestants, observing them closely and prodding or poking whichever ones he felt weren't producing the goods. He was the referee. He tapped people on the leg with the black cane or stick in his hand which meant they were disqualified. He nipped in and out, dodging the threshing torsos and knees and elbows. He looked so cool, with the white suit and that panama hat on his head and all.

The talent of contestants shrank and soon there were only 2 left; Edward, and the girl he was with, and another couple. People were taking bets who'd win. He wasn't with Vanessa. He was with a girl I'd never seen before, a tall skinny girl with glasses. She was pretty good at the moves too. Edward spun her in a cartwheel. I was wondering who "She" was.

Bobby waved his arms in the air. The music stopped. He led Edward and the other male contestant to the middle of the dance floor where they gathered in a nervous huddle to what was being said while the girls were sent to join the mob surrounding the dancefloor. We couldn't hear what Bobby was saying but I could see Edward mouthing, 'No way, man, no way!'. He was shaking his head and throwing his arms up in despair.

The music started again, sort of comical tunes repeating themselves. The other male contestant started stripping off his clothes! The place went wild.

"Go on Edward, screw them!", I shouted. At first I was embarrassed for him, how prudish he could be. He wouldn't even take his jacket off. He just stood there saying, "No way, man, no way.", with his hands to his head.

He ran up to the tight wall of the crowd and tried to force a hole through it. The wall of bodies contracted and laughed and mocked him. He ran again towards the laughing throng of heads that permitted no escape. They pushed him back out. If you'd just come in by time machine you'd think you were in a coliseum rather than a nightclub. They contracted and laughed and howled and taunted him like a unified pack of hyenas. I get mirth at another person's chagrin, how failure can be funny, but I thought at least one person would say, "Come on, let's call it a day.", and stop the torment and let him through, but they didn't.

What happened next is something I'll never forget. He started stripping off his clothes too! "Go on Edward you legend!" I couldn't believe it. Something clicked in him. If you'd told him earlier in the day that before the night was out he'd be running around a nightclub in his underwear he'd have baulked at the idea. So would everyone else. He took off his jacket and lay it on the floor and feverishly opened the buttons on his shirt and tossed it on the ground. Then he prised the heel of each shoe with the toes of the other foot and tossed the shoes aside. He tore open his belt. You'd have thought his pants was on fire. He pulled his trousers off, using his toes again to stand on each opposing leg, and then yanking his leg through. Then he took off his socks. Peer pressure got the better of him, I reckoned. It did him good to strip off like that. There's nothing more therapeutic than jumping out of your comfort zone.

By the end of it, the dance floor was like a battlefield strewn with socks and shoes and trousers and t-shirts and tops. He walked up and down the length of the dance floor and said rhetorically to random people in the crowd, "Are you happy now, huh?". When they looked at the fruits of their defilement and humiliation in the eye, they would feel shame at the ordeal they'd put him through, he believed, but they just laughed all the more. Just with his chin raised defiantly, and his bandy white legs sticking out of his underpants. At least the other contestant was wearing boxer shorts. Edward was wearing y-fronts. He had his leather jacket folded over his arm. He wouldn't let that jacket out of his sight.

Bobby led them, their hands full of clothes and shoes and socks, and the two girls, fully dressed, away some place. The pumping techno beats resumed and the sea of revellers came crashing back onto the dance floor. It was like nothing had even happened.

Then, Juliana and her buddies really did leave. I gave her a kiss on the cheek and herself and the rest of the bunch started towards the steps of the balcony. She was really stunning. Just when she was stepping off the balcony and I was standing there by myself again, she turned around and gave me this nice wave, with a smile. It was the prettiest thing I'd seen all day.

Good old Edward. I was delighted for him. Before I'd known him I'd have had trouble telling a good dancer from a bad one – unless they were completely crap – but Edward had taught me a few inside tricks of the trade. Academically, anyway. Most of it is about confidence. That's what he told me, and he was right. If you have good posture – keep your chin up and don't slouch forwards – you're halfway to being a good dancer. The other half is having the moves, obviously. Edward had both.

Chapter 22

The Exclusive Zone

The temptation to go down and try to follow him was quickly rendered void by the tortuous reality of such an endeavour, so I took a position on the balcony again with my eyes peeled on that door like a fire escape for if he returned, but it was dark in that part of the room which the pulsating beams of light that pivoted and bobbed on the ceiling couldn't reach. The place was chockablock. As it turned out, he came to me. I'd been leaning on the balcony pondering everything that was going on and I felt a nudge on the shoulder and I turned around and he was standing there. Fully dressed, for a change. The buttons on his shirt were opened all the way down, showing his belly and chest. He looked like one of those Spanish blokes in the holiday brochures with the gold medallion hanging over their hairy bellies who say, "Welcome to my beautiful country!"

"Hey, Kev. I've been lookin' for you everywhere! Where the hell you been?"

"Edward!"

"Get your hairy ass over here! Come on, I got a surprise for you!" He was dragging me by the arm some place.

"Edward you legend!... What the hell was that about?... you've got more balls than I thought... Where the hell we going? Where'd you get the cap?" He was wearing a black cap that said *Chez Bobby's* in red writing.

"I won it. You like it?"

He dragged me all the way through the nightclub, through all the crowds and up some more steps and then down a little series of steps, and then up some more. There was bunting on the bannisters saying "Happy Engagement". There were balloons and tinsel decorations. We ended up at what appeared to be the "Exclusive Zone" of the nightclub. It was the same set up as the balcony section but more trendy and in a room all of its own, like its own separate little nightclub. There was a floor to ceiling glass window overlooking the dance floor, which I remember being very impressed with. It would have been impressive even today. I don't think floor to ceiling windows were as common back then. It was a novelty. There were designated round frosted tables with numbers on them. There was a little stand on each table with a piece of laminated paper saying, "1" and "2" and so on. On the walls were paintings and mirrors, behind the crimson sofas and pouffes. There was a chandelier on the ceiling, but it wasn't turned on. Roving disco beams were the source of light, less aggressive than those outside, and the music wasn't as loud either, and with less techno beats, perhaps more amenable to some of the older folk in the room.

Edward pulled me through the room to our designated frosted table, the number 7. He stood besides it, his arms outstretched, up in the air. "Come on! Make yourself at home!"

"What the hell is this? Where's Vanessa?", I asked. I couldn't see her anywhere. There were glasses full of drink and a jug of coke with ice cubes and bowls of peanuts and crisps on the frosted table. And envelopes, too, which he'd tell me later were two £10

Eason vouchers, one for him and one for Cecilia, who was the girl he'd been dancing with, who was sitting on the sofa besides where he'd been sitting before coming to look for me and who was giving me a big wide smile and saying hello. She had buckteeth.

"We got split up at the competition. That referee was splitting everybody up and fixing them with new partners in case they were pros or something. It's a shame. We would have won hands down if we hadn't been split up – after all those new moves I'd shown her." He shook his head regretfully, but forgot about it very quickly. "Come on! Make yourself at home!", he said, snapping out of it.

"I mean seriously, what the hell is all this?"

There was the blonde, the brunette, Jim, Arlene in the wheelchair, who I wondered for a while how she got up, there was Bobby and all their friends, sitting at frosted tables. Some danced on a little dance floor. There was a girl in her thirties I'd say talking to the brunette at one of the tables and she had a white dress and blotchy fake tan which I noticed in the light as we passed – either that or she was badly sunburnt. She was with a chubby bloke a good bit older, smoking a cigar.

Edward started getting all excited, as electric as the Edward of yesteryear ever had been. "Man, did you see me out there? Did you see me!? I can't believe I was running around stark naked on that dance floor." Stark naked – that cracked me up. I sat on one of the pouffes. He sat on the velvety crimson settee on the other side. I noticed he was holding a bottle by the neck, that dazzled and glistened like a brick of gold.

"What's that?"

"It's a bottle of whiskey! Wild Turkey! I – *We,* won all this stuff. Can you believe it!? Hah! I just can't believe it!"

"Jesus, good man!", I said. "Technically it's bourbon but... good man!" I'd had some great sessions with Wild Turkey. Out of respect I was compelled to apply the correct nomenclature.

"Are you drinking too?" He raised a glass to his lips and took a swig. I'd never seen him touch alcohol. He spent his time rebuking the rest of us for drinking so much.

"Yes, Kevin. I am drinking too. Uisce beatha. The water of life."

"Now you're talking! Welcome to the club. You're a legend, Edward. A *legend. Look* at this. I mean, *look* at it!" I swung an arc with my arm, taking in the grandiloquent surroundings of the room. To my right was the full-length glass wall with a view on the crowded, sweaty broth of regular nightclub goers below, who, judging by the jealous tint in their eyes that ogled up at us through the thick glass, had yearnings for our exclusive VIP section.

"I mean... what the hell was that all about though? You were practically running around stark naked, like you said."

The other contestant who'd stripped down to his underwear, Thomas, from Cork, was sitting at the frosted table next to us. He looked over as Edward explained what had happened. I'd say he was 21 or 22. My initial impression was of a quiet man by nature. He had the quality of a startled hare about him. His eyes were glossed over like he didn't quite believe he'd been awarded a place at the Exclusive Zone. Intermingled with this confusion was a touch of modest pride at what he'd pulled off, his clothes, an act of bravado at odds with who he truly was. He had a delicate, almost quivering little smile; nervous, but daring to congratulate himself at the same time.

He crouched forwards diffidently on his crimson pouffe to hear Edward embellish the good points so they were even more amazing, from how he and Vanessa had gone out hand in hand and then the "ref" decided to mix it all up by pairing them with new partners and the excitement that ensued when the music came on, and soon Thomas pulled his pouffe over altogether as did the girl he was with, Andrea, so bubbling with enthusiasm they were to hear Edward talk, and as he did so, you could see Thomas' mood visibly change, cutting loose the shackles that held him back. By the end he was clapping and laughing in high pitched giggles and clinking glasses boisterously with everybody, more like a person feeling exhilarated after their first skydive, far from the frightened boy in a foreign land, quiet and subdued, which is how he'd greeted me initially. Edward opined on Bobby's naturally generous disposition and shrewdness, saying how the act of rewarding the two last couples, rather than singling out just one winner, was a very classy, empathetic gesture, an acknowledgement that anybody who humiliates themselves for laughs in a crowded room deserves a prize rather than the double humiliation of having to leave empty handed in nothing but a pair of underpants. Edward praised Bobby's astute business sense, as evinced by the packed club of people who'd all paid two pounds in. He must've been making a fortune. We lowered our heads and nodded in respect of Bobby and business sense but the act of solemnity was short-lived. Soon Thomas, Andrea, Cecilia, Edward and me were all clinking our glasses to uproarious chants of, "To Bobby! To Bobby!"

"This is just... so cool. Chandeliers and all. Look... that over there is a Van Gogh. And there... with all the colours... that bloke with all his bright colours... Paul Tahiti? Or he went to live in Tahiti?"

"Yes, it's pretty cool alright.", Edward said, his chin raised and scanning his head slowly at the pictures on the walls like they were works he'd personally bequeathed to a museum. "It's like an art gallery, isn't it? *Life* is like an art gallery. There is only one art and that is the art of living. Jack B Yeats. Have you ever experienced pure, total love, Kevin?"

"Yes, just a few minutes ago. There was a girl here shortly before you came along."

"Love is like an ocean.", he said, followed by words in French, or German or something.

"Are you drunk?"

"It's highly possible. You know this is my first time ever getting drunk? You know that? I just never saw the point in alcohol. It feels good. *Real* good." We high-fived and clinked glasses. "I remember one day I was off to lectures and all you guys were in the front room, drinking beer. This was morning time. I came back from my lectures in the evening and you were all still there, the five of you. The whole day. Losers, I thought. Who's the bigger loser though? The one chilling out on a sofa from dawn til dusk with his friends or the one repairing an attic door on the roof? That's what I was doing. Fixing the attic door. You know what my new ambition is?" He was slouching a bit too much to his right towards Andrea. I was afraid he'd rest his head on her shoulder. She was talking to Thomas. Cecelia was talking to the guy on her left.

"I don't know. Lean forwards, I can't hear you."

"My ambition is to do nothing. Absolutely nothing. It's such a gift. For you it might be easy but for me it's like... I mean I'm not criticising you... it sounds terrible the way I'm saying it, doesn't it, basically calling you a piss head?" I laughed at how he was embarrassed to talk about our laziness, knowing he meant nothing offensive. "I'm envious of you. That's what I'm trying to say. To be able to sit on your ass and do nothing is a gift!"

"I know!" We laughed loud and clinked our glasses together, a bit too hard, sending gushes of booze over the edges, and which had me checking later if I'd cracked the glass.

"A woman is like the flickering flame of a candle, Kev. Your heart rises like the swell of a wave and you just want to shroud that thing, to throw a blanket over it and hold it for eternity. At some stage in a person's life..." He leapt up like he'd sat on a thumbtack. "Where the hell is Vanessa?", he said.

"I don't know. I'm just after asking you the same bloody question. Sit back and relax, man."

"You're right. You did just ask me that question. Oh man, I am toasted. *Toasted.*" He guzzled from his glass like an alcoholic just in from rehab, deciding abstinence wasn't his thing. He reached for the jug of coke and poured some into his glass.

"What are you doing?"

"Mix it with coke. You can hardly taste the alcohol."

"Mix it with coke*?*" I looked at his glass. It was indeed a browner colour than the golden hue of Wild Turkey. "No wonder you're so bolloxed if you keep knocking it back at that rate. You're supposed to swirl it in your mouth, you're supposed to let it sit on your palate." He laughed and took another swig. He passed me the bowl of crisps from the table. I took a handful but didn't put them in my mouth straight away as I was serious about the Wild Turkey.

"Seriously. Slow down. Mixing Wild Turkey with coke is sacrilege. Do you think poets and artists in times gone by mixed it with coke? Van Gogh with his absinth, Caravaggio with his... I would have thought with your haut-cuisine -

He threw his eyes to heaven, no time for my highfalutin rubbish. "Eat your crisps and shut up." He stretched his neck out and scanned about the room covertly like ensuring it was free from assassins.

"What's wrong? What's wrong?" He had a stern and serious look on his face, all of a sudden. He looked surreptitiously left and right at Thomas and Andrea on one side of the sofa and Cecilia on the other, who were indulged in conversation with the person next to them.

"What is it?"

He started that, "Hmmm" business, grumbling, stroking his chin, contemplating whether I deserved to know what exactly was going through his head. "You know what I have to say, Kevin. You know what it is."

"I don't have a clue what you have to say." I hate that; acting like he wants to tell me something, then considers changing his mind at the last minute. "Don't tell me if you don't want to, I don't care."

"Now if you see her, you tell me, ok?" He sat up and scanned the far reaches of the Exclusive Zone to ensure the coast was indeed completely clear. He winked at me. "Sit in here beside me." I left my pouffe for the spot of crimson velour sofa he'd been sitting in, which was nice and warm with him there, as he'd nudged closer to Cecilia, making a space for me.

He poked me in the chest. "Who do I love?"

"Vanessa, I suppose."

"Exactly. I – love – Vanessa.", he said, which I was relieved to hear, because for a while I was afraid he'd say me.

He folded his jacket neatly in his lap and opened the zip on the inside right breast pocket, knowing exactly what he was going for. He put his hand deep into the pocket.

Something didn't feel right. He froze. "Holy shit.", he said. "What's wrong?", I said. He turned the jacket over frantically. His eyes widened in distress. He rummaged through the pockets. Each newly searched pocket came up as empty as the last. Even in the poor light I noticed the transition on his face from apoplectic with terror to quickly plummeting until it was white like a sheet of A4 paper.

He took a deep breath to recollect himself. He restarted the process - going back to the original breast pocket, putting his hand in and rummaging around, this time extremely thoroughly.

He felt what he was looking for. He left his hand in the pocket for a longer time than normal, like its presence was reassuring. He threw his head back in relief and looked up at the ceiling. "Jesus, Mary and Joseph, thank you God." He zipped the pocket up again, without taking whatever it was out.

"Are you not going to show me what it is?"

"Wouldn't you think I'd learn? Wouldn't you think I'd *learn?*" He slapped his forehead with his hand and laughed. "Mothers are great but on the passport debate, she's wrong. Dead wrong. You really have to take what they say with a pinch of salt."

"The what?" I was keen to see the thing in his pocket but also curious about the passport debate.

"The passport debate. The mother-son ritual every teenager goes through. If you're abroad, and you go out, should you carry your passport with you, or should you leave it behind in the hotel. Ok, granted, I'm not staying in a hotel, but even if I was I think I'd leave it in the hotel. It's ingrained in my system. I can't understand how anyone can genuinely say it's safer carrying it on your person rather than stashed away somewhere in your hotel room, in a drawer or somewhere, or left at home." He shook his head resentfully on the adversaries of the great passport debate. "Come in closer." I shifted in even more. He unzipped the inner breast pocket again and put his hand in and scanned around the room while his hand was in the pocket. At the last instant with his other hand he gripped my arm, to denote grave importance. "Now, if you see Vanessa, you tell me, ok? You got that? I shouldn't even have brought it out. If she suddenly walks around the corner or in here -

"Yeah, yeah, I get it."

He placed a square little velvety navy or black box into my hand.

"What's this?" I already had a good idea what it was but asked anyway.

"Open it. Take a peek inside. Don't take it out please."

I lowered the box into my lap, under the table. The way Edward was acting, I felt we were doing something illegal, like we were a pair of undercover plutonium dealers. I opened it. The top flipped open. It gave me a fright. I was afraid stuff might fall out. Mounted in felt padding was a ring; two diamonds set on each side of a ruby which, as I would learn in later years, is indeed an unconventional engagement ring, as Edward would point out.

"Do you see what it says?" He pointed along the inner band of the ring, still in the padding. I could hardly see the ruby and the diamond and he was asking could I see writing. "On the band. Look." I squinted in the dusky luminance with little success. We perched our heads down. The girl in the white dress and blotchy fake tan was looking over, analysing whatever it was we were up to, or at least I felt she was.

By this stage, Cecelia, Andrea, and then Thomas had noticed our clandestine behaviour. It would have been rude if he didn't explain. When he was assured the coast was clear he said with controlled excitement, "It's an engagement ring. I'm going to ask my girlfriend to marry me." The girls exploded with the excitement of it all. Edward raised his finger to his lips, imploring calm. "Can you see it?", he whispered to me. Cecila leaned across Edward's lap and Andrea leaned into me, looking into the box on my lap which I tilted in various directions to try make out something discernable on the inner band. With his blessing, I passed it to Andrea, who also asked for his blessing and passed it to Thomas, who did likewise and passed it to Cecelia. "Don't take it out.", he'd say each time. "I don't want to risk it getting lost." Andrea said "Oh yeah!" like she could read something. I was thinking she was caught up in the whole excitement of it all. "I see numbers."

Edward took the box and tilted it in the air to try get the right light to see it himself, which he couldn't. "Screw it.", he said. He was about to take the ring out. We pleaded with him not to. If it fell on the sticky carpet and got stuck on the sole of someone's shoe or something and disappeared forever, that would have been a nightmare.

"It says, 'Vanessa 12/6/199-'. Which is the date we'll be in Rome together. It's a bit unconventional, I know... but she loves rubies." He was chuffed with himself. There were congratulations and splashes of Wild Turkey all round, the girls remarking how romantic it was that it was only a week away. The furore might have reverberated further along the sofa and gathered quite a crowd had Edward not made reminders to please keep the matter under wraps, his eyes constantly darting about the room lest Vanessa suddenly appear.

So it was no joke. He was for real. He was drunk now but the fundamentals were there – he'd bought the ring and thought it through in advance. I was speechless.

"Wow. Congratulations, man." I was still digesting it all. It was hard to get your head around.

"And you know what else is happening?"

"What?"

"Give a guess."

"Just tell me."

"I only found this out a few hours ago. Vanessa's parents are coming to the States."

"Fuck off!"

"I'm serious! It's so fecking freaky. They'll be travelling around but they'll be with Vanessa for a good while. Isn't that mad? Her parents meeting my parents."

"Wow. That is going to be some Summer, man."

"I wonder where we'll even get married. If she says yes, of course. Here or at home. Hopefully Vanessa would like to have a big wedding. It would be her choice. I'd expect you to be there, Kev. If it's a wedding like the one I'd like to have, there'll be hundreds at it. It would be some party."

We clinked glasses.

"Salud!"

"Santé!"

Before flipping the velvety box closed on the ring and returning it to his pocket, he had a personal moment with it. A smile played on his lips, but it wasn't an altogether happy expression. It was like the ring was the child he'd nurtured. Seeking out engravers and agreeing on prices - he adored her even before her conception. He had changed nappies and guided her through nursery rhymes and lullabies to the fine strapping specimen she was today, enjoying every step of that journey, but despite her startling beauty, if he could go back in time, he would make her different. He would make one irrevocable change to her, if he could. "When I was getting it engraved, if I knew then what I know now, I might have put a different date. I'd have put a date in August. They'll be over the whole month. Maybe I could change the 6 to an 8. These engraver guys, they can engrave anything." He leaned forwards and splashed a bit more Wild Turkey into each of our glasses.

I was delighted for him, yet I felt it's something I should be talking him *out* of.

"Edward, you know how much I love Vanessa. She's a great girl. If she was single I'd marry her myself. But are you sure you're doing the right thing?"

"What do you mean?"

"You want to prolong all that stuff as long as you can into the future. Make the most out of life. It's like what you were saying earlier about the art gallery. Or about sitting on the sofa. *Enjoy* those things. Grab the bull by the horns. I know grabbing the bull by the horns sounds like a strange way to describe doing absolutely nothing but as you said, you have a problem with it. It's like me going for a 10 mile hike, instead of sitting on the sofa, which is easy for me. You won't be able to do nothing forever. Enjoy life, then get married. There's plenty of time for having kids. As Andrea said, you're talking next week, like."

"Not soon enough."

"What age are you again? 23?"

"Yes. And I'm not getting any younger." I laughed - so serious, with that cap on his head.

"And why do you have to have loads of people around? Would you love her less if you were stranded on a desert island?"

"What? No."

"So what's the big deal about having people around? I'm just playing devil's advocate here. It looks like you've thought it through but I want to be sure you've considered it. Big fancy weddings and stuff. If you were stranded on a desert island, the two of you, and you loved her, and you wanted to marry her, is *appearances* really what you would think about? Would you not love her as much on a desert island? It doesn't matter when or where you pop the question as long as you love her."

"Appearances... no... appearances don't matter at all, Kev.", he mused. The way he was staring vacantly at somewhere outside the big window gave me confidence my words were having an effect so I continued quickly, "It doesn't matter where you ask her to marry you as long as you're together, forever. And think about yourself, too. You're 23 years old. I don't mean to be disrespectful or anything but... are you sure you want to be chained to the same woman your whole life? Like I said, life is like a bull. You only have one chance. Live it to the full. Try everything. Do everything. And then... when you're happy you've given everything a shot, get married."

"Grab it by the horns... Appearances don't matter...", he said slowly to himself. His demeanour was serious compared to the jubilance of earlier. I couldn't resist saying, "By the way, did I say congratulations?" We laughed and clinked our glasses again. "We're going to be so locked, man.", I said.

We gazed through the glass down onto the dancefloor and my attention shifted from a long-legged girl in black leggings and high heels to two girls who I was sure were looking up at us the odd time, and giggling. They were leaning on a tall table near the dance floor and looking up at us. "Check out three o'clock.", I said. They were looking at Edward, more like. Probably because he won the dance competition.

"Where?", Edward said.

"Just there, look. Don't make it so obvious." I didn't want to point.

"Oooh yeah", Edward said, scratching his chin.

"Come on. Let's go down and talk to them, man. Stop staring." He was making it so obvious he was looking at them.

"Aw. Jee, Kev. I don't know. What about Vanessa?" He didn't look too happy.

"It's not as if we're going to bloody marry them. Come on."

I started to get up, pulling at his sleeve, the same way he was pulling at me earlier to join the exclusive zone.

"Come on, man."

He got up very slowly, with this real bored look on his face, but I think secretly he was happy to leave. Vanessa would show up eventually, as time went on, and with a number of us in on the secret, the chance of something slipping was multiplied. Cecilia insisted Edward take what was left of the Wild Turkey. She'd hardly been drinking it herself. Thomas and Andrea had won a bottle too, in case she did want any. Amid thank yous on our part and congratulations again on theirs, we said our goodbyes, Edward trudging along behind me, with the subtlety of a bowling ball rolling down a stairs.

The girls knew we were coming for them the moment we left our table. You could tell a mile away. One minute they were looking straight at us through the glass. Then when we join them they give us this surprised stare and say, "Aaaah!!", as if we're the last people on the face of the planet they expect to see. One of the girls was tall, and the other was a bit smaller than me. The smaller one, Reyna, who I spent most of the time talking to, was very good looking. They told us they were going home the next day. They were from Madrid. We all had a glass of Wild Turkey together and swapped email addresses. I did all the talking between myself and Edward. He was too busy looking around the nightclub for Vanessa, with his eyes wide open, and his leather jacket buttoned up to his chin. Then she turned up, all of a sudden. We were just standing there drinking and chatting and she turned up. She looked lost – I mean in a total daze. Edward asked her what was wrong. He had his arms wide open to accept her. He asked her if she wanted a glass of Wild Turkey. She said she was exhausted and wanted to go home so eventually we left. There was still a bit of Wild Turkey left in the bottle and we let those two Spanish girls polish it off.

Chapter 23

Vanessa

From around the time we'd met the girls on the dance floor Edward hadn't been talking much, and now as we walked along the path in the direction of home, on the path along the road, Edward with his jacket buttoned to his chin and his teeth chattering, I noticed a pensive, quizzical expression develop on his face. Lots of people were walking on the path in the same direction. Vanessa was walking a bit ahead with a friend of hers. Edward observed the ground that preceded his steps which were not in a straight line like each step helped formulate the conclusion he was coming to.

"I've been thinking about what you were saying, Kev, about grabbing life by the horns."

"Yes?", I said, proud I'd said something intelligent, flattered my words were worthy of his consideration. He was a clever guy, Edward. It was always him who came up with ideas. "It's a good comparison, isn't it?", I said, wallowing in the moment, delighted how my insights of worldly wisdom had made him ponder to such a degree. "It's so true. Things disappear so quickly. You have to just grab it. Before you know it, it's gone. Settle down and do that sofa thing. Follow your dream. That's my advice anyway."

"Follow your dream. And appearances. Appearances don't matter. What matters is just... two people who love each other."

"Exactly."

"The time is now, Kevin."

"What do you mean?"

"The time to ask Vanessa to marry me is now. Right here, right now, right this moment." He leaned his head within centimetres of my own, to convey utmost sincerity. "Tonight I am going to ask Vanessa to marry me."

"It was John who came up with that bull by the horns stuff. It's probably not that wise." I pulled him to a stop so I could have a good look at him. He nearly made me laugh. He was just in no way befitting for the job of proposing to someone - with that silly smile, his hair ruffled and unkempt and his teeth chattering.

"Are you sure tonight is the right time?", I said, laughter tickling my throat.

"Never more sure of anything in my life." He started to walk quicker to catch up with Vanessa but I held his arm.

"No, I'm serious, Edward. Maybe tomorrow or something. This is ridiculous. Any time but now. You're completely locked." People walked past us.

With gritted teeth he looked into the dark sky and raised a clenched fist - like a plea to God for strength or courage to do what he had to do - and he said, "Tonight, Kevin, I might just be the luckiest man in the world. Fingers crossed." He took steps forwards and then stopped. He turned suddenly and came back to me. "Do us a favour, Kev... will you... This might take a few minutes... I need to get myself psyched up just to get my frame of mind clear and all... I mean I mightn't just walk right up and say straight out, 'Hey, baby, marry me!' You know what I'm saying? I'd like to do the whole down on one knee thing. I need to get my head cleared with as little interference as possible and psyched up. It could take the whole walk home. Meet you back at the house for a bit of a celebration?"

"This is your moment, man. Whatever you want me to do but... Jesus, is this even real?" I put my hands to my head to clear my mind and when I looked back at him I saw it was indeed him standing there, assuring me it was all indeed as I believed it to be. "Whatever you want me to do, consider it done... but are you sure... I mean... come here for a second." Vanessa was a few paces ahead but dangerously within earshot. I didn't want to take any risks and get the blame for a cock up. We took a few steps back. When I saw Vanessa was still walking I said, "The ring says the 12th of June. Today is the 5th of June. Does it not make more sense to do it on the 12th of June? I'm not trying to be a smartarse but normally if you have the date on the ring that's the date you ask a person to marry you. You've got the wrong date. Or even doing it in August, like you were saying. Or else just wait for bloody Venice and do it on the right date, or whatever, anytime but now. You're locked, man. If you bent down on one knee you'd fall over."

"The ring is only a thing. You were right about that. The ring is only a thing. It's an appearance. Only love is eternal. Maybe this is just a test run, but it feels right doing it now. Maybe I'll be asking her again on the 12th. Maybe I'll be asking her on the 12th of June *and* the 12th of August. Third time lucky. This could be the warm up act." He laughed. "No, seriously. I'm feeling positive vibes right now. I feel like I'm on fire! Divine providence has intervened." I tried to protest more but he insisted I let him go, so I did, and he walked on to catch up with Vanessa.

God has a sick sense of humour when doing his divine providence for the trek towards Vanessa came to a sudden halt. He lurched for the grey stone wall along the path. He leaned into the bramble bush growing from behind. There was a heaving sound.

He wasn't quite puking, but he was on the verge of doing so. "Put pressure on your ankles, tighten your ankles.", I said in a whisper, trying to avoid attracting Vanessa's attention, but it was too late. I shut up. I know those few seconds when you're about to puke your guts up, the spinners. How he coped with those spinning demons with his head in the bush in the space of those short few seconds determined whether he puked all night or plucked up the courage to fend them off and do what he had to do. My intervention would tilt it towards puking so I shut up and stayed back. It was an old trick an old man in a pub toilet taught me a year or two earlier. It really works, reminding you there's solid earth under your feet when the world is spinning, spinning, spinning.

When Vanessa saw him with his head in the bush, she rushed over to him.

"I can't believe you let him drink so much, Kevin.", she said, while patting him on the back, consoling him.

Between stomach wrenches, Edward came to my defence.

"Not his fault... had a load before he even got here... it's just nerves... "

"What are you nervous about?", Vanessa asked.

"Nothing to worry about", I interjected. And then louder, so Edward would take the hint, "You'll find out *tomorrow*, when he's feeling better. Isn't that right, Edward?" I nearly said "You'll find out on the 12th." Thank God I didn't. "We'll all go home now and have a good night's sleep." He was in no state to propose right now.

Vanessa took one side of him and I took the other and after some struggle to lift his arms around our shoulders - they were like pipes of lead - we proceeded on the journey homewards. "Thank you so much for this, Kevin – sorry for snapping at you.", Vanessa said, "There's no way he'd be able to make it home without our help."

And it was with those words of recognition and appreciation, I think, that for a few minutes I fell in dreadful love with Vanessa.

Edward was right. As he said in the nightclub, he was a very lucky person. Vanessa was fantastic. She had all the traits that a man could ask for in a woman. Pretty. Kind. Genuine. Fun to be with. And now, catching glimpses of her under Edward's chin as we made our way up the road, that chin which rose and fell like a braying donkey, I witnessed that tender, once in a million beauty of which he would likely be the sole custodian, and the urge to have a similar gift for myself, a soul mate – how readily she jumped to his defence against John in the house earlier on!, nestled in my heart. Seeing Edward and Vanessa together, with that love that never tired, that spark that never quenched... it really stunted my cynicism. All those films with the couple riding off into the sunset. Fantasy tales sanctioned by governments to placate the masses. That's my usual mindset. I'm very cynical. But now, thinking of Edward and Vanessa together... me and... I thought of Juliana... her wave from the step, the warmth of her cheek pressed against mine on the dance floor... that kiss on the cheek and stepping off the balcony and me on that bench by myself again... and her nice wave with a smile at the end... I looked up into the starry sky. It was a beautiful, yet sad, image. Like those stars, I would only ever have Juliana from afar, never close to me. Yes, that's what I wanted, right then, at that point in time, with Edward about to propose to Vanessa; I wanted a soul mate, someone permanent.

Edward limped along between us, Vanessa carrying one side and me the other. Sometimes his feet dragged with the sluggish velocity of a rake's deadweight on the ground. "Oh guys..." His words mashed together like food in a liquidiser. He resisted our efforts to carry him forwards and tried to struggle free. "I'm so sorry about this. This is mortifying. This is embarrassing.", he slurred. He attempted another escape, determined to defeat his clumsiness, and this time we let him go. His whole arm of leather jacket rubbed on my right cheek and flipped my ear forwards but his hand was still touching my neck when he thought it best to not look a gift horse in the mouth and he returned his arms to our shoulders, deeming it the most sensible thing to do, and this time I took adequate care to duck my head well down to give him plenty of room to return his arm to where it had been, to avoid heat rash on my face, or a finger in my eye. Vanessa had her arm around his waist, as did I, and I enjoyed the little bounces of pressure her arm made on my arm, with each step. I was tempted to place my palm on the top of her hand but I would have had to twist my arm into a funny position to do so and besides, I thought it might have appeared vulgar, or louche - too physical, too soon, and right behind Edward's back.

"It's ok, darling, it's ok.", Vanessa said.

The wind was like frustrating whispers in my ear. There were ghosts behind the bushes and the trees. They fleeted in front of my face, teasing me, putting ideas in my head. What on earth was Vanessa doing with a bloke like this?, I found myself asking. Could she not have done any better? Vanessa was a work of art in the making. Like a sculptor with a chisel I started rehashing and reliving past experiences we had shared together, smoothing them out, making them perfect. There was the time, before St Patrick's day, when I cooked for everyone in the house. It was a rare occasion, but I did it. Edward made a bet with me. "This is better than Edward's dinner last week.", she joked. A smile like a candle lit on her face, a flame of laughter rippled through her body.

All those times she called to the house, those times I chatted to her from the stairs as Edward got ready in his room. One day, she gave me flowers. A massive bouquet. I remember she rang the door and there she was on the doorstep holding a straw bouquet bulging with flowers. She was wearing a beige dress. She had on those irresistible black tights. Her lips were like flowers, too, with that shiny red lipstick... and her teeth, pearls within a blossoming rose. Vanessa worked part-time at a solicitor's office on Mondays and Wednesdays. She was studying Law. Edward was out, playing squash or something. There had been a mix up where the office had ordered flowers for a client but they never arrived at the destination and the flower company sent the bouquet back to the solicitors. The boss gave the bouquet to Vanessa and she gave them to me.

To me! Why did she even wear lipstick, or makeup, I was thinking now, as we walked up the path, assisting Edward. Her beauty didn't need embellishments. Her mum was French. In the computer lab one day I asked if she could help me with a problem I was having. She was sitting at the row across from me. She leaned over my shoulder looking at my computer screen with her neck close to my cheek and her hair on my shoulder for what I was sure was longer than was necessary. She said she had a project to finish that very evening. Her deadline is only a few hours away, and she's with me!

Edward's head shot up in an attempt to restore dignity and his arms pushed down. Man, he was heavy. I thought how heavy it must be for poor Vanessa, who was holding him on the other side.

"Look! I'll cook dinner for you guys tomorrow!", Edward said now, remorse being displaced by an attempt to regain self-respect, for in his eyes he believed he was an embarrassment to us, which he wasn't at all. "You really don't have to carry me like this."

"We're leaving tomorrow, Edward. You can't cook dinner. Our car is booked and we have to get ready to go.", said Vanessa, ever the realist.

"Well..." He bit his lip, caught in a dilemma. Then another enthusiastic spurt; "You come with us!" - he almost bit my nose. "Drive to Galway? Travel around with us 'til Monday?" Through fumes of alcohol I replied, "I'm broke, man. Can't afford it."

"Here, come on. Let me go. I can walk. I can walk." A skirmish was easily resisted.

"It's dangerous, Edward."

"It's dangerous? How? We're on a sidewalk. It's ok, I'm fine... I'm an idiot."

"Look, there's nothing wrong with getting drunk.", Vanessa said, her voice a festoon of sweet intonations to quell his remorse. "It's not as if you get plastered that often and... now's as good a night as any – your last night."

"How do you mean?"

"I mean with your friends. Realistically, you might never *see* Kevin again." She pondered what she had said and as if her last words had been a bit harsh she added, 'Ok, perhaps sometime, in the future... but you might never experience *this* again - the three of us, walking down a road on the last night of college. It's important to celebrate times like this."

The words hit him like stones. "What? Of course we will see each other again. Won't we, Kev? I got Kev's number and address." His eyes fastened on my own; a sober interlude in a drunken stupor.

"You bet! With that pool table in your gaff, I'm there, man.", I said jovially, trying to resist the growing strain of temptation that was burdening my head.

"Kev, we'll support you. Come on, come with us tomorrow."

The offer was tempting.

"Don't be silly Edward. We can't afford that." It was cold water over our drunken aspirations. And then she leaned forwards and looked at me across Edward's chest and smiled and said, "No offence, Kevin. We just can't afford it. But you're more than welcome otherwise." At that moment, in the haze of booze and fantasy, it was a smile I recognized instantly. I had seen it many times but until now had been afraid to acknowledge what it truly meant; it was a smile whose lips the first declaration of love could never pass. For too long, ever since we had first met, Vanessa and me had to act in Edward's shadow; his presence and our respect for him dictated what could and could not be said to each other, both of us walking on eggshells around him. It was a smile that illuminated one's secret thoughts and desires, threw them into the external world and dared to hope against hope that "the one" might catch them and set them free. She secretly loved me and I secretly loved her. I'd be damned if I'd let that secret go to the grave with us. Soon, we would all be split up. I'd probably never see Edward again. She was right. He was off to the States after his European travels, permanently. We'd agreed to keep in touch, but long distance relationships rarely work out. To ascertain the possibility of a future between Vanessa and me, to apply myself to seeing if a relationship could be forged between us, once and for all, was a must. To do otherwise would be cowardly, and selfish. It would be a dereliction of manly duty. What could have been, but never was. If Edward made his proposal, before I made any mention of my feelings, we'd end up like the characters in a sad love story. Not only might I be saving them humiliation and trauma, particularly for Edward, in case she said "No" outright, but there was always the chance she fancied Edward intensely, and might be tempted, mistakenly, to say yes. I'd be condemning Vanessa and I to days and nights of grinding teeth in anguish, knowing a life together of joy and fecundity could have happened with only a few small words. It would be condemning Edward to a moribund existence, too. There are few things more painful than realising the person you're married to doesn't love you back as much as you love them. It was on my shoulders to intervene and make fate right.

My mind was bouncing about like a ball in a pinball machine. Things were happening in slow motion. I had twice the amount of time to absorb stuff. The sum of all my educated estimations and philosophical conclusions which I had twice the normal time to calculate in this acid inspired love fest of lucidity was that Vanessa wanted me as much as I wanted her, and it would be criminal to not act on my impulses, to not grab the bull by the horns. We crossed the road. The breeze was cold. I let it hit my face, hoping to refresh carnal thoughts and images with positive wholesome ones. In a pub someone once said to me, "What a woman really wants, Kev, when they look at a man, the question they ask themselves is, 'Will this man give me healthy babies?'" What women really want in a man is carnal instinct. I would have to fight for the prize. That's all that matters. Mr Nice Guy doesn't work.

I was so out of it, I didn't notice Vanessa had taken Edward's place in the centre and was guiding us along the path, with an arm around our waists. I had been reduced from joint guardian to fumbling toddler without even knowing it! Man, I was wasted. She couldn't carry both of us. *She* was the one who needed our protection... especially on this cold dark night. I moved swiftly to regain my status and to position Edward back in the middle. "It's ok, Kevin, stay where you are.", she said. I continued to wrest my arm from poor Vanessa's shoulder but then I thought better of it. Perhaps there was an ulterior motive; she wanted to be closer to me for another reason?

"I'll make you a lovely hot cup of cocoa when we get back, darling.", she whispered in his ear. "And then straight to bed.", she said, with authority.

I tried to resist turning her words of comfort for Edward that flowed like honey for myself, but couldn't. I pictured the two of us later on, in the same bed she was talking about - Edward's bed, waking up together, her lying in my arm. She would acknowledge with whispers in my ear that, compared to me, her love for Edward could never exceed that of a close, dear friendship. She would tell me that, even though she did feel a sharp sadness for Edward, nothing made her happier than to discover she was on this earth for me and not for him. She'd feel guilty for leading him on. I'd tell her her feelings were completely natural. I'd hug her tightly and console her. I'd tell her that this night, which we had yearned for so long but avoided until now out of respect for our mutual friend, was one to celebrate with all our hearts, not to be regretted by even a little inch, like a speck of sand compared to a beach of love, and she would agree, and we would make love all over again, wallowing in the satisfying mischievousness of our adulterous fling while also feeling eternal gratitude for being able to share the rest of our lives together. We'd have another glass of wine, two bottles of which I'd purchased in the 24 hour Esso station when Edward fell asleep on the sofa. "Where... where am I? What happened last night?", he'd ask in the morning, eyes squinted and hand raised against a throbbing forehead. "Why, poor Edward", we'd say. "You just conked out. We had to leave you lying there. You big ninny. You really must control yourself in future. Kevin and I were so worried about you last night. Weren't we, Kevin?" She'd wink at me. It would be our debaucherous little secret. No one ever need know about the night before we made our love public. Passion, and love, would win the day.

"I have to go." I broke away and made an about turn and stepped towards solitude, away from the light-hearted crowds, hoping dark thoughts would recede with Edward and Vanessa.

Vanessa's groin-sizzling words followed a second later, coming back for me.

"Are you ok? Where are you going?"

"I'm ok, Vanessa." My pace slackened, yet I didn't look back. We'd come too far, me and Edward, to risk losing it all. I tried to have uplifting thoughts. In a way, he was his own worst enemy. The relationship between him and the rest of us in the house, it was like the story of the little red hen, without the ending; he'd do all the work all along, but at the very end he'd share the spoils with everybody else, rather than keep it for himself. All I want to remember is the good Edward, so I'll do that in one more chapter, and then call it a day.

Chapter 24

The End

Now that my story is coming to a close, I'll say first of all that I had a lot of fun writing all this. I don't know what I'm going to do when it's finished, to be honest. I know nostalgia plays a part, especially straight after writing it. They were a cool bunch of people, and so much comes back, talking about it. The weird thing is, I talked to him about writing this book. It was a different idea back then obviously, not having the information that would transpire. We were coming back from town on the bus, after seeing the Fugitive. We were saying what a cool film it was. They did something new in the cinema. The sound of the waterfall made the room vibrate. I told him I'd write a book one day. Enid Blyton; what happened to the 6? There was the Famous Five, the Secret Seven... I thought there was an opportunity there with the 6 of us in the house with all our stories.

I suppose that's where my story ends, then. There's a lot more I could write, but I don't think it's helpful. The reason I wrote all this is I thought it would be cathartic. I thought it would have the same effect that a trial has on the family of a loved one sitting in the courtroom, listening to his last moments, imagining being there to hold that person's hand in their time of need. It's painful to listen to, or write about, but it's redeeming, and necessary. Lately I've taken to drawing, as well as writing. Stuff I remember from back then. It's like a penance. It's strangely satisfying doing stuff passionately, no matter how inconvenient it is. I think how a knight must feel. The wily stratagems I make at work to overcome boredom are like his singing of ballads in lonely fields. I apply myself wholeheartedly to my day, like he does in his battles against giants, facing them with candour and patience, and discipline, knowing they'll fall into insignificance when he finds his bride; my bride being that time in the night where I sit in peace and quiet when I'm home from work and write this. Actually, the knight is a bad analogy - me doing the dishwasher and him severing heads. I can't compare my elation to his, with his bride. I love it though, even if it's just for 30 minutes. I'll look over all this and it will probably be gibberish but I don't really care. As long as *I* understand it.

It makes me think of another time. I think I told you I was never away from the house for more than 2 days but in fact there was a week around Christmas I went for 4 or 5 days to Cork with my mum and dad and sister. He asked me to send a postcard to the house. I had full intentions of doing so. I'd taken a mental note of a shop where I could buy a card but the break went so fast. "It's the thought that counts.", I said, when I got back to the house. He laughed. It's the thought that counts. Most of the time I just think of the stuff he said, rather than do it. I want to remember only the good Edward. The student doctor coming over, the crowd gathering... it's like going into those grisly details isn't worthy of being in the same story as him. Writing about that would only achieve the opposite to what I want to achieve. I want to remember only the eternal optimist.

With the clickety click of Vanessa's high heels approaching me as I walked away, every miniscule interaction in my relationship with her was scrutinised at lightning speed. New insights into her subtle mannerisms and gestures were revealed. Going bowling in town with Vanessa and Edward, how I helped her stick her fingers in the ball, the Saturday afternoon she slurped from her mug of tea in a way that made me giggle and she giggled back, her chin tucked into her chest with a little embarrassed grin on her face. Edward, my dear friend, that engineer of happiness, that fountain of generosity, having the unpalatable truth foisted upon him! For a long time he would awaken brokenhearted in the night. The dreams, or nightmares, would be vivid; me handing gifts to her on her birthday, walking along the beach with her, laughing and hugging tightly as the dog ran ahead in the breaking waves. He had believed her his lighthouse, his guiding star, instead she was a mermaid, singing, drawing him towards the rocks. Her nest would be feathered not with the kind, noble Robin, but rather with the dirty Eagle who had pretended to be the Robin's friend, who had plotted from the sidelines and had snatched the golden egg at the last instant.

When the deed of delivering the news was done and had receded in the rear view mirror, Vanessa and I would get married ourselves. All the glories of our future rolled out before my eyes. We would have 2 children; Connor, who would have my fair hair and blue eyes and Irish skin, and Hannah, who would be of a more sallow complexion, like her mother. She would have Vanessa's eyes; little flares erupting on the circumference of the dark pupil, like an inverted photo of the surface of the sun; at intervals a courageous streak of dark brown broke from the little flares and sped across the sky of iris which turned progressively greener, like displays of fireworks over Amazonian rain forests. Conor would be good at maths in primary school. He'd have a proclivity for board games. Hannah, two years Connor's junior, would excel on the track and field. Vanessa and I, always preferring a candle lit dinner over being thrust into the glare of high and brash society, would at first attend reluctantly the charity dos and gala dinners we were invited to, but soon we would come to relish these occasions for the source was our children, and their achievements. Hannah's prowess for javelin throwing would take her to the Olympics where she would win a medal. Connor would win the title of chess "GrandMaster". They would be famous but not too famous to be burdensome; a Johnny Logan or a Michael Carruth rather than a Lionel Messi; contestants on Dancing with the Stars or found in the pages of The RTE Guide rather than hitting the international mainstream - which is a joke I would make a bit too regularly at my speeches, and which Vanessa would ask me to desist from doing, more than once, but they would be the apple in the eye of households throughout the country, a local phenomenon, and we would only be happy to regale our gleamy eyed listeners with stories of what it was that made "the Farrington kids" what they were, and how proud we were of them.

    The amazing children we had produced would not have been without anguish, and in the early days we would speak publicly of this too - the exhaustion of transporting kids to training sessions, the turning down of promotions at work, but we would learn that discourse verging on self-pity makes the audience uncomfortable, so we would concentrate instead on finely worded, upbeat eulogies. As the beaming faces applauded the parents whose dedication had given them the prodigies they celebrated now, Vanessa and I would share a smile over the mic, acknowledging all that had happened, which nobody else could know. Our love had mellowed fondly with age yet was as ardent as ever. Despite the hardships, our love never deviated from a steady line. As the applause continued, getting stronger rather than abating, we would cuddle, as warmly and fondly as on that first day, our hearts somersaulting with glee and giddiness. I walked on briskly in the dark, hoping to dispel the fantastical stellar achievements of our fictional children to the outer regions they deserved, but rather, the intermingled futures accelerated to the point I could almost touch them. We would take two family holidays a year, one in the summer to Paris to visit Vanessa's parents, and a Winter holiday, too. I would never be able to get Edward out of my head, sometimes to the extent I could hardly breathe. We realised the panic attacks were more pronounced when we were sharing romantic moments together. Vanessa would suggest I write to him. He would be hardly able to breathe himself when he received that letter, inviting him to our holiday home in Galway. Many years would pass before he would take up the offer.

 As I walked away from the crowds I could hear Vanessa calling out to me. My feelings oscillated from confusion to clarity and back again. Sometimes it sounded like she was singing out prophecies of our future, then I heard her yells for what they were - demands to not be silly and to follow her. At the end of the day, Edward would be happy with his lot. The monotonous lonely life he accepted back in America and became resigned to was broken one day by a grateful happenstance at the local library. He would marry and have 4 children, themselves bright young sparks who'd achieve remarkable heights.

Years later, when Vanessa and I were married, and he was married too, he'd take up the offer to visit us in our lodge in Galway. We'd observe something that, after a moment of considerable solemnity, it must be said, would make us laugh. It was coming close to Christmas. We'd returned to the house after a Winter's day of hiking with our families. We were standing on the far side of the room in regal fashion with our elbows perched on the ledge that extended over the marble fireplace, a pleasant aroma of burning ash logs rising to our noses. Vanessa and Marion were getting on like a house on fire. Our children laughed and played. I opened a bottle of Wild Turkey. Without saying anything to each other, we would smile into each other's eyes, pondering the arrows that life throws in our way; that despite the unbearable prodding and taunting of the human heart, things really do turn out for the best.

Vanessa tugged me by the wrist in the other direction where everybody else was walking and towards Edward who was slumped on the wall, his head bowed like he was transfixed on some spectacle between his feet.

"Oh, Kevin. Come on. You can't go anywhere in your current state." I tried to resist the warm bracelet of her fingers and those light-floating whispers of encouragement to follow her.

"Vanessa." I stopped abruptly. She stopped too, still holding my wrist. The declaration I had to make was beautiful, and brutal, but causing offence is a meagre price to pay if the prize is spending your days with the one you adore. I was acutely aware of opportunity's brittle window. Time is too precious to risk lost love, now was the chance to see if a spark existed which could be kindled into a blossoming union, the heavenly scribes had allotted me the pen, the narrative for the future into which we were being summoned was in my hands; one stroke, one word, an evocation of all those unspoken sentiments on the doorstep –

"Vanessa... I love you.", I said.

"What?" She looked confused. I was disappointed. I felt guilty at my lust alongside her innocence. Yet my hopes were far from dashed. If anything they confirmed my beliefs.

"Je t'aime." She was looking right into my eyes. "What are you talking about? And keep your voice down."

"Think, Vanessa, think back over all the moments we shared together." What an idiot I was.

"What moments?"

"That flower pot you gave me, for example. When you won those flowers from work or whatever. There were like -

"The bouquet?"

"Yes, whatever it was. The straw yoke. Your boss gave them to you or you won them or something..." She remembered and nodded. "Well, you remember when I accepted them?" Edward was pacing a short diameter back and forth on the path, absorbed in his own thoughts. "If I'd rejected the flowers it was like, 'No, I am not available.' But I took them. I took them. You were happy when I took them. You remember that? On the doorstep?'

"Yes, I do. It was a luxury bouquet of roses and tulips. Really beautiful."

"Exactly. What I'm trying to say is... I keep thinking of my granny before she died. We'd see her every weekend. She lived in Carlow. Her dream was to go to Corsica. We'd be watching, 'The Bridge on the River Kwai' or something and she'd say 'Oh I'd love to go to Corsica.' My Dad said she was like that too, when he was a kid. She never went to Corsica. Ever. I don't want to be one of these people who look back on their life in 80 years and go, 'I wish I'd gone to Corsica.'" Her eyes searched my own, flitting from one to the other, seemingly entertaining what I was saying.

"Let's talk it over dinner. On me.", I said. Prawn cocktail for starters. Rump steak for main course. Melons for dessert. I'd been hoping to see at least a vague recognition of mutual feelings by this stage. In fact, she was bamboozled by what was happening and dismissed it out of hand.

"I can't believe I'm having this conversation. How many fingers am I holding up?"

"Two." Pause. "Three?"

"How many hands am I holding up?", she asked, like one whose patience has been breached dealing with a hopeless case. She threw her eyes to heaven. "Come on, let's go. We're all going home to bed." Her tone was decisive. The voice of leadership, sufficient to make me obey her command and follow. Edward turned to face us, wiping a froth from his mouth with the back of his hand. There weren't any more people behind me. Maybe once again seeing the old Edward, apparently sober and alert, acted as a wakeup call, or maybe it's because Vanessa had departed my side, but at that point my protestations of love came to an end. Vanessa walked right past him to catch up with some friends. There were some words of criticism – I couldn't hear what – but I caught the cold look of reproach she gave him as she was walking by. "Now that you're on your own two feet, you can fend for yourself.", she seemed to be saying.

I chatted with Edward as Vanessa walked on, just the two of us. He closed his eyes and extended out his arms towards me, like a sleepwalker standing on the spot. "Ok. Take a deep breath. There is only fresh, cool air around me, blowing pleasantly into my face. Breath through your nose.", he said to himself. He stood like this for about 10 seconds, breathing in and out slowly through his nose.

He opened his eyes. "Wow. I'm suddenly fine now."

"You still going to ask her?"

"To marry me? Now? No way. Would you believe it, Kev, you've talked some sense into me."

"Thank you."

"I know. Very strange. I'd say the right words, I'd do the right actions – getting down on one knee, but she'd be looking back wondering if I was actually drunk when I said it, that would always be at the back of her head." He looked into the sky. "Who could ask for more than a night like this, eh?" The rain clouds were well and truly gone, made pitiful by what had replaced them: the unending black canopy of the sky filled with its loyal servants, the stars. Millions of them. We arched our heads back and peered up at it all, just the two of us. I cherished the moment and the silence with the two of us looking up, appreciating how it could indeed be one of our last times together. "It has everything a person could ask for, doesn't it?"

"Sure does. Look at that, look." I'd just spotted a satellite, zooming across the sky.

He stopped. "What?" He'd started to walk on, to catch up with Vanessa, and now he came back and looked into the sky, trying to see what I was looking at. "A satellite. You see it? Just there." I pointed as specifically as I could. It was hard to pick out unless you really knew what you were looking for.

"A satellite?"

"Swear to God.", I assured him, as he sounded sceptical, as was I when my cousin first pointed one out to me on a beach in Wexford, years earlier. "You'll believe it when you see it. Look, you see it? Right there." He was squinting, following the line of my pointed finger. "There's no flashing lights or anything so it can't be a plane. You see it? It's a little dot. Like a star. Just there, look."

The little pin prick had broken away from a cluster so it was easier to pick out. "Ohh yeah... I see it! A satellite? Is it not a shooting star?"

"A shooting star burns and fades. This is just, like, a steady spot moving across the sky. Mad, eh?"

"Wow. Mad. There has to be another earth out there somewhere, man. How many?... trillions, gazillions of suns out there. Each one with maybe ten planets on average going around it. Ok, let's get a move on. Lots of stuff to be done..." He clapped his hands to awaken his faculties, to dispel those horrible spinners for good, and made a move.

Only a few seconds later, he was hit by a truck, and killed. There we are talking about America and shooting stars and in a puff of smoke, he's gone. 23 years old. Less than half my life ago. The truck driver said he'd been driving slowly with so many people coming out of the nightclub and with Edward near to the curb he slowed down even more. He saw me at the last instant, he said, trying to grab hold of him, but it was too late, and he fell out on the road.

I hardly talked to Vanessa again after that day. His parents came over to Ireland. We all met at the house. I'd hoped to meet his sister, but she didn't come. The funeral was going to be in America. I wanted to tell Vanessa things she couldn't know, like in the "Exclusive Zone" how happy he was with his two diamonds and a ruby, and the thought he'd given to the engraving, and maybe how he had plans to go to France. My heart was pounding in preparation to say these things. I was wondering whether to tell her he was thinking of proposing to her that night, that if I managed to deliver it in a delicate way there'd be a bit of humour in there, but I decided it would be too risky, causing more upset than good. I thought that, considering what had happened, and what we'd been through together, he warranted a shared moment of happy reflection between us, but it never happened. We were showing Edward's parents the location clearly on a map for where we'd meet later and then, quite suddenly, we just seemed to go our separate ways. She already knew about the ring. She went on the ambulance with him. They gave her his items.

On the ambulance with him! I was gone before it even arrived. Scumbag and coward that I am, I thought it wise to put time and space between me and the deed.

I didn't even stick around long enough to see the truck driver. I only saw him the next day. There was the sound of "phssst" from the brakes, air cylinders or something. I'll never forget that noise.

That's a question I was asked by some councillor my folks paid for in the following days. "Why did you run?", he asked. I told him the truth. I was afraid. You're there having an in-depth chat with your best friend and then he's gone. On acid, too. He's the one who suggested I write about my feelings. He said putting your emotions on paper is a good way to work through your thought processes. I wrote those few notes I found at the end of my bed before he'd even said this to me, but since then, I've done nothing. Until now.

When I was kneeling beside him on the road, he held my hand in a firm grip. I knew by the way he was looking at me he was happy he'd come to Ireland, where he'd met Vanessa, and me – even after what had happened. The notes aren't the catalyst that got me writing all this, even though I couldn't get them out of my head. That was a while later, at a funeral. The priest was saying - St Paul to the Corinthians, "our time is growing short, those who have to deal with the world should not become engrossed in it... because the world as we know it is passing away." That's when I decided I'd start writing, a recompense for what I'd done, lame as it is. I'm like the hotshot jet setter I saw interviewed on tv. The whole thing seemed a bit deceitful to me. He flies around the world constantly and gives out about climate change but it's all ok because he donates to a green charity. I should be wearing sackcloth and ashes for the rest of my life, but by writing this, I'm offsetting my carbon usage.

Vanessa must have felt angry that I was the last one with him, that she never got to hear what he wanted to say, but I'm pretty sure she didn't consider me as someone instrumental to his demise; rather, I was a buffoon, a drunk in the wrong place at the wrong time. I doubt she remembers me at all now, to be honest. She never came back to Limerick. I'd have become a vanishing footnote in her mind, unworthy of competing for space against the happy memories she wanted to preserve.

So that's it. That's my snivelling, pathetic apology. When I imagine the course his life might have taken and what might have become of him, those thoughts come with a tint of sadness, being a future that can't happen, so I prefer to reminisce over stuff we actually did together. Simple things, like playing kerbs on the road in front of the house; a pastime that gave us hours of free fun, especially when the evenings were getting longer coming into the Summer. He was crap at running back from the middle line. I'd hit him every time and get the points. I told him he should walk backwards, instead of bolting for it. He'd be better off looking at me, and seeing where I'm about to throw the ball, rather than just going for broke. He took my advice, and then he started winning. I should have told him nothing. One day we played for about 5 hours. At first we said we'd play to 30, then we said we'd play to 50... we must have played to 500. We'd given up counting at that stage. We only came in when it was dark. Edward suggested next time we should have the points in tens and fives rather than sixes and threes. That was a good idea.

They'd definitely have gotten married. They'd got through the stage of writing to each other under a directional lamp, that's for sure. She could have gone to college for a year over there, maybe he could have done another year here... time would fly. I could see him being a very successful businessman, the head of the company. He could fit in with all sorts of people. That was his gift. He had a naturally congenial quality about him. He'd rise to the top that way. Or, maybe he'd have been too nice to get ahead, I don't know. You have to be ruthless to get to the top and stay there. He wouldn't have done so good at that part.

Sometimes now on clear nights I lay out on my back in the little park across from my flat and look up at the stars. The sky is never as dark as it was that night in Limerick. Yellow light diffuses around the park throughout the sky. I imagine a raging fire. The cars on the M50 are its thunderous hum. I think of Edward and me looking into the sky that night. Whatever would have happened in Venice or later in August or whenever, Vanessa's answer didn't really matter – "Yes" or "No"; no matter what hurdles blocked the way, the starry sky would shine for him tomorrow, and the next day, and the next, and he'd shine straight back up.

I'm going to keep talking about him. If I stop to take a breath, I won't get back to it. It's mostly for myself, and because I'm enjoying writing it, but if you suffered my rants and are still with me, if you actually read this far, then I owe it to you, too, to keep talking. The stuff that happened afterwards is worth writing about. In a way I went to hell that night, then purgatory, then heaven. If I can finish this I might get to stay in heaven. "He lived. He died. That's the end of my story." It's too blunt. I'm going to keep going, while the iron is hot. But for the moment I'm going to show you what I've written now.

I probably would have gone to Galway with them. They'd have told me to feck off if I'd strong-armed my way to accompany them around Europe, but I think Galway was feasible, for one last hurrah. I can imagine Vanessa being impressed that I actually had money, buying my own McDonalds and beer. The college doesn't even look the same as it did back then. I went back recently. They've built a new library. The Kremlin is different. They got rid of those tiles, like Grafton street. There's a glass ceiling over where the open air terrace was. That's what we'd be celebrating if we met each other again - how we still had that zest for life; how we had something permanent, even though everything had changed. It's been 30 years since I saw or heard from any of them. If we ever bumped into each other again, there wouldn't be enough hours in the day to catch up on those intervening decades since that day on the 5th of June.

We might have tried to keep it as our own private joke from Vanessa but our giggles would be irrepressible and she'd notice and we'd muster the courage to tell her - that the reason I had money is because Edward gave me a loan of 40 quid. The 5 of us sitting in John's Volvo, spinning pool cues like ninjas in the Hangman... I look back on those days and see some of the best days of my life so far. I wouldn't have added "so far" were it not for him. He made me into an optimist. The two of us dancing in the room that day. He'd be the same now, if he was around. Deep down, we all would.

Printed in Great Britain
by Amazon